Rise and Fall

Casey kelleher

Editing and proofreading by Sam Szanto: http://www.samszanto.co.uk

Cover Design by Leanne Phillips: http://www.leannephillips.co.uk

Casey's Website: http://caseykelleher.wordpress.com

www.facebook.com/officialcaseykelleher.co.uk

Twitter: @caseykelleher

For my family

For always encouraging me to rise,
and for catching me when I fell.
x

"Some rise by sin, and some by virtue fall."

~ William Shakespeare

Chapter 1

"Why ain't you at school?" Maura Finch leant forward with exaggerated effort as she switched on the TV guide to check what the time was on the telly; her son, Jamie, had normally left for school by now.

Jamie Finch stood, feeling awkward, in the middle of the lounge, where his mum was sitting. The curtains were still drawn, and the place had a familiar musty stale smell. He could see his mum's flabby belly poking out from under the threadbare top she was wearing, and she had her early morning fag on the go already. Smoke poured out of her mouth as she spoke.

Jamie looked over at Kevin in his playpen, trying to divert his attention to anything he could so that he didn't actually have to make eye contact with his mother.

Maura had bred four kids, including Jamie and Kevin: each had been born to a different man, none of whom she had managed to hold onto. Jamie felt that his mother wasn't exactly what you would class as a catch.

Jamie's father had been just like his siblings' dads. He had only stuck around long enough to impregnate her, and God knows how she had managed to even get that far. Jamie had never witnessed a flirty, womanly side to his rough, intimidating mother and couldn't imagine her with a man in her bed.

Jamie's dad had scarpered long before Jamie was born and hadn't been heard from since. Jamie couldn't blame the bloke, really; he had obviously cottoned on to what a nasty, vindictive woman he had got himself involved with.

Jamie wasn't that bothered by the fact that he never had his father around when he was growing up. He had never known it any other way and had always reasoned that you can't miss what you've never had. He couldn't imagine a man with a strong enough backbone who would be willing or able to endure this miserable existence with his mum. Jamie knew that first hand.

Maura was a beast of a woman, a complete tomboy. She was nothing like the other mums at Jamie's school. She never bothered to wear make-up or to go to any kind of effort with her appearance and her feminine mannerisms were non-existent: she would sooner be sitting in a pub downing a few pints with the local lads and shouting encouragement at the big screen for her team, Fulham. Maura loved football, she lived for it; it was her religion. Jamie and his siblings had practically grown up in pubs, even as small children they had been forced to endure their mum's passion. There had been many nights when they had had their dinner substituted for crisps and fizzy pop, and they had been left to fall asleep on grotty pub chairs, with nothing but their coats to keep them warm, instead of being tucked up at home, snug in their beds where most normal children were. When the football was on they were ignored by their pissed-up mother who was always too busy trying to ponce drinks from the locals who mainly gave her a wide berth, all too familiar with her blagging ways and her foul mouth if she didn't get what she wanted. It was because of that, that Jamie hated football.

Even when Jamie had been younger, he had taken on the role of man of the house, and because of this he felt wise beyond his years, and more than capable of looking after the lot of them. At fifteen, Jamie was the eldest of his siblings. He had two sisters, Fliss and Kara, who were thirteen and eleven, and he could pretty much take or leave the pair of them; they were selfish cows, two little clones of his mum.

Standing in the lounge, he smiled over at his little dribbling brother Kevin. He could sense his mum getting agitated with him for not answering her, and he knew what would happen when she heard his news. He hadn't wanted to tell her last night as he really couldn't be bothered with the earache she would no doubt inflict upon him. She loved an argument.

Jamie couldn't get over how much things had changed since Kevin had come along. Jamie had only just turned fourteen when he had found out his mum was up the duff again. This time there wasn't even a man on the scene, and it disgusted Jamie to realise that his mother had probably got herself pregnant through some cheap and nasty one-night-stand. Probably with someone too pissed to remember what he had done the next day. The idea of having a screaming baby around the house again really hadn't appealed to Jamie. It just meant another mouth to feed and more hassle for him in the long run, especially seeing as his mother was such a lazy cow; he had known that she would leave many of the chores that came with a needy baby to him and his sisters. But as soon as his mother had come home from the hospital with little Kevin wrapped in his blue blanket all such thoughts had instantly disappeared. Jamie fell in love with the gorgeous, tiny baby.

Jamie adored Kevin; he hadn't in a million years expected to feel so protective over the little thing, nor had he anticipated feeling so much love for the boy. Kevin had been so small and vulnerable-looking that Jamie had felt an instinctive protectiveness towards the little fellow: he had never known a feeling quite like it.

"Jamie, I asked you a question; why ain't you at school?" his mum said.

As cocky as Jamie could be, he could admit that his mum scared the shit out of him, especially when she was in one of her moods. She was like the anti-Christ then. She was as wide as she was tall and had a mouth twice the size of the

Dartford Tunnel. You would hear her before you would see her, and boy, did she always have plenty to say.

"I'm not going back to school." He shrugged as he spoke, knowing this would infuriate her even more.

"What do you mean you're not going back?" Maura looked at him suspiciously, she had barely taken a sip of her first cup of tea of the morning and Jamie's forthright attitude was pissing her off. "Are you sick?" He didn't look very sick. Jamie was a slip of a boy, five foot six and paler than milk. He had a sprinkle of freckles over his nose and just looked like an average kid of fifteen. Although unlike most fifteen year olds he could more than handle himself if he needed to. Chip off the old block he was, she always thought to herself, quick with his fists when he needed to be, and even quicker with his tongue; he had been blessed with the 'gift of the gab' and could pretty much talk himself out of wet cement.

"Am I sick? Yeah, as a matter of fact I am. I'm sick of bloody school. I've jacked it in; I told Mr Rudgewick where he can bloody well shove it yesterday, and I ain't going back."

Jamie knew that sugar-coating his words was pointless; she was going to be angry about him leaving school, so he may as well tell it to her like it was. He knew why she would be so cross, too; she wanted him to do well at school so that he would get a good job, and he only had a year left until his GCSEs. Although mothers usually hoped that their kids would do well, Jamie knew that his mum's wish for him to be successful was driven by selfish motives. She had drummed it into him from a very young age that he would be helping support her and the kids when he left school; she had made it seem like it was his duty as the eldest. He needed good grades so that he could get himself a decent job. She didn't want him ending up working somewhere like their local chippy, like Janice's boy who lived next door; that spotty little git worked all the hours God sent and barely made the minimum wage. No, her Jamie would do better than that. Maura wanted Jamie to earn big money and went on about him getting himself a job at one of the posh offices down by the river, overlooking the Thames. She had seen all those snobby-looking pen-pusher types making their way to work in the mornings, when she had been out early herself, on the rare occasions she had to go and fetch her own fags. That lot strutted around like they thought they were the dog's doo-dahs, all suited and booted, chatting away on expensive mobiles. Maura knew that they must earn a fortune. Jamie could do that and support her and his brother and sisters with the money.

Jamie had other ideas; if his mother had bothered to ask him what they were, he would have gladly told her. But his mum was too wrapped up in herself to even realise that he had no intention of following her plans. She practically lived like she was disabled; in fact Jamie was pretty sure that she had actually declared that she was disabled to the Social, so that she would be able to claim more benefits. She wanted anything she could get her hands on. From as far back as he could remember, Jamie couldn't recall ever seeing his mum do a full day's work. As far as he could make out, the only real thing his mother suffered from was terminal 'lazyitous'. Watching football matches in the pub and cashing her giros in at the post office were just about the only physical activities that Maura did when she wasn't slobbing out at home thinking she was Lady Muck.

Jamie had much bigger plans for himself than this kind of a life; he wasn't going back to school, and there was no way he was sticking around in this dump any longer than he had to either. His mum could think again if she imagined he was going to go out and make a living so that she could continue to sit on her arse all day long.

"Er, no, I don't bloody think so, Jamie." Maura laughed at her son's audacity. He had lost the plot if he thought that he could jack school in. Those teachers at that school might claim that the boy was clever, but he didn't half come out with some stupid bloody things sometimes, she thought.

"You're going back now," she insisted.

"No, Mum, I'm not, I've just told you…" Jamie barely got his sentence out before his mum bellowed at him, her patience gone: "You will do as you're fucking told, my boy. Go and get changed into your school uniform right now and get your arse down to that fucking school, and tell Mr Rudgewick that you're back. Do whatever it takes. Get on your hands and knees and bloody beg him if you have to."

Maura's face was beetroot red with rage as she glared at her son as he stood in front of her. Jamie may be stubborn as hell, but he had got that trait from her and there was no way she was going to back down on this one. She was depending on him, and there was no way that he was going to fuck up her plans.

Jamie was furious; how dare she think that she had any right to try and control his life; all she did was sit on her fat arse all day long, smoking fags and watching crap on telly.

"I said I ain't going back." Jamie gritted his teeth in annoyance and glared back at his mother defiantly as she sat looking gobsmacked.

Jamie was done with school. He knew that he was clever: really clever. His grades were the highest in his class, and that was without him ever really bothering to try. His teachers had always told him that if he had made more of an effort, he would be able to get into a good university. The problem was Jamie didn't want to make an effort; the whole school thing bored him to tears.

"Well, you can't just fucking leave, what would we do? What about bringing some money in, Jamie? We haven't got a pot to piss in."

Leaning forward to stub her fag out, Maura pulled up her leggings which had sunk down to reveal her arse crack. Her blonde hair was lank and greasy as always, and her skin was red and blotchy. She looked a mess.

As Jamie looked at her, a familiar feeling of disgust washed over him. His mother was a lazy fat pig who was content to just sit in her flat all day, every day, festering in her own filth. She was right; they didn't have a pot to piss in: they had barely any food in the cupboards and the carpets were stained and worn. Fair enough if they didn't have any money, but it didn't cost anything to run a vacuum cleaner about the place or empty an overflowing bin: as far as he was concerned that was just pure laziness.

He looked over to his little brother, sitting happily in his playpen. The poor little thing didn't have any idea of what was in store for him; he cooed and smiled at any attention he was given while he wore a filthy babygrow and no doubt a nappy that was probably full to the brim with shit from the night before. It was all the poor mite knew.

His sisters were just as bad as his mum, lazy mares the pair of them, probably still asleep in their pits upstairs, when they should have been up and getting ready for school. His mum never bothered to moan at those two to get their arses to school, probably because she knew they were both thick as shit anyway and would end up just like her. Why bother wasting her breath?

They had never had money from what Jamie could remember; their food barely lasted the week and they had to live off toast or cereal half the time; every once in a while his mum would really push the boat out and do them all a microwave meal as a bit of a treat, although that didn't happen very often.

It was the way it had always been. Jamie saw so many kids at school with flash phones and cool trainers. He had neither. He was lucky if his trousers weren't swinging up around his ankles, or his school shoes weren't pinching his toes, as they were always a size too small for him. Luckily, unlike some of the weaker kids who got bullied for being poor, or having short trousers, or pretty much anything that made them stand out against being 'normal' like everyone else, Jamie had never been a victim. He had an air about him that he wouldn't stand for bullying, and he reckoned it was because of that no-one had messed with him.

Even so, there had been many occasions when, despite the brave face he had put on, he had felt mortified that his clothes were dirty, or that he had to go to school wearing ankle-swinging trousers. However, he had gone to school, no matter how he looked or what he had been wearing, and he had always kept his head held high and made out if he needed to that it didn't bother him.

He wasn't prepared to do that anymore. This life might be enough for his mother, but it was a far cry from what he wanted for himself.

Jamie felt a pang of anguish as he looked over at Kevin again. Poor little Kevin. The kid had it all to come. The screaming matches, the guilt trips, the demands. Jamie hated the thought that when he left, Kevin may be next in line for his mother's plotting and scheming, but Jamie just couldn't do it anymore; if he stayed here even a second longer he would lose his mind.

Jamie had made a plan last night as he lay in bed thinking about his new life, which would be a better one, and he had made a vow that he would make sure that Kevin was alright. He would get himself sorted out and then come back for him.

Jamie walked past a garage on the way to school each day. It was near the high street. The owner looked like he earned a few bob, Jamie had seen him getting out of his flash motor all suited and booted, and Jamie had decided that this morning he was going to go there and see if he could sort himself out some sort of a job. He fancied having a go at learning the motor trade and had high hopes that even though he was young he would be able to start at the bottom and work his way up, even if it meant just cleaning cars and sweeping floors, he was prepared to do anything if it meant getting away from his mother.

Kevin smiled up at Jamie and held out his little chubby arms, wanting to be lifted out of the playpen, but Jamie couldn't pick him up. He knew if he held his baby brother even for a second, he'd end up staying out of pure guilt.

"What are you doing standing there looking gormless? Go and put your uniform on. Get your arse into gear, boy," his mum demanded. Maura thought she had won, as Jamie seemed to have nothing to say for himself.

"Yep, you're right, Mum." He nodded.

Smiling at the thought of Jamie finally doing what he was told, Maura picked up the TV remote ready to turn the volume up; one of her favourite programmes was about to start.

"You take care, Mum, I'm off." Jamie walked out of the room, ignoring Kevin's cries as the poor little sod realised he wasn't going to get picked up.

As Jamie grabbed the bags that he had left by the front door, his mother hoisted herself out of her chair and made it out to him in the hallway in record-breaking time.

Grabbing him by the scruff of his neck, she dragged him in close so that their faces were almost touching; the stench of stale cigarettes on her breath hit him full in the face, making him recoil.

"You're off? What the fuck is that supposed to mean?" Maura was seething. Jamie would do as he was fucking told, she thought.

It was a step too far for Jamie; he was fifteen now, and his mother still felt she could control him; with every bit of balls he could muster, he let her have it.

"It means, Mother, I'm off," Jamie spat back. "I'm leaving. I've had enough of your fat fucking gob and your constant fucking demands. I can't bear to even look at you. You fucking disgust me. Now what part of that do you not understand you fat, lazy bitch?"

Jamie spat the words with as much venom as there was truth. For the first time in his life, he witnessed his mum rendered speechless. Shrugging off his now silent mother, he pushed past her and slammed the front door.

Breathing in the cool fresh air, he felt a surge of relief wash over him. This was the moment he had dreamt of for so long. He had finally broken away from her; at last, he had told her what he thought of her. He was the master of his own destiny now, instead of his mother's mule, and for the first time ever Jamie Finch felt free to be his own man.

Chapter 2

Shay drummed his fingers loudly on the dash-board, his agitation getting the better of him. They had been watching this house for hours, and his patience was beginning to wear thin.

This was the swankiest road Shay had ever been to. It was a private lane in the middle of Oxshott in Surrey, and it had the most luxurious-looking houses he had ever set eyes on. Each house was immaculate, from the pristine manicured lawns to the gleam of the sparkling windows: there was not as much as a leaf out of place around here. As for the cars: well, they were in a whole other league. Porches, Range Rovers and Audis were parked in most of the driveways. These people must be swimming in money, Shay thought. It was a far cry from what he had to call home back in Lambeth; the only things that lined his street were fag packets and overflowing bin bags and plenty of them at that.

Normally their jobs were quite straightforward, but this one was proving more difficult. When they had followed this bird back to her gaff earlier, they hadn't anticipated the extent of the wealth in the neighbourhood nor the tall, wrought-iron gates standing in their way.

They would have to take their time before they made their move. The fact that they were squished into a crappy little blue Ford Escort that had seen better days, probably wasn't aiding them much in their plan of keeping a low profile. The car stood out like a sore thumb, and it stunk, or rather Gavin's arse stunk.

"Ah, man; has a fucking rat crawled up your arse and died, or what?" Shay's words were muffled as his hand was clasped over his mouth and nose trying to block out the stench.

"Sorry, mate, I think it was that doner kebab I had last night." Gavin had the good grace to look shame-faced, as Shay wound down the window for about the tenth time that morning.

Shay couldn't help but notice that when Gavin spoke his breath actually smelt worse than his arse; feeling queasy, Shay turned his head in order to avoid the smell.

Out of the corner of his eye, he saw the blonde woman finally come out of the house they had been watching just across the road. He watched as she tottered down the long driveway towards the brand new Range Rover that, a few hours ago, they had followed back to this street.

"Okay, here we go." Shay sat bolt upright to get a better view. He was relieved that they could hopefully get moving, as they had already wasted enough time today. He had been bored shitless waiting, and he wanted to get out of here before someone noticed them.

Shay watched the girl walk to her car. She was hot, he'd give her that, blondes were his weakness when it came to women, and this one was something else: a real stunner.

Nudging Gavin to get his arse into gear, Shay's mind went back to the task in hand; no matter how hot the bird was, the Range Rover that she was about to get into was hotter and that was their main priority right now.

Turning on the ignition, Gavin knew what they had to do; there was a secluded lay-by at the entrance of the lane, lined with hedges. It was going to be much easier to do it there, they had figured, much less chance of being spotted. All the houses seemed to be gathered in one cluster at this end of the lane.

Driving on ahead, they had a few minutes to gather their thoughts and get themselves motivated for the task ahead.

Looking into her rear-view mirror, Saskia Frost reapplied her lipstick, rubbing a pink smudge from her teeth with her finger. Then, she checked around her eyes for crows' feet.

She was only twenty-four, but in the harsh light of day and without her usual thick layer of foundation, she was sure that she could see the start of one or two little lines forming at the outside edges of her eyes and between her brows. She might book herself in to see that Botox doctor some of her girlfriends went to, Doctor Nutley-Rowe. His prices were probably high end, but his reputation preceded him, unlike some of the syringe cowboys she had heard horror stories about. The girls had told her that this doctor was so good that he had a list of celebrity clientele longer than her legs.

Making a mental note to call one of her friends to get the doctor's phone number, Saskia started the engine, trying to put the depressing thought of her newly found wrinkles out of her mind. She pulled off down the lane. Turning up the radio, she had just started to relax as she hummed along to a new dance track, when a blue Ford Escort pulled out in front of her, blocking the lane forcing her to brake suddenly.

"What the fu...?" Her head flung forward, as her car screeched to a halt.

She barely had time to clock what was going on when a man wearing a balaclava jumped out of the car and leapt in through her car's passenger door, opening it with such force he almost pulled it off the hinges.

"Get out of the fucking car," he bellowed.

Saskia couldn't think straight, her ears were ringing and she felt like she was going to pass out. She stared at the man in the balaclava, as if in a trance. She could see his lips moving, but she couldn't hear any words, there was just a dull ringing in her ears as she tried to make sense of what was going on.

"I said get out of the fucking car: now." The man pointed a gun straight at her.

Everything seemed to be in slow motion. This can't be happening, Saskia thought.

Seeing the daft bitch's blank expression, Shay realised she was going into shock; he yanked off her seatbelt, leant over her and opened the driver's door then pushed her out onto the road.

As she landed with a thump on the road, thick dust flew up into Saskia's eyes; seconds later, the tyres screeched as the two vehicles pulled off at full speed. Saskia heard someone scream; dazed and confused as she was, it took her a few moments to realise that the sound was in fact coming from her mouth.

Tears rolled down her cheeks as she watched both the cars disappear from sight as they left the lane.

"Are you okay?" a man asked. Saskia recognised him as a busy-body from up the lane; he had obviously come out to see what was going on. "Have they just stolen your car?" he asked, shocked, as things like this just didn't happen where he lived. This was a sought-after area. They had Neighbourhood Watch.

Saskia glared at the nosey neighbour, the shock of her beautiful car being stolen now turning into pure anger, talk about stating the fucking obvious!

Chapter 3

The blue escort pulled into West's Garage forty minutes later. It was closely followed by the gleaming black Range Rover.

"Ah mate, that was a fucking heavy one." A sweaty Shay jumped out of the four-by-four, relieved that they had finally completed the job.

Jamie walked over to inspect the car that he had spent the morning waiting for. It was perfect. They needed to get this out pronto; their client had been in a hurry with this order, and they were way behind.

"Fucking bird wouldn't get out of the motor, would she?" Shay's pulse was racing as he told Jamie what had happened.

Stealing cars used to be child's play for them; motors could be broken into and hotwired in seconds, but the contract they were handling now was for luxury cars and their main client insisted on having the keys for every motor he ordered, otherwise the cars weren't worth shit as far as he was concerned, and that always made their jobs of stealing the cars tricky. They now had to make sure that they nicked the keys as well as the motors, which doubled the chances of them getting caught. They would have to break into homes and steal the keys or like today, they would have to spend hours waiting for an opportunity to get the occupant out of the motor so that they could get in, which was even more tricky. The risks were much higher now.

Shay had felt a second of panic earlier when the blonde bird hadn't got out of the motor when he had first told her to. People could go either way when they were dealing with their instincts in circumstances like that, especially if they went in shock mode, like she had, there was no telling how some people would react. Luckily Shay hadn't encountered anyone brave enough to argue with him in the heat of the moment, especially when he had a loaded piece pointed in their direction. His adrenaline had been pumping today, but thankfully it had all gone to plan and the motor had been delivered in one piece. Satisfied with the boys' job, Jamie told Shay and Gavin to go for lunch.

Ignoring Jamie lording it around the garage like he was the boss, just because the boys had managed to bring in another motor for him, Les Patterson couldn't disguise the fact that once again his nose was firmly out of joint. He inspected every inch of the motor himself too. It had taken most of the morning to get it here, yet Jamie seemed to have once again come up trumps; it was immaculate.

Les had worked at West's Garage for nearly thirteen years, and he loved his job. The location, a small side road in the centre of Lambeth, just off the high street, was spot on.

Under the boss Gary's strict orders, they only ever took on as much work as they needed to from real punters, so the books would tally up at the end of each month. They needed to make sure they were keeping up appearances should anyone get suspicious that the garage was being used for anything dodgy and demanded to see paperwork. It was a great front and worked a treat as a cover for the dodgy motors that passed through the rusty garage doors. To anyone on the outside, they looked like another small-time garage.

Les knew that there was nothing small time about his boss, Gary West, though. Gary was the brains of the outfit. He had managed to set up a big contract with some Ugandans that had turned out to be a nice little earner for them all. All they had to do was supply to order and shift top-end motors out of the country. Gary had so many customs officials in his pockets that he barely had room in there for loose change, so that was actually the easy bit.

Most days Les loved his job, but today wasn't one of them; today, his patience was being tested to the limit. He glared at Jamie. He couldn't stand the bloke, his attitude stank and he had a knack of rubbing Les up the wrong way. How they had managed to work together for the past ten years without killing each other remained a mystery, but on Gary's request Les put up with Jamie.

"Wonder what Gary will make of this little beauty, huh? Should put a smile back on the miserable git's mush." Jamie noticed that the comments he had been making all morning about Gary were doing the trick and winding up Les nicely. Les was never happy with anything Jamie said or did, so he enjoyed adding fuel to the fire and riling Les.

Les, loyal to Gary, didn't want to listen to him being cut down by Jamie. He ignored him and got to work, glad to get his teeth into sorting out the Range Rover. He loved keeping busy, especially if it meant he didn't have to listen to Jamie spouting anymore of his shit. Les climbed into the driver's seat to take a closer look at the interior, thinking that if it had been up to him, they would never have taken on Jamie. Les had always thought that Jamie was trouble, but Gary had taken an instant liking to the kid and had taken a chance on him by letting him into the firm. Gary was normally a shrewd man who made the right choices and they had certainly raked in a nice amount of cash over the years, but Les had never been able to get his head around why Gary had taken on the little scroat; and as the years had passed, Les's dislike for Jamie had grown.

Yes, Jamie was good at stealing motors, Les would give him his due: he had a way of finding the top-end motors they needed, and he was smoother than butter when it came to hotwiring them and getting them back to the garage in record time. But Gary had made a massive gamble in taking him on, ignoring Les' reservations about the boy. Jamie had only been fifteen when he had walked in and brazenly asked for a job. Les couldn't believe the balls of the kid, nor could he believe it when Gary had seemed impressed at the young boy's confidence. Walking in as a complete unknown and being given an 'in': it was unheard of. Of course Jamie had only walked into what he thought was a legit car garage back then, but he had seemed clued up on who Gary was and what he would be getting himself involved in. The way that Jamie had handled the situation had made a good impression on their boss.

The boy was strong and had youth on his side, but Les had experience and he had been at the garage since day one, and as the years had gone on he had been incensed as he watched the kid get all the kudos. It really irked Les that Gary seemed to be acting all proud of Jamie, like Jamie was his main man, when it was Les who had worked at the garage the longest. The whole situation left a sour taste in Les' mouth.

Whatever Les thought of Jamie, though, from the start he had been made to swallow it. Whatever Gary said, went, and after all these years of working for him, Les didn't need that explained twice. Trying his hardest not to cause a fuss, especially seeing as Gary seemed adamant about his decision Les had swallowed his pride and just let things be.

When things started really taking off for the firm, a few years back, they had taken on Shay and Gavin. They had been mainly employed as runners, helping Jamie to get the motors in, and also as an extra bit of muscle when they were needed, but Les never really had an opinion on either of them. They were a pair of Muppets as far as he was concerned; he never saw them as a threat the way he did Jamie.

It was fair to say that Les had never been the brainiest, and he knew it too. Jamie got the motors in and Les worked his magic on changing the chassis numbers and matching up the paperwork they had collected from their contacts. Then the cars were out of their hands, which generally meant they were loaded straight onto a container and shipped to Uganda. It was an easy setup, which had made them all a small fortune.

"What do you think then, Les; this one got what it takes to make Gary happy?"

Jamie's question was innocent enough, but it still had an unmistakably shitty tone to it, and Les was barely able to keep his patience with the boy's sarcasm as he demanded: "What's your problem, Jamie? Gary does nothing but sing your fucking praises. All bloody week you've done nothing but bad mouth him, and I'm getting sick of listening to it."

"Me bad mouthing Gary? I wonder why... You can't bloody tell me that you haven't noticed that there's something going on, Les. Gary seems to be going soft; look at the state of him, the man's a right mess. I've never seen him look so frigging miserable. What, am I not allowed to state the fucking obvious?" Jamie threw back his remark, frustrated that Les wasn't able to see what he so clearly could.

Jamie was entitled to his opinion and if Les couldn't see what was staring them both in the face, he was even more stupid than he looked. Jamie couldn't help the way he felt; Gary was going down in his estimation after the events of the last week, and the more Jamie mulled the situation over the more pissed off he felt about it all. Les was right about one thing though; Gary did think that the sun shone out of Jamie's backside. The man had taken him under his wing, so to speak, and had taught him everything he knew. That didn't make him any the less pissed off about things, though.

Over the years, Gary had even helped Jamie through his driving test by footing up the money for his lessons and had sorted him out with his own sporty little Volkswagen Golf. Jamie was also paid a good wage, which had enabled him to be able to afford his own flat over-looking the river. He had been living the dream thanks to the opportunity his boss had given him, and he was grateful for all of it. Gary had gone above and beyond over the years, teaching Jamie everything there was to know about the business. He could practically run the show if he needed to, which was what Jamie had a sneaky suspicion Gary had wanted all along.

Jamie knew that he was being out of order talking disrespectfully about Gary, but he was so angry about the way that Gary was acting; it was a side of him that he hadn't seen before. Gary had always been such a strong bloke and to see him weak and vulnerable had really thrown Jamie. Jamie had never had a father figure in his life, but he was guessing from the way that Gary acted towards him, that he was more or less treated like a son. They had so much in common and spent hours chatting about all kinds of things, and Gary often commented that Jamie was a chip off the old block, like a younger and fierier version of himself, and Jamie had happily noted the pride in the man's voice when he had said it.

Jamie liked the thought of having someone like Gary watching his back, it made him feel secure. Using the break that he had been given, wanting to prove that he was worthy of it and to make Gary proud, Jamie had slowly worked his way up over the years. He had worked hard and learnt every part of the trade. Gary had hinted on several occasions that one day, when he was too old for all this, he would need someone to take over. Of course that was all way off in the future, so the comments had been subtle and left to hang in the air, but the intention had been there all the same. Having someone who watched out for him was something Jamie had never experienced. He often thought of his younger brother, Kevin. He would be twelve now: how time had flown. He regretted that Kevin would probably now no longer know, or else no longer care, who Jamie was; he had left it too long now to go back for him. Jamie hadn't realised, when he walked out on his vile mother all those years ago, that he would never be going back, he really hadn't thought that far ahead. Ten years had flown by, and he had a new life. The Jamie he had once been was better left in the past.

Jamie's thoughts returned to the present when he caught Les smirking at him. He could almost see the cogs turning in the man's transparent head as he realised how Gary would react, once Les informed him of all the shit Jamie had been spouting about him. Jamie tried to control his rising temper. Les was a prick. He had made it very clear that he didn't like Jamie, and for the most part Jamie ignored him. Jamie couldn't be arsed to give the bloke any reason to go running back to Gary, complaining about him. Besides, the more Les showed his apparent one-sided hatred towards Jamie, the more Les confirmed to everyone that he was the one with the issue and not Jamie.

"Look, Les, I know you don't like me, you've made that more than clear over the years, and to tell you the truth, I don't really give a flying shit that there's no love lost between the two of us. I ain't here to be your mate; I'm here to earn a living. But come on, even you must be able to see that Gary's losing it lately. Look at the deal we did last week: we're a fucking laughing stock," Jamie persisted.

Les knew that there had been more to Jamie's bad attitude that day, finally they were getting somewhere, Les thought. All the shitty little comments about Gary, which Les had felt had been uncalled for, were because of this. Even Les could see there was some truth in what Jamie was saying. Of course he had noticed that Gary hadn't been himself lately; you would have had to have a guide dog and a white stick not to see it. Gary had been acting in a way that was completely out of character and the past week had been a nightmare for them all, but there was still no need for Jamie to be so narky about him.

The deal Jamie had referred to had been with a Jamaican bloke. He was supposed to be the first of many of the new contacts that Gary had made recently. This Yardie bloke was new on the scene but had started to get a reputation for ripping off people, so Jamie and Les had been wary at first.

Gary had insisted that the deal was kosher, however; he was adamant that, despite the man's reputation, his contact that had put his name forward was reliable and that the deal would pay off. Gary had assured the two men that it was all under control.

It had turned out to be a set-up, much to Gary's cost. The motors.they had bought were junk, and Jamie had figured that not even that Dynamo magician bloke would be able to transform the pieces of crap they had been stuck with. They were like baked-bean cans on wheels, probably the worst cut and shut cars Jamie had seen since he started in the business. They were worthless; the only place they were fit for was the local scrap yard. They had been shafted for thousands. When Jamie had told Gary, he had expected to start a war. There was no way that they could be mugged off so publicly like this by this Jamaican bloke, especially after their source had given them their word on him. The bloke seemed to be taking over a lot of the firms around here, and Jamie thought that Gary needed to put a stop to him trying to do them over, or they would be the ones out of business next. Who would want to deal with a bunch of mugs? Once that piss-taking Yardie bloke thought that he could lord it over them, they would be screwed. Jamie couldn't have been any firmer about his thoughts on them needing to sort this situation out and pronto.

Jamie was prepared for violence; it came with the job. He had come across more than a few sticky situations since he had worked for Gary and Les, and he could handle himself, especially if they went in tooled up. He knew as soon as you showed a tiny crack of weakness, they would be crawling all over the yard like sewer rats.

Gary's reaction, however, had not been what Jamie had anticipated at all.

Jamie had stormed into his office, furious about all the shit cars they had been stitched up with, and after telling Gary how bad the motors they had been shafted with really were, he had been left speechless by Gary's reaction, or rather lack of one. He had just sat there and swallowed it. Seeing his boss looking so worried and out of his depth had knocked the stuffing out of Jamie. He had seen for the first time that Gary was no longer in control, the Yardie had clearly got one over on him, and Gary didn't look like he had any intention of fighting back. Gary had told Jamie, in no uncertain terms, to leave the situation well alone. Jamie had been riled about the whole thing and had spent the past week going over the whole conversation time and time again in his head. As the days had gone on, he had noticed that Gary seemed more and more shaken up. The more Jamie stewed on it, the more he had come to the conclusion that it was time to take matters into his own hands; if Gary wasn't prepared to sort this mess out, then Jamie would be left with no choice. He would walk. He couldn't work for this firm any longer if they were going to sit here and take it from this Jamaican bloke. Jamie was not one to let people have anything over him; that he would always remain in control was something he had promised himself ten years ago when he walked out on his mother. The way that Jamie saw it, they had two options, either he made Gary see sense and they both sorted this mess out once and for all or Jamie would leave. It was as simple as that, as far as he was concerned.

Les had a point, though; Jamie shouldn't be bad mouthing Gary, not after everything he had done for Jamie. But he felt so angry with Gary for not doing what he had always instilled in Jamie: standing up and fighting back.

"You know what, Les? For once in your life, you're absolutely right…" Jamie slung down his tools. "I shouldn't be standing here harping on about him to you. I should be saying it to his face, and you know what? I think I might just go and do that." And with that, Jamie marched to the office where he assumed Gary would once again be skulking. Les could jog on if he thought for a second he would have any hold over Jamie, the bloke had another think coming if he thought that he would be the one to tell Gary what Jamie's thoughts were. Jamie was more than capable of doing that himself.

Jamie stepped into the small, cramped office and was surprised to see his boss looking even more pale than usual. He could smell alcohol and noticed the slight shake in Gary's hand as he put down his pen and looked up at Jamie. It was the sort of shake that implied Gary had been up all night drinking.

"Gary, can we talk? Is everything all right?" As bad as things had been lately, it worried Jamie to see Gary looking ill.

"Why wouldn't I be okay?" Gary snapped, as Jamie took a seat. Gary had a horrible feeling that he knew what was coming.

Jamie wasn't sure how to say it. "Gary, we need to talk. I don't know what's going on..."

"You want out, don't you?" Gary didn't have to wait for Jamie's answer; the way the boy hung his head answered his question. "Well, to be honest, son, I'm surprised you stuck around this long." Gary smiled affectionately at Jamie. Jamie couldn't mask his surprise, and Gary laughed at the younger man's expression. "What did you think I'd do, shoot your kneecaps off to prevent you leaving?"

Jamie smiled back but felt shame wash over him. He realised now, sitting opposite Gary that this was a man who had done nothing but look out for him over the past ten years and, as much as he had worked hard, he was in Gary's debt for giving him his chance.

As if reading Jamie's thoughts, Gary said: "This ship is well and truly sinking, mate, so if I was you, I would have jumped overboard like yesterday. I've lost it all, Jamie. I'm in deep shit." Gary reached into his desk drawer and pulled out the remaining dregs of Scotch that were left in the bottle he had managed to put away last night. All night he had sat at his desk, pondering every avenue of options he could think of, but there was nothing he could do to sort the mess out. Things had changed too much in the past decade. People no longer played fair, and the game was too dangerous now: it was more trouble than it was worth. The fire he had had his belly when he first started the garage was burning out. The money and the kudos all came with a whole world of shit these days.

"What do you mean, you've lost it? What's going on? We haven't lost the garage?" Jamie felt bad that things had gone this far, that Gary had been left to shoulder whatever had been going on alone. He felt guilty that he hadn't been there for his boss when he had clearly needed him.

"No, not the garage," Gary said. "Not yet, anyway. But I've lost the deals; I've lost the fucking lot." He rubbed his temples. Jamie noticed that he had a few days' worth of stubble on his chin, and that his suit looked crumpled, like he had slept in it, although Gary's under-eye bags told the tale that there had been no sleep achieved lately either. Gary normally prided himself on his smart appearance. The severity of the situation was dawning on Jamie, this was beyond bad.

"They've taken over our contract with the Ugandans." Gary looked at Jamie. "Fuck knows how. We've been working with those men for years. We offered them the best prices, but they must have undercut us or got to them somehow."

"Who're you talking about?" Jamie asked.

"The contacts that fitted us up with those motors," Gary said. "There's some real nasty bastard running the show now. His name's Jerell Morgan. Trust me on this, kid; he's one fucker not to be messed with."

Shaking his head, as he tried to take in what he was being told, Jamie couldn't believe what he was hearing. The Ugandan contract was their main earner; it took up most of their time and resources and was practically their sole source of income. They would be royally screwed without it.

"Well, what are we going to do about it?" Jamie couldn't let Gary sort this out on his own. He felt ashamed that he had thought about walking. At least now he understood why Gary had been the way he had this week: the man had the weight of the world on his shoulders. The way Jamie saw it, they had two options. They could let that thieving Rasta bloke walk all over them, or they could take back what was rightfully theirs. And Jamie had no intention of letting the piss-taking fucker walk all over them.

Despite his misery and worry, Gary smiled as he recognised the fury and fight in the kid before him; he reminded him of how he used to be when he started out all those years ago. Who would have thought back then that at the grand old age of fifty-two, he would be thinking of jacking it all in.

"Look, kid, I know you want to help and all that, but I really don't think we're going to come back from this one. I've been wheeling and dealing for years, and never in all my time have I witnessed such a sorry state of affairs. There are so many foreigners getting in on the game nowadays, it feels like we don't stand a chance anymore, we're totally outnumbered. We can't match their prices. It's a whole other world out there now."

Jamie could see where Gary was coming from. Gary's main rival, when Jamie had started at the garage, had been the Turkish gangs in North London. But over the years, the Turks had lost interest in cars and shifted their attention to shifting drugs. Drugs seemed to be the main earner everywhere these days. But it wasn't something that Gary had been keen on getting involved in. The money to be made was vast, but the risk involved was far greater.

Gary had been fortunate enough to have been left with free rein with his business dealings around Lambeth with the motors and had become so well known for his astute business sense that he had managed to secure a very large contract shipping out high-end motors to a bigwig in Uganda. Gary had sealed the deal by offering prices that they couldn't refuse: money in this game always talked.

The Yardies had been coming over to England in their droves in the past year and were fast becoming prominent players, but they were right nasty fuckers and like no-one Gary had ever encountered. Unlike the Turks, they didn't want to blend in and stay on their own turf to do their deals. The Jamaicans wanted the lot: the cars, the drugs, everything. Whatever was making the money, they wanted a piece of it. Instead of working their way up, they were just taking whatever they wanted, muscling in on the bigger firms and putting them out of business. And being the vicious fuckers that they were, they seemed to be getting away with it; no-one seemed to be capable of stopping them. They had already managed to muscle in on their contract, and the junk cars they had stuck them with had just been their way of fucking with their heads. Gary knew they had done it to antagonise him. They were giving him a chance to back down quietly.

"What if I can get the Ugandan contract back?" Jamie's voice was filled with enthusiasm, as he thought how they could turn the situation around.

"You're not listening, Jamie. This Jerell bloke is supposed to be a fucking animal. He eats people like us for breakfast. The word out there is he's taking over the streets. Cars, drugs, the lot; he seems to have everyone in his pocket. The Turks only really wanted the drugs, and they keep to their own: always have. They have their own battles to sort out; even they don't want to get involved with this fucker. We have no back up. We all have our roles to play, but these Yardies are fucking ruthless, and a ruck with them becomes personal; you pick one wrong fight and that's when wars start." Gary sighed.

"There's only one thing for it then, isn't there?" Jamie had a glint in his eye but spoke in a cold, serious tone. "We don't pick a fight."

Gary stared at Jamie in confusion, as he continued: "This Jerell Morgan... we're going to have to take the fucker out."

Chapter 4

It was almost three o'clock in the morning and, once again, it was cold and wet. The temperature gauge in the car had shown that it was minus one, probably the average temperature for an icy January morning in England, but even after being here for almost two months, Jerell's hot Jamaican blood still wasn't used to how cold it could get.

Just a few minutes' drive up the Thames, the clubs would be closing and the last of the drunken partygoers falling out onto Lambeth's busy lamp-lit streets. He could see the long stretch of the Lambeth Bridge far off in the distance further up the river, and beyond that he could just about make out the twinkling lights of the famous Houses of Parliament reflecting down onto the rippling murky waters of the Thames. The isolated spot he had driven to, this far down the river, felt like a million miles away from London's infamous tourist spot. There was no one around; even the broken streetlamp next to where he pulled up was in darkness. In fact he couldn't have planned it better; the eerily quiet, muddy verge was perfect for what he needed to do.

He dragged the suitcase from the boot of his flashy new Beamer 3-Series. His car was his pride and joy, the first thing he had bought with his newfound wealth. He saw it as investing into the image he wanted to portray; the boys back home in Jamaica would give their right arms to have a car as flash as this. In fact, he had seen a few boys take a bullet for much less.

He hoisted the bag out of the car using all the muscle power he could muster. He loved the way that he could intimidate people with his massive six-foot-tall frame; his huge body was pure muscle and his bulging arms had a way of doing the talking for him.

He had taken the time earlier to line the boot of the car with plastic sheeting; there was no way he was risking getting it messed up: it had cost thirty-five grand, more money than he had ever seen; until now.

How quickly things had changed for him. It was a far cry from his backyard. England was definitely where the money was at.

Jerell was smartly dressed in a pinstripe grey Armani suit, although because of what had happened earlier it was ruined now. He would have to burn it when he was done here. Overalls would have been a more practical option, but he had got caught up in the moment this evening and the suit he had been wearing hadn't factored into the events that had taken place; besides, he had plenty more get-up where this one had come from.

He shivered once again, as the icy winds from the river swept over him as he walked. The verge was slippery and he struggled to steady his body, to stop himself from falling; the weight of the case pulled him down, but he managed to stay upright as he dragged it along the dirt track that led to the water's edge.

He had always known that he would love England, and he had been right. The two months that he had been here had flown by, and he had developed a taste for the lifestyle, even if the weather was shit; being cold was a small price to pay.

His grandma back home in Kingston would not be happy if she could see what he was doing. She had raised him to be a good boy, after his mother had upped and abandoned him just days after giving birth to him, claiming she was too young for the responsibility of looking after a child.

His grandma had been strict. She lived by the words of the Bible, believing: 'If you spare the rod, you spoil the child.' Jerell had religion drummed into his ears from the minute he was born, and as a mischievous child, he had been whipped more times than he could remember.

His grandma's efforts had been wasted on him, though; no matter how many times she had shoved the Bible down his throat while he was growing up, evil was in his bones.

As a boy, Jerell had been an inquisitive child, his energy boundless. On many occasions, he had wondered out loud what the shores of England would be like to visit: he had been obsessed with the place.

His grandma had disagreed. "England is too cold, only white skins can live there. We Jamaicans need sunshine on our bones, boy; we is black for a reason." She made it her mission to drum it into him that being Jamaican was a privilege, and that he must grow to respect his black heritage and his culture. "A man without knowledge of his own history is like a tree without roots, never be ignorant 'bout where you is from boy, dat is God's truth."

The last few weeks before he left Jamaica had been difficult for Jerell. He felt bad that he couldn't tell his grandma that he was finally going to the place he had grown up dreaming about, but he knew it would be against her wishes. Things were looking a whole lot better for him now than that he was here, though, and he was sure that she would understand one day why he had just upped and left without saying goodbye. He felt that he had made the right choice. Things seemed brighter for him on this side of the world. So the bad weather, as far as he was concerned, was a small sacrifice to make in return for the big money that was to be made here. England was a money pit, unlike back home where all the Rasta men sat around in the sun, stoned out of their minds, drinking rum all day and preaching shit to each other. No-one got rich by sitting around talking shit, he thought, that was for sure.

The options for a man like him were limited, back home: there were two main paths that he had watched many others follow. You could live your life preaching the Lord's good name, dedicating your life to being a chilled-out religious brother, but after spending a lifetime listening to his Grandma's preaching it wasn't a route that he favoured. He had taken the other path, the more common amongst his like-minded peers, going in the opposite direction of working his way up the ranks in Jamaica's ghetto as a soldier. Although they all thought they were bad men dealing with guns and drugs, he had learnt early on that he was just a soldier. He was always lining some top man's pockets while putting himself in the firing line, stealing and fighting on someone else's behalf and never getting anywhere himself. Violence and sometimes death were always present, and the rewards were relatively small considering the lengths he had to go to earn them. The wealthy ranks of Jamaica didn't do their own dirty work; they got their soldiers to do that for them, and there were plenty willing to do it.

Bringing his mind back to the task in hand, Jerell gave the area another once over, making sure that there was no-one around to witness his actions. In future, he would be getting one of the others to do this type of shitty work for him. Jerell was good at dishing out even the most heinous acts of violence; this was a first for him regarding a clean-up operation, but he had wanted to see this through until the very end.

Inside the suitcase was the mangled body of some junkie Polish bloke. The idiot Pole had found out to his ultimate cost that he should have kept his mouth shut. The stupid fucker should have thought twice about running his mouth off to the police when he got pulled in for being found in possession. He clearly hadn't realised that his loyalties should have lain with Jerell and not tried to strike a deal with the pigs to save his sorry arse. The police would never be able to enforce a punishment anywhere near what Jerell was capable of, and the Pole should have known that.

Jerell was now certain, after torturing it out of him, that the Pole had kept his name out of it with the police; he promised Jerell that he had given false leads trying to cut himself a deal and had made up names.

Jerell had finally believed the man; no-one could go through that amount of pain without telling the truth. Looking at the mess he had made of the man, though, Jerell had had no choice but to finish him off. It had been a massive fuck-up on the Pole's behalf that he had talked in the first place, and Jerell couldn't afford that level of distrust now he knew what the man was capable of when desperate to get himself off the hook, especially at this crucial moment when Jerell was busy establishing his reputation.

Jerell had really gone to town on the bloke; he wanted maximum impact now that he was beginning to make a name for himself.

Tonight had been essential in the next stage of his game plan. Jerell had shown the stunned boys who worked for him exactly what kind of level he was operating on. They had stood and watched, horrified, as Jerell had carved the Polish bloke up. As the Polish man had cried and begged him to stop, Jerell had enjoyed the show he was providing for his boys, loving the reaction he was getting from them all. They all looked shit scared of what was happening in front of them.

He had wanted to let everyone know he was the boss, the man in charge. No-one would fuck with him now. He knew they thought he had lost the plot, but he didn't care. Killing the man so brutally was a complete over-reaction, he knew, but a well-timed one.

This man's slaying had been a lesson, on a grand scale, for everyone present. They were all in fear of him now. The gruesomeness of the man's death wouldn't be forgotten any time soon.

The sight of the derelict warehouse floor lined with plastic had made the Polish man's bowels loosen in fear at what he knew was coming, as he had been dragged into the large empty room earlier that evening. Blood had oozed across the sheeting as Jerell had set to work carving and slicing, as the man fell unconscious from the shock and pain, while the boys had watched in shocked silence. Jerell's finale had been slicing off the man's head with a machete. He must sharpen it up, he thought now, as he lowered the bag down into the filthy water; the blade had been blunt and the boys had watched horrified at the ruthlessness displayed before them as Jerell had hacked through the dead man's neck like a piece of butchered meat.

There was an almighty splash as Jerell let go of the case. The weight of the corpse, along with the bricks he had used to weigh it down, made it plunge straight down to the riverbed.

Jerell smiled at how successfully tonight had turned out. As far as he was concerned, if you want something doing right you do it yourself. He had proved himself tonight. He wanted his boys to fear him; through fear he would have his own army of dedicated soldiers. It was exactly what he had

wanted: now they would do whatever he told them.

Chapter 5

At just gone six o'clock, Les had been all ready to down tools and set off for the boozer, when Gary had called a last-minute meeting. He had said he had things to discuss and the tone in his voice told Les that whatever Gary had to say was going to be serious; however, it seemed to be Jamie who was doing all of the talking now that the meeting had begun.

Les was trying to take in what he had just been told. Ever since earlier on today, when Jamie had gone to speak to Gary about the situation with the Jamaican fella and the cars, the mood round here had lifted slightly, and now he knew why.

Jamie had come back from his little chat with Gary without saying a word to Les about what had transpired, and Les had been too proud to show Jamie that he was curious. Not wanting Jamie to know that he was bothered, Les had ignored Jamie and the two men had done their work in silence for the rest of the afternoon.

Les had expected Gary to be annoyed with Jamie for the things that he had been saying, but it seemed the opposite was true: Gary appeared more chipper.

Les looked around the room; even Shay and Gavin seemed to be more in the know about what was going on than he was. He watched them nod their heads in agreement with Jamie's plan, their expressions indicating that they were drinking everything in without so much as a question. It would have to be Les who burst the bubble.

"That's your plan, is it?" Les laughed. "You just expect us to walk up to him, tap him on the shoulder and then blow his brains out? As easy as that, is it? Then what: problem solved? Cos if that's what you think, then you must be completely fucking crazy. Great one, Jamie. Round two to us, yeah?"

Jamie rolled his eyes at the sarcasm; trust Les to be difficult, throwing his two pence worth in at the last minute.

Les couldn't help feeling rattled; the decision had clearly already been made, and made without him. He had been left out of the loop again. He was now being informed of their plans like he was an afterthought.

"It's not quite like that, Les." Gary sensed that Les might need convincing. Les could be a stubborn old sod, and Gary was more than aware of his personal vendetta against Jamie. "But Jamie does have a point. We only have two choices: we either let them stamp us into the ground, or we take back what's ours and take them out of the game."

Gary tried to sound more convincing than he felt; he agreed with Jamie about what needed to be done, but he couldn't shake the feeling that they were way out of their depth. He had heard nothing but bad things about this Jerell bloke, and letting his men get involved with this animal was something that Gary was wary of doing, he really didn't want to put them all at such risk.

Lifting himself up onto the dusty garage counter to sit next to Shay, Les tried to get comfortable; now he knew what the meeting was about, he had a feeling that they were going to be at work for a while. He felt his forehead start to throb, signalling the start of another one of his headaches; he always got headaches when he was stressed out, he really wasn't very good at coping with such high drama. He had wanted to finish early tonight as there was a fishing documentary on TV that he had really wanted to watch, and he had fancied getting a couple of cheeky beers in at the pub first. He loved his creature comforts, did Les, it was the simple pleasures in life that did it for him, that and routine. Tonight he had wanted to put his feet up, order a pizza and watch a bit of telly. But instead here he was, sitting with four men who had all clearly lost the plot, and who were now arranging to start World War

Three by murdering a big Jamaican psychopath. Les felt uneasy about the entire thing. They had had more than a few rucks in the past with other firms, it went with the territory in this game, but Les was getting a bit old for it all now, and for the past year or so, it had barely felt like they had been doing anything even remotely criminal. There had been almost no drama. Gary was the one who dealt with the Ugandan contract, and all Les had to do was what he was told, which was just how he liked it; it was all part of his routine.

"Look, there really isn't a choice, mate." Jamie hoped that his friendlier than usual manner towards Les might persuade him into coming around to his way of thinking. "If we don't take this Jerell out, we may as well shut these doors now and skulk off out of here with our tails between our legs." Jamie couldn't put it any more bluntly.

Gavin nodded; he was certainly up for dishing out retribution. In fact he would have great pleasure in inflicting some damage on the black bastards; he'd had enough of the fuckers lording it over the place, thinking they were untouchable; as far as he was concerned, there were way too many around already for his liking.

Les felt Gary's stare burn into him; he knew that he meant business, and there was no way he would back down now that he had made his mind up, as always. Les knew that Gary must be serious, especially if this was the best plan they could come up with. Les couldn't bear to think about what would happen if they closed the garage, it was his life. He wouldn't have a clue what to do with himself.

Catching Gary's eye once more before Gary quickly looked away, Les could see a glint of hesitation in his boss' face as he listened to Jamie speak.

Jamie and Gavin seemed to be the only ones out of the five of them to be confident about the plan; Jamie in particular appeared certain of how they should play this, and it angered Les that once again he was going to have to do what Jamie said.

"And what if it all backfires, huh; what if one of us gets caught up in the crossfire?" Les was sweating at the thought of it. Dodgy cars he could handle, the police, customs... none of that fazed him. Les was good at denial; he knew what type of business they were involved in, but his part seemed so small that he had never really felt like anything he was doing was illegal. Even though he spent his days etching numbers off chassis' and matching up dodgy paperwork, to him it was just a job his boss asked him to do. Ignorance, where Les was concerned, was most definitely bliss. These days, he didn't have to deal with any of the contacts or get involved with much that happened outside of the garage doors. This plan was different. A crazed, machete-wielding lunatic was someone he really did not want to get mixed up with.

"We're already in the middle of it all, Les, look around you. We've just lost our biggest contract to that fucker. And not only that, he's tucked us up tighter than a mental patient in a straitjacket with those dodgy fucking motors he sold us; we look like a fucking laughing stock." Jaime got more vexed as he spoke. "We either do this together once and for all, or we're out of the game."

Jamie let his words hang in the air, as he took a swig from his mug; the coffee he had made earlier was now stone cold, but he drank it regardless, quenching the dryness that lingered in the back of his throat. He looked over to Gary for reassurance, he needed him to back him up; his silence hadn't gone unnoticed. Jamie was only going to fight if there was something to fight for. If Gary wanted this business to keep working, then Jamie needed to hear it; otherwise, what was the point?

Gary had thought about nothing other than Jamie's plan since their chat earlier, and although he was uneasy about what they may be starting if it backfired, the thought of losing what he had worked so hard at building up over all these years scared him more.

Jamie was right. They didn't have a choice.

Meeting Jamie's gaze, Gary then turned to Les and said: "Well, what's it to be, are you in? Or are you out?"

Les thought that this was a stupid question; he would be loyal to Gary to the day he died; if Gary needed his help with this then there was no question, he would be there for him no matter what shit it might bring them all. He hated the thought that Jamie was the mastermind behind it all, though, and as petty as it was he made a point of only looking at Gary when he replied: "Well, looks like I'm in, then, don't it?"

Shay jumped down off the table he was sitting on. He was happy to go along with any plan; it was what he had signed up for when he joined the team. He gathered the empty mugs; he fancied another coffee, he had been trying to suppress yawns in the meeting as he didn't want to look like he was sleeping on his feet while all this was going on, it was far too important. They had a lot of ground to cover.

Gavin was also happy with the plan; he had fancied getting a piece of some action since he had started working at the garage, and now it seemed he would finally have his chance to get some. He loved the thrill he got from nicking cars, but inflicting violence was what he was all about, it was definitely more his thing. He loved a good fight.

Passing Shay his mug, Les was pissed off that they now had a long night ahead of them as they figured out how to execute their plan. Pushing away his former thoughts of a few chilled beers and a relaxed night in front of the telly, Les geared himself up to spend the evening listening to Jamie harp on with his grand plan of arranging the hit.

The men were all agreed.

Chapter 6

The music blared out of the speakers, muffling the sound of the chatter in the

room and filling the air with the sweet sound of Caribbean vibes. He was a

long way from home, but as Jerell lay back on the sofa inhaling his spliff deep

into his lungs, he closed his eyes and let his mind drift. When he smoked his

gear and listened to his music, he was transported back to Kingston.

Jerell had come to England with fake papers; he had no intention of returning

to Jamaica. It hadn't taken him long to get lost in London, to feel that he could

make a go of starting a new life for himself. Meeting Reagan had been fated.

The flat they shared was chaotic. Jerell's boys came and went all day long; he

was never alone and that was exactly how he liked it. He couldn't help feeling

smug about how everything had seemed to have fallen into place.

Reagan sat at the table counting out some money, as he skinned up a joint.

The musical vibe was contagious; he tapped his foot along to the beat; these

days, he felt like a king.

When Reagan had left the care home that he had grown up in, a couple of years ago when he was sixteen, he had wondered what was going on inside the head of his social worker who had sorted this place out for him. The system had landed him his very own council flat bang in the middle of the crime-riddled Stockwell Estate, one of the roughest areas of South London, notorious for gang crime. It made him laugh how this social worker claimed she was there to help him, preaching to him about how to better his life and then dumping him in a place like this, before fucking off back to her two-point-four kids in her own idyllic little house. It was a joke. People who worked for the system had no idea what it was like in the real world.

Reagan would have been happy to live in a shed; he didn't give a shit where his flat was, he had just been chuffed that for the first time in his life he had a home of his own. He was used to shitholes, he had grown up in these kinds of places, so he knew he would fit in.

Having a flat of his own, at such a young age, had made Reagan a popular boy and wanting his mates to stick around he had always encouraged them to treat the place like it was theirs too. Reagan's mates had been more than happy to oblige; this place, where they could bring back the girls, was a pussy magnet and there had been many a crazy party until all hours of the mornings, tearing it up to the latest tunes whilst they got drunk and stoned.

The parties were great, but it hadn't taken Reagan long to realise that he had been missing a trick. What he actually had was a base. If he was clever enough, this place would be perfect for him to use to start his own little money-making factory, where he could concentrate on getting some gear out onto the streets. He named his gang the Larkhall Boys and they had quickly started to become known on the estate.

The main thing Reagan cared about was that the boys he surrounded himself with respected him, and as he was the one who owned the flat and had set up the nice earner for everyone with the drugs he was pushing out, respect was something he had no trouble getting from them. He had relied only on himself: until he met Jerell.

Reagan couldn't believe his luck when Jerell befriended him. A mutual friend had introduced them, and Reagan had instantly been in awe of the man. Jerell wasn't some messed-up kid with a chip on his shoulder wanting to make a few pounds, he was a proper gangster. The man was unhinged, everything about him was intimidating. Reagan had quickly realised that with Jerell by his side, they were going to make some serious money.

Reagan had fallen over himself trying to impress Jerell and had been prepared to do whatever the man asked so that he could get an in with him. When Jerell had finally taken him up on his offer of a place to stay, things had

59

started to progress for the two men. Jerell moving in had been the opportunity Reagan had been looking for, and now he wanted Jerell to see what he was capable of.

Jerell's operation made Reagan's little cannabis factory look like a pathetic gardening hobby. The first thing that Jerell had said, when he came on board, was that they were to stop selling gear from the flat. As far as he was concerned, that was a fucking capture waiting to happen.

One of the Reagan's mates, Louise, had also been given a place by the social around the same time as Reagan, just across the estate, so Jerell had moved all their drugs there. Louise had been apprehensive about having all the gear moved to her place, at first; it was a massive responsibility, and she would be in charge of overseeing the operation from her end. She was frightened that she would get caught, and be the one that ended up taking the rap. She was a smart girl, though, and knew that it was the only way the gang would take her seriously. If she was careful, then she would be okay. Jerell had assured her that if she did things his way then she would be fine and the generous cut of money he had offered for her services had helped her put any worries to the back of her mind.

Jerell was ready to flood the streets of Lambeth with more than just ganja.

The set up was simple. Reagan made sure, as he always had, that his boys knew their roles. No-one was to go to Jerell for petty problems. Reagan wanted Jerell to know that he was capable of keeping everyone in line and letting the operation run as smoothly as possible. Jerell was the top man now and Reagan was his second-in-command, a role he was happy with.

Jerell made sure that none of the other boys went in and out of Louise's flat as they did in Reagan's house. He didn't want to draw attention to the place; he wanted it kept low-key.

Louise had slipped into the role of the main courier. She picked up the gear and dropped off the supplies. No-one would suspect that a pretty girl like Louise was the main runner; with her big eyes, she looked like butter wouldn't melt. Any of the nosey neighbours who spotted her frequently coming and going would just assume that she was some pretty young thing who lived there.

Reagan was strict with the boys about taking drugs; Jerell insisted on it. At the flat, the most they had was a few spliffs on the go; they made sure that if the heavies ever suspected them for dealing and raided their flat, they would find nothing.

"No one touches crack, man. Weed is fine; I appreciate that a brother needs to chill from time to time, but save the crack for the skanks on the street. If these boys wanna be part of dis operation, then they need to keep their heads clear so dat we make some serious money." Jerell didn't want to be working with scummy crackheads. As far as he was concerned, crack was for his customers not his crew. He knew he would be setting himself up to lose if he surrounded himself with addicts, it was something that he had witnessed time and time again with other bad-ass wannabes and in his book it was a guaranteed way to fail. This was a business, and everyone around him needed to keep a clear head and always be one step ahead of the game. Jerell had it all sorted: business as they say, was booming.

Jerell tapped his foot to the music; it was the first time since he had arrived in England that he could put his feet up and chill out for a few hours. He listened to the boys sitting across the room, having a heated debate about the rioters who had terrorised the capital back in August. The boys talked amongst themselves like they were hard done by, and Jerell couldn't help but grin as he listened to the conversation; the boys all spoke as if the country owed them something. Employment was at an all-time low, and judging from nearly everyone Jerell had met since he had been here, crime was the only thing that paid. These boys were young; they had a lot to learn. Most of them had been born into crime, working the streets from young ages: dealing drugs, carrying knives and some even using them.

Jerell had the knack of being able to tap into the boys' pent-up anger and twist it around so that they would use it to his advantage. They hung on his every word. Even now, as they sat there chatting shit to each other, they all thought that it was their right to make money by nicking cars and selling drugs. The system didn't care about them, they said, they could only rely on the people in this room.

Only ignorant people were stupid enough to assume that gangs were just bored kids who had nothing better to do than to hang around causing trouble, Jerell knew. Gangs were an established part of organised crime in London. The boys may be kids, but they were part of the bigger picture.

Sitting down on the floor, bored with the conversation that was now going on around her, Louise interrupted Jerell's thoughts. "Jerell, any chance I could have a little drag of that?" Leaning with her back against the sofa on which Jerell was sprawled across, his legs hanging off the end, Louise fluttered her eyelashes in the hope he would share his spliff with her. She waited patiently and ignored the looks she was getting from the younger boys sitting opposite her. One of them shook his head at her obvious flirting with Jerell. She smirked at them defiantly as Jerell took another long deep drag and then passed the spliff to her.

Jerell smiled, as he thought of another thing the boys back home had been right about. English girls were easy meat. Louise made it obvious that she had a thing for Jerell, she made constant advances towards him, and he knew she was available should he want her.

The girl curled her lips around the spliff and looked at him as she took a long drag. He looked back. She was a pretty girl with her flawless white skin and long blonde hair. But he had no interest in her. She was too easy for his liking and as they said back home: easy come easy go. For his own amusement, he let her have a quick puff of the joint, before he snatched it back out of her grasp and lay back down on the sofa.

"Hey, I've only just got it," Louise protested, miffed he had only let her have one toke and embarrassed that the boys had seen Jerell make her look like a prat.

"Dat all you got to worry about, girl, smoking my gear?" He laughed at Louise's expression, which conveyed her rejection. "You came round for your money, girl, buy your own gear." He raised his eyebrows to let her know not to ask him again. Jerell paid the girl well, she had no need to ponce gear off him. "And you better not be robbing any of the gear over at your place either. You know what they do to thieves that steal off their own, back in my yard? They cut their hands off."

Louise was mortified. She had thought that, after all she was doing, Jerell would treat her with more recognition. She was practically running things at her flat. Unsure of how to save face, noticing that some of the boys were laughing at her now, Louise giggled, trying to pretend that she wasn't bothered by Jerell's rudeness. Feeling her cheeks burn red, as she pretended not to notice the mocking glance he sent her way, she realised that Jerell had absolutely no interest in her at all. She hadn't really fancied him anyway. It had been the idea of him that she had liked. He had a presence about him, unlike all the stupid little rude boys round here. She was embarrassed by his blatant disrespect towards her, though. She wasn't used to being rejected; in fact if anyone did the brushing off around here, it was normally her.

Shamed by how easy she must have come across to him, and feeling stupid that she had been throwing herself at him Louise got up and grabbed her jacket. Taking the cash from Reagan, she let her hair fall around her cheeks so that she could mask the humiliation burning her face, as she made her way to the door.

"Shut the door on your way out, girl." Jerell laughed in amusement at how much he had got to the young thing. He inhaled some more of the spliff, thinking that he had no time for shit with young girls like that. They were more trouble than they were worth. Louise was another one who thought she was owed something. She was doing the lion's share of the work, he knew that. But it didn't hurt to bring the girl down a peg or two and remind her that it was he who was in charge. She would do well to remember that in future.

Closing his eyes, he let the music carry him back to simpler days of growing up in sunny Jamaica.

Chapter 7

Tapping his fingers on the table in the shabby little cafe, Gary couldn't shake

the feeling that something bad was going to happen.

The normally busy greasy spoon was unusually quiet for this time of the

morning, giving Gary more time to be alone with his thoughts, which right

now he could have done without. In the cold light of day the worries that had

kept him up all night seemed magnified. Gary lived by his intuition, and the

fear that had kept him awake most of the night was sitting uneasily in his gut.

What if they had bitten off more than they could chew? Maybe it was just

nerves at what they were about to do, but he couldn't suppress the feeling

that they were getting involved in something that they should be leaving well

alone.

But a vote had been cast, and although it had ultimately been Gary's decision

to make, in the end he had seen no other way but to agree with Jamie that they would go ahead with their plan. Sitting here alone now, though, every bone in his body was telling him to call the hit off.

What would Jamie and the others think of him if he did that, though; they were already acting like they thought he was losing his bottle. He didn't want them to think he was going soft, but how could he explain what his intuition was telling him without sounding like a complete nut-job? They would think he was bailing out on them, and who could blame them for thinking that; after all, they were all more than aware of what this Jerell Morgan was capable of.

Wiping away the sweat trickling down his forehead, Gary tried to remain calm. The waitress came over, and he asked for a full English breakfast and a pint of orange juice. As soon as she had left, he wished he hadn't ordered it; his appetite had gone.

The others would be at the cafe in about ten minutes, and to show he was still in control Gary had wanted to be the first to arrive. He had wanted to use the extra time to think things through and get his head straight.

He was glad when Shay walked through the door a minute or so later, as he realised that the more he sat on his tod, the more time he had to think things over and the more he was becoming certain that he was losing his nerve.

"You alright, mate?" Shay asked, barely waiting for an answer, continuing to talk as he picked up a menu: "Tell you what, I'm bloody starving. I only got home about three hours ago. I met a right sort last night. She helped me work up a nice little appetite, if you know what I mean." Shay smiled cheekily at Gary, not realising the annoyance that he was causing nor picking up on the fact that things clearly were far from "alright".

Gary shook his head, although Shay didn't notice as he was scrutinising the menu, his rumbling belly the main thing on his mind.

Gary was fuming; they had a crucial job to do today, a job that they had planned for the best part of a week, and Shay had decided to spend the night before shagging some bird until the early hours, treating their plan like it was some kind of joke.

The waitress came over and put a plate of steaming hot food down in front of Gary. He pushed it over to Shay. "Here, you may as well have mine."

Shay picked up a fork and then, giving the waitress a wink, asked her to bring over a pot of tea. Barely looking up, as he shovelled the food into his mouth, and with the yolk of the fried egg dripping down his chin, Shay was oblivious to Gary's anger building across the table. Shay didn't have a clue what they were about to go up against, by the looks of it, and once again Gary wondered if it was only him that had thought any of this through. It took every ounce of his restraint to stop him from leaning over the rickety cafe table and grabbing Shay by the scruff of his selfish, scrawny little neck.

Seeing Jamie and Gavin arriving, Gary tried to shrug off his mood.

Jamie, taking a seat next to Shay, and as always quick on the ball, picked up on the atmosphere. "You alright, Gary?" A frown was etched on his boss's forehead; he looked stressed. It had taken a lot of persuading by Jamie for Gary to go along with this plan; he wondered now if Gary was once again having second thoughts.

"Mmm, that looks handsome." Gavin said as he leant over the table and took a piece of fried bread from Shay's plate, before dipping it in ketchup.

"Oi, get your own bleeding grub, Gav, I'm bloody starving," Shay protested, knocking Gavin's hand away.

"Yeah, I can tell you're hungry, mate, you're eating that fry-up like you ain't ever seen a plate of food before," Gavin replied, put out that he would now have to wait for his own food to arrive while Shay tucked in greedily in front of him.

Rolling his eyes at Jamie, as if the two Muppets next to them had just said it all, Gary forced a smile. "See what I've had to put up with? Old gannet-guts here has been up all night shagging some poor bloody girl, and now he's acting like he's been invited out for a friggin' three-course meal." Gary tried to make light of the situation; he knew that he had to put on a front and reassure his men if they were going to go ahead as planned. If they thought for a minute that he was still unsure about what they were going to do, it could all go to pot.

Ordering another full breakfast for Gavin and a coffee for Jamie when the waitress came over with Shay's tea, Gary leant back in his chair.

Shay finished his breakfast and let out a loud and gratuitous burp. "Hey, where's Les?"

"Fuck knows." Gary had been wondering the same thing. Les knew he was supposed to be here at seven sharp; he would be really pushing his luck if he didn't pull his finger out and get his arse in gear for their meeting: he knew it was crucial.

"I've been thinking..." Jamie said. If Les couldn't get himself here on time like the rest of them had, then Jamie wasn't going to waste his time waiting for him. They needed to get down to business. "I know what we agreed but I think it's going to be better if I do this myself." He had been awake all night too, tossing and turning with a myriad scenarios running through his mind.

Knowing that it was him that had masterminded all of this, he felt it fair that he would be the one to carry out the hit, alone, so that they had more chance of getting away with it undetected.

"No way, Jamie, you're not going it alone on this one." Gary was adamant that they were in this together, until the end.

"Besides," Gavin chipped in, not wanting to be excluded from the action that he had been looking forward to, as taking out coons was a sport as far as he was concerned, "we don't know who's going to be with him when we do the job. He might be alone, but chances are those boys he has hanging around him won't be too far away. There's no way that I'm letting you do it on your own, Jamie, you can't face him single-handed."

Jamie knew they were right, but he felt responsible for putting them in this situation, especially Gary, who had wanted no trouble. Jamie couldn't see the point of dragging everyone else into it. No matter how big and scary this Jerell nutter was supposed to be, when faced with a loaded gun, surely he would cry and beg just like any other bastard.

"We're in it together, Jamie, and I ain't discussing it with you again." The finality in Gary's voice was loud and clear. "I've got the guns out in the motor, it's all sorted. We stick to the plan. Today we wait it out… watch the flat and gauge how many fuckers he has in there with him. Then tonight we strike."

As Gary spoke, the other three men nodded; it was, after all, what they had agreed to. They had spent the majority of the week digging up every ounce of information they could get their hands on about Jerell Morgan, and had come up with a good bit of background on the bloke, and some knowledge on the group of scroats he had running all over London for him. More importantly, they now had an address.

Jerell was as nasty as they got; Jamie knew that they had never been up against anyone as ruthless. The bloke seemed to have made a lot of enemies in the short time he had been on the scene, so getting people to talk about him hadn't been too much of an issue. Jerell was taking over the streets and had been severely pissing people off in the process. Jerell seemed to dabble in all sorts, from what they had managed to gather, but drugs were mainly his thing. The man seemed to be on a power trip, taking out other people's businesses purely because he thought that he could. Jamie knew that starting a war with the bloke would be dangerous, ultimately, so they may as well go straight in for the kill. They would be doing a lot of people a favour by taking the man off the scene.

The garage was all they had, and Jamie knew that Gary and the others had never been tempted to get involved with the drug-dealing that so many of the other firms were involved with. All they wanted was their contract back; they needed it, and Jamie was going to see to it they got it. He said: "Yeah, I know you're right, I'm just trying to work out the best way of doing it. Hopefully, we'll get a chance to take that sorry fucker out when he's alone, preferably out of the flat, on the street, to make it look more anonymous. It'll make our lives a whole lot easier if there's not much bloodshed."

The table fell silent as the waitress returned with Gavin's breakfast and the coffee for Jamie.

"Where the fuck's Les? He's almost half an hour late," Gary said, as he threw down his mobile onto the table. It had gone straight to Les' answer-machine. Being late wasn't Les' usual style. Les always did what was asked of him. But the meeting was over, and he was still nowhere to be seen. It just wasn't like him.

"Finish up your breakfast, boys; we can fly by Les' place on the way. See what the silly bugger thinks he's playing at." Gary was sure that Les was feeling even more nervous than he had been, but even so, if you agreed to a job, there were no excuses for not turning up. Nervous or not, he should be here; he was just as much a part of this as they were.

Chapter 8

Les had been quiet all morning, which as far as Jamie was concerned was a bonus. Having picked up on the vibes from Gary, he had guessed that Les was feeling anxious, so he and Gary had let him be as they sat in silence staring out the windows of Gary's Jaguar watching Jerell's flat.

Les was knackered. He was also in the last place in the world he wanted to be right now, but he had promised Gary he would see this through, and he would.

The knock on Les' front door had come with such force earlier that morning that he had thought that someone was trying to break the bloody thing down. The banging had jolted him awake. For the first time in years, Les had slept in and had been mortified when he had realised that he had missed the meeting; he never slept in. He guessed that it hadn't helped that last night had been one of the worst night's sleep he had ever had. He had been dreading today so much that thoughts of what he was getting himself involved in had kept him awake with worry all night.

Les was fearful that he was too old for this kind of stuff now; he was scared he wouldn't be able to keep up with the others if it kicked off. First of all, they were all much younger than he was and secondly, they were a lot fitter. He was out of shape; his beer-belly and the fact that he couldn't make it up the three flights of steps to his flat most nights, without feeling out of breath was a painful reminder of that. The thought of getting old, and not being as capable as he used to be, was a depressing thought to be left alone with. Getting old meant one thing as far as Les was concerned: dying. Stuff like that in his head at silly o'clock in the early hours had added to his anxiety about what would happen in the morning.

Les was petrified of the fact that one day his cold, lifeless body would be lowered six foot under the soil, and that his corpse would be left there all alone, to be eaten by the maggots. He couldn't get his head around the fact that he would no longer be on Earth. When he wasn't tormenting himself in the early hours with thoughts of death, he drove himself demented with imagining the ways that he might die. The still of the night always brought out his terrors, and last night had been worse than ever with this all hanging over him.

When he had finally managed to nod off, sometime around five o'clock in the morning, he had been plagued with nightmares. He could only vaguely remember the details of his vivid dreams, but the terrifying feelings they had provoked had left him feeling uneasy.

Despite his fears, the last thing Les wanted to do was piss off Gary. He knew how much planning had gone into this whole thing and had been so embarrassed when he had realised that he had let Gary down by missing the meeting. He couldn't have apologised more when he finally dragged himself out of his bed to the sound of his door being bashed in, realising that he had overslept and that Gary must have come to get him. He had opened the door, exposing his fuming boss to the sight of himself half-asleep and thus barely coherent, donning a pair of grey Y-fronts.

"Fucking hell, Les, you're a sight for sore eyes." Gary was relieved that Les was okay, all sorts of things had run through his mind when Les hadn't turned up and he could sense instantly by Les' apologetic expression that he was genuinely sorry for letting him down. "What the fuck are you doing, Les? We were waiting in the cafe for over forty-five minutes for you," Gary said, as he followed Les down his pokey hallway. The curtains were drawn and the musty smell was powerful: Gary could barely breathe.

"Go and stick some trousers on," Gary ordered, as he pulled back the curtains and then opened a window to let some fresh air in. Seeing the flat in the harsh daylight, Gary could see that it looked as bad as it smelt. Les' furniture had been his late mum's, and the flat had a real fifties feel to it. Retro may have been fashionable, but Les' flat looked like it had run through a car-boot sale and had been hit every stall; there was junk everywhere. Piles of DVDs were stacked up in front of the TV. Tacky trinkets and ornaments covered in dust lined every bit of shelf space on an old mahogany wall unit. The large unit took up most of the back wall of the lounge, making the already small room feel claustrophobic. Together with the mustard-coloured sofas, that looked so worn and tired you'd almost feel guilty for sitting on them, the room looked dire. And the carpet, Jesus! It had a large, faded floral print; the sort of carpet that only vomit or a lit match could improve. Gary knew that Les had kept everything exactly as his dear old mum had left it; he had taken his mother's death hard, and the place was clearly still a shrine to the woman.

"I'm so sorry that I overslept, boss. I was staring at my alarm clock 'til the early hours so God knows how..." Les called from the bedroom, as he pulled on a pair of jeans, not wanting to hold Gary up any longer.

Gary knew that feeling. Les wasn't the only one who had lost sleep last night.

"When I finally did nod off, I had nothing but bloody nightmares." Les' voice was muffled through the sweater he was pulling over his head, as he came back into the lounge where Gary stood.

Gary knew that feeling too; the past week had been full of nightmares. It was only right that they were all nervous about what they were about to get involved with, but Gary picked up from Les' jittery body language that he was actually really scared. This was going to be a big job; they weren't playing games. This was as real as it was going to get.

"You know you don't have to be there later on tonight, don't you, Les? The main thing is that we all stick together this morning, and watch this Jerell's every movement. When it comes down to it later, and we get our opportunity to strike, you don't have to be there if you think you're not up to it, mate." Gary tried to play his words down. He didn't want Les to think that he was implying that he wouldn't be able to cope. Les had been an asset to him over the years, and Gary knew that no matter what, the man had always had his back. But Les wasn't made out of the same stuff as Gary and Jamie. They were fiery and gutsy, they had built themselves up from nothing, and that was what Gary had instantly recognised in Jamie when he had walked into his garage all those years ago. Gary still had some of that fire burning away, but Les didn't anymore, and it showed. The man wanted a quiet life; he had no fight left and Gary could understand that. But Les worked hard at the garage, which was all that Gary required of him these days.

"No, honest, Gary, I'm good for it." Les was adamant that he would see the thing through to the end. There was no way he was going to sit this one out; no way that Jamie would be able to say that he was a coward.

Gary shook his head at Les' stubbornness but understood that he was resolutely loyal.

"They don't make them like me and you anymore, you know." Gary laughed. "Come on, we'd better get our arses down to the motor, I've left Jamie with the two Muppets. He'll be ready to kill them if we leave him alone with them for too much longer."

When Gary and Les had joined the others at the car, the men decided to stick with the plan and split up, taking the two cars.

Shay was miffed. The Jag was a beast of a motor, it was full-on leather and luxury, and had Shay been able to go in that car, it would have made sitting on his arse for the next eight hours a much more pleasant experience. Instead he was going to have to sit in the shitty Escort with Gavin and his dodgy guts all day long. He always drew the short straw: Gavin was an animal who was constantly full of wind, and the smells that came out of him were so potent they could strip paint from a wall.

Les stayed with Jamie and Gary at the opposite end of the street to Shay and Gavin. They had been there for a good few hours and Les had hardly said a word; the fact that Jamie was sitting in the front next to Gary spoke volumes, as far as he was concerned, about the pecking order. At least he had a bit of space in the back, he thought moodily, as he stretched out his legs along the back seat and leant his head back while he watched the flat. So far there had been a lot of coming and goings: Jerell must be an extremely busy man.

The flat was on the ground floor. There were two BMX bikes outside it, locked to a drainpipe. The door was brown and shabby-looking, just like the blinds at the windows. It looked as dull and depressing as every other flat on this estate. If the Earth had an arsehole, Jamie reckoned that they were now sitting in it.

"Is it me, or has anyone else noticed that the majority of people going in and out of that flat are little fucking kids?" Jamie was shocked at how young the boy that had just left the flat appeared to be. He was wearing a bomber jacket and a baseball cap, but Jamie guessed he was only about twelve.

"Kids are born into this kind of shit these days," Gary replied; he understood how shocked Jamie was by the kids' youth, but that was how it was these days: the children were worse than their parents.

"But what's a fucking psycho like Jerell doing hanging round with a group of kids?" Jamie hadn't signed up to start a turf war with a bunch of children, and the weapons in the boot of the car were making him feel uneasy. Shooting kids had not factored into Jamie's equation; he had been expecting tooled-up men.

"Well, I guess kids are easy to control and manipulate, and Jerell's probably paying them a pittance and raking in all the readies for himself. From what I've heard, the bloke ain't stupid," Gary reasoned, although even he would have expected older teenagers. "Don't let their looks deceive you, Jamie. Most of those little scroats would murder their own mothers if the price was right." Gary nodded over to the group of hoodies hanging around the steps next to Jerell's front door. The kids were clearly trying to portray big-man personas: smoking, spitting and, looking at the average age of them, bunking off school too. "They might look young, but this is all they know. This is one of the roughest estates going and those kids over there fucking run it. Trust me; you wouldn't wanna walk around here late at night on your own. Don't matter how hard you think you are, or how much you think you can handle yourself, one of you against a group of these nasty bastards and you wouldn't stand a fucking chance, mate. These kids play dirty." Gary smiled before adding: "Besides, you seem to be forgetting, Jamie, you were only a boy yourself when you rocked up at the garage, mate, you were as cocky as you like back then: you forgetting that in your old age, are ya?"

Jamie supposed this was true, although he had felt older than his fifteen years back then, but he expected that was how all teenagers felt. At fifteen, Jamie had been sure he knew best, when the reality was, he had known jack-shit; he made it up as he went along, and had got lucky by meeting Gary. Jamie guessed that putting up with his mother's endless bullying and constant demands back then, and also taking on the responsibility of looking after his younger sisters and brother, had forced him to grow up quicker than most people his age. He pushed back the thoughts of his family back out of his head as quickly as they had come in; his mum probably hadn't given him a second thought in the last ten years, so why should he consider her now?

Jamie continued to look out of the window in disbelief. Gary was right that the kids looked rough, they were like mini-gangsters with massive chips on their shoulders. He had never seen so many kids in one place. Some of them were rapping and beat boxing, some pulling tricks on their bikes. There was a group of girls in one corner, their faces painted heavily with make-up and wearing tiny skirts.

The hours ticked by, as the men continued to watch. There was no sign of Jerell.

Looking at the clock on the dashboard, Gary saw that it was nearly five. The day had dragged by, and even though there had been more than enough going on to keep them from getting bored, the day had ultimately been unsuccessful. They didn't even know if Jerell was in the vicinity. The man clearly had no need to leave the flat, judging by the amount of kids he had running around for him. At five o'clock, it was starting to get dark, and they needed to get a move on. No doubt the amount of movement in and out of the flat would only increase as darkness fell; it went with the territory.

"Right then, that's us done for now," Gary said. "We'll leave Gavin and Shay here to keep watching while we grab a bite to eat; we can bring them something back."

Les was hungry after missing breakfast but hadn't wanted to mention it to Gary as he had felt so guilty about missing the meeting, so he brightened up at Gary's words. He had been trying to muffle the sounds of his belly rumbling for the past half hour without success.

"I'll give the boys a bell and let them know." Jamie picked up his mobile. As he waited for Gavin to answer, he added: "We can get some food in us, then we can mull over what we're going to do when we get back. If we're lucky enough, maybe we'll be able to get him on his own sometime tonight if he decides to venture out of his flat, but I'd say going by how unsuccessful today's been, we might have to go and pay him a little visit after all." Jamie

was disappointed that they hadn't so much as caught a glimpse of Jerell. They

had seen boys come and go all day long, and one had even had the cheek to

walk up to the window and take a proper look at their motor up close,

brazenly peering in, having a right good stare. At first Jamie had thought that

maybe the kid had sussed out that they were watching the flat, but Gary was

convinced that the little shit was more than likely trying to see if he could

have a go at breaking in. After a few seconds of the boy staring boldly through

the windows, so close that his breath left patches of condensation on the

glass, Jamie locked eyes with him. With only a thin pane of blackened-out

glass between them, the boy had stared in, unable to see through the glass;

Jamie had felt that the kid knew they were in there. The three men had sat as

still as statues, afraid to breathe; finally, all of them felt relieved as the kid had

eventually given up on whatever it was that he was trying to look at and gone

over to the flat. Jamie had tried to figure out if it was one of the kids who had

come out of the flat earlier, he looked familiar. There were so many dodgy

little gits around here, all wearing oversized baseball caps and riding little

BMXs, that they all looked the same to Jamie; he was probably just another

little toe rag that he had seen about that day.

Starting the engine, Gary felt the uneasy feeling wash over him once more. But they had come this far now, there would be no backing out. Jamie was determined. Gary had a feeling that even if he called the whole thing off, Jamie would see it through now with or without him.

Driving off to get food, the men were oblivious to the fact that the Jag was now the hot topic of conversation in the flat that they had just spent the whole day watching.

Chapter 9

Reagan had the hump. Tyler always liked to cause a stir, and it wound Reagan up so much that at times he had to try his hardest to keep his cool. Tyler was a pain in the arse. He was only twelve, so a lot of the crap that he spoke was down to his immaturity but even though Reagan knew that, it didn't make him less annoying to listen to.

Jerell had assured Reagan that the road to success for them was to use the younger boys as mules to drop off the drugs to their dealers, as there was less chance that the police would be suspicious of them. The younger the boys the better, he insisted. There was no way that little ten year olds riding around on BMXs would look suspicious, it was hardly what you would call unusual behaviour.

Jerell's plan had been ingenious, and so far it was working well for them, apart from the fact that dealing with young boys meant dealing with the bullshit that came with them.

Tyler often bunked off school so that he could hang out at the flat, wanting to fit in with the other boys in the group, and he had been pleased when he had even been given the responsibility of making a few drops for Jerell and Reagan. Working for the two men had made Tyler feel, for the first time in his life, that he had a function. He listened to every instruction that he was given and followed the men's orders to the letter. He wanted to make a good impression.

Tyler's only real downfall was his lies. He told so many that he had earned himself a reputation as a compulsive liar, and not only were most of the Larkhall Boys slowly losing their patience with Tyler but they were also losing their trust. Tyler had tried hard to stop the stories, but it was like he had no control over what came out of his mouth: the lies just seemed to pour out.

Reagan wondered if Tyler had been left in front of a telly watching soaps for most of his early childhood, because not only did he sense that he craved attention but the boy seemed obsessed with far-fetched stories that seemed like EastEnders' plots.

"Give it a rest, man." Reagan flashed a warning glare at Tyler, who had done nothing but jabber on with his tales since he had arrived fifteen minutes ago.

Reagan glanced over to the table where Jerell was sitting; he seemed deep in conversation with two of the other lads, going over a few important jobs they were organising for that evening, but Reagan could sense Jerell's tension even with his back to him, the man's shoulders were hunched up tightly. It wouldn't take much for Jerell to get pissed off with yet another of the boy's make-believe dramas, and Reagan was trying his best to diffuse the situation as quickly as he could before Jerell had a chance to react to it. Everything had been running so smoothly for them all and they were so busy at the moment, their whole operation just seemed to be going from strength to strength. Reagan had made sure that he was indispensable to Jerell, and worked hard to keep all the boys in order, so that Jerell had one less thing to think about.

The table was cluttered with take-away boxes and cans of drinks, and even though Jerell seemed to be caught up in the discussion he was having, Reagan knew that the man never missed a trick and probably had one ear on his and Tyler's conversation. Wanting to show that he was capable of sorting out any of the little problems that arose, Reagan didn't need this bullshit from Tyler right now.

"But I'm telling you the truth. Someone's on to us. They've been out there all day, Reagan, honest." Tyler's eyes bulged like saucers, as he continued to insist that a posh car with blacked-out windows was watching them. "Maybe it's the police? Maybe they're keeping tabs on the flat, before they make their move and try and bust us later," Tyler suggested, getting frustrated with the lack of reaction he was receiving; he had assumed that warning the men would have earned him a pat on the back at least and had not been expecting this amount of grief. Getting Reagan to believe him was proving almost impossible and Tyler knew it was mainly his own fault. He knew that he always elaborated slightly with his stories; generally just because he wanted them to be more interesting, and it did feel good having people actually want to listen to him for a change. Who didn't tell a few white lies? He knew that most people didn't believe a word that came out of his mouth the majority of the time, but how could he make Reagan see that he wasn't lying this time.

"The police don't generally stake out neighbourhoods like this one in swanky motors, Tyler, they'd stick out like a sore bloody thumb around here; even the pigs aren't that stupid," Reagan reasoned.

"Look, I know you don't believe me, but I'm telling the truth. When I went out this morning to do that drop down at Brockwell Park, it was sitting out there. It's gone five o'clock now and it's still there. It's been out there all day. I swear on my life Reagan, I'm not lying." Tyler paused for breath; he hoped Reagan would finally realise that he was telling the truth.

"A car has been parked up outside all day? So what? Just in case you haven't noticed, Tyler, this is a massive block of flats we're in, and that road out there..." Reagan waited a second so that the sarcasm would be more obvious to Tyler, who let's face it, he thought, really wasn't acting like the sharpest

tool in the box right now. "Wait for it... is where people park their cars."
Reagan said the last sentence in a slow patronising voice to emphasise to
Tyler how ridiculous he sounded. His patience was disappearing.

"So, some posh git has left his motor out on the street while he visits his bird
or something; why does there always seem to have to be a drama with you?"
Reagan added.

Feeling totally frustrated, Tyler spoke up with even more determination to get
Reagan to believe him: "I thought that too, Reagan, but I just got a weird
feeling, like I was being watched, so when I came back just then, I rode my
bike up real close to the motor and tried to get a good old look in the
windows. You can't see anything through that glass, though. But I could feel
them eyeballing me, I'm telling ya, they were in there watching me, and if
they're watching me, then they're probably watching this flat too."

Tyler was so persistent with his story, and seemed so certain that he was
right, that Reagan started to feel the smallest inkling of doubt sneak in. What
if the police were watching the flat? It wasn't unheard of. But it would be
stupid turning up in a motor that was going to sit there screaming out for
attention like the one Tyler had described, surely the police would be more
low-key. Jerell had a blinding motor that was worth a fortune, and he
wouldn't park it outside the flat. He kept it around the corner in a private

garage that he had rented; only a mug would park a car like his out there in this estate, anything half-decent would end up with its windows smashed and its radio swiped, or even worse, it would be nicked by some little rude boy for a joyride, although they'd have to have a death wish if they even looked at Jerell's motor.

"And I'll tell ya something else, Reagan, it's a well posh motor, it must have cost a mint! Look, it's still sitting out there now if you don't believe me." Tyler lifted the blinds, tangling the cord in his haste to prove to Reagan that he was really telling the truth this time.

Seeing how adamant Tyler was, and not wanting to anger Jerell if there was any chance that there was even a glimmer of truth to Tyler's latest spiel, Reagan thought he had better check it out, just to be on the safe side. Reluctantly standing at the window, he glanced in the direction Tyler was pointing. Looking out across the darkened street he could see there were a few cars scattered in the parking bays. His eyes scanned the length of the road as he took in every detail. A group of kids were all hanging around outside a phone booth at the end of the estate. Two of the boys were fighting, wrestling each other onto the pavement; it was a playful fight, not like the normal violent scuffles he witnessed on almost a daily basis on the estate. There was clearly an element of competition involved with this one, though, as Reagan watched the two boys trying to out-do each other as the three girls standing around them smoked cigarettes and watched on in amusement, intermittently cheering for one of the boys. Further down the road were two guys sitting in a clapped-out Escort; one of the windows was rolled down; they looked like a pair of dossers smoking a bit of weed from what he could make out through the darkness. It was a familiar sight round here, people hanging out doing that. There was fuck all else for anyone to do in these parts.

A few cars up from the Escort, Reagan could see a woman from an upstairs flat getting into a little red Mini. He had bumped into her on a few occasions when he had been leaving the flat but she always ignored him and on the rare time when she had seemed to notice him she had come across like she had been looking down her nose at him; the kind of look that told him in no uncertain terms that she was way out of his league. He knew that he would never stand a chance with someone like her, and even though she looked at him like he was worthless, he couldn't help but fancy her. Watching her bend over through the driver's door, she leant over to the passenger's side to place her bag on the floor. Reagan smiled to himself as he watched her skirt ride up high, above her toned thighs revealing her peach of an arse and the tiniest thong he had ever set his eyes on; talk about flash the gash, that girl was fit.

As he watched the girl get into her car and drive off, Reagan remembered that he was supposed to be looking out of the window for a reason. Giving the street a final once-over, he saw that the rest of the cars were parked up like normal and there didn't seem to be anyone else about. And as for a 'posh motor with blacked-out windows', there was nothing that fit that description. Either it had been out there earlier and had gone, or Tyler's imagination had once again run away with itself. Reagan had a feeling that it was probably the latter.

Closing the blinds, Reagan turned and gave Tyler a clout around the back of his head that sent the yelping boy flying across the room, landing in a heap on the floor. Reagan sat down, rolling his eyes to Jerell, who had turned to see what the crash was; clearly he had been listening to the whole charade the entire time, as Reagan had suspected that he would be.

"You got to seriously stop making up stories, boy," Jerell bellowed. "Ain't you heard of the boy who cried wolf?" Jerell's voice always seemed to boom out when he spoke; his Jamaican accent was rich and deep and only added to the air of menace around him. Jerell remembered the story well, it was one of his grandma's favourite tales, and she had used it on more than one occasion when Jerell was a boy. He may have told a few lies back when he was a young boy, but Tyler was on a scale of his own and he was pushing his luck. Jerell had no patience for this type of shit; he couldn't understand why this boy felt the need to make up so many lies.

"No-one gunna believe a word that comes from your lying mouth, if you keep spouting this made-up shit all the time." Tyler couldn't be trusted: he was just a stupid little boy with a big mouth, and his mouth was going to land him in a whole lot of trouble. Jerell wasn't prepared to risk being dragged into the boy's dramas any longer. "Reagan, get the boy out of here now, before I teach him where his lies are gunna get him." Jerell spoke calmly, but Reagan recognised the anger flashing in his eyes; he was getting accustomed to Jerell's low-tolerance level. It was like the man had a built-in bullshit detector.

"Oh please, Jerell, honestly I was telling the truth, I swear on my life I was." Tyler felt a flush of embarrassment, as his cheeks flared a deep crimson, as he desperately tried to stop the tears that stung his eyes from falling. Being a liar was one thing, but getting himself the reputation of a cry-baby would be something he would never be capable of living down; the boys round here would rip him to pieces. He had loved helping Jerell and Reagan out these past few months and could not imagine not being part of their world. This place had kept him busy and given him a purpose, and even though he had more money than he knew what to do with for a kid his age, he didn't care about the cash, he just wanted to be part of something; anything to keep him away from his shitty existence back at home. He avoided his home like the plague. His mum had no time for him, and in the very few rare moments that she did acknowledge him, she did nothing but shout abuse at him, telling him what a loser he was and that he would never amount to anything. It hurt Tyler that his own mother was like that, he had seen how his friends' mums were towards their kids, and even as stressed-out and as tested as they were by them, they were nowhere near as nasty as his mum was to him. She hated him, and as much as he tried to hate her back, he just couldn't find it in him.

These boys had become a family to him in the last few months, and Jerell and Reagan had given him a glimpse of another way of life: he was gutted that he had messed it up.

"I'm sorry, Jerell, I really am, I know I sometimes tell lies, but I won't anymore, I promise. Please don't make me go," Tyler pleaded.

Jerell leant back in his chair and glared at Tyler. The boy was short for his age and looked younger than his twelve years. Unlike many of the other boys who hung out around here, Tyler's tough guy attitude didn't really cut it, he couldn't carry it off. The boy was too soft. He needed toughening up. Jerell could see that Tyler was desperate to be given one more chance; he would do anything to redeem himself. Looking at the pathetic boy before him, Jerell couldn't help himself. Getting up from his seat, he clicked his fingers towards the sofa, indicating to Tyler to sit. "Reagan, you take the boys and go make tonight's drops. Me and Tyler here are gunna have a little conversation about a few things, the boy needs to learn a thing or two about where his lies are gunna get him."

Reagan didn't like the way that Jerell was looking at the boy; he could see anger in Jerell's face, but something else, which was more sinister, flashed there too. He looked like a man possessed, and even though Reagan felt uneasy about leaving Tyler alone with Jerell he knew that he would be a fool to get involved. Jerell called the shots around here, so Reagan giving his five pence worth wouldn't have gone down well at all; he figured that he should just do as he was told. Getting up quickly, sensing the bad atmosphere that Tyler had created, the lads gathered their jackets so that they could go and meet Louise to collect the gear ready for tonight's drops. Reagan, who was going with them, also got up. He glanced over in Tyler's direction as he walked towards the front door, reluctant to leave. Tyler sat back on the sofa; he seemed to have calmed down. The silly boy was looking relieved, perhaps in his assumption that he had won Jerell over as he had been told that he could stay. Sitting there all smug, thinking that Jerell was going to have a chat with him and it would all be okay: how gullible could he be?

Reagan felt the bile rise up from his stomach, he had a bad feeling.

Nodding to Jerell as he left, but unable to meet his eyes or speak, knowing that if he opened his mouth he wouldn't be capable of finding words, he closed the front door, leaving Tyler to his fate.

Tyler was so young and naive. Reagan knew, if his instincts were right, that in just a short space of time, Jerell would ruin the poor boy's life.

Chapter 10

Seeing the glare of the headlights of Gary's Jaguar behind them, Gavin and

Shay couldn't have been more chuffed with the timing. They had both been

desperate for a proper smoke all day, and had lit up another sneaky joint as

soon as Gary had finally gone off to get food with the others, and now they

both had the severe munchies. Gavin had insisted that they had to hurry up as

they took turns taking drags, knowing that it wouldn't have gone down too

well if Gary found out that they had both been smoking a bit of gear whilst on

the job. The stuff that Gavin got was always shit-hot, and because they had

both hurriedly taken long, swift pulls on the joint, the drug had gone straight

to their heads, and Shay was starting to feel so laid back he was almost

horizontal. The day had dragged on, and even though they knew that Gary

would go mental if he caught them, it had been a risk they had both been

willing to take, anything to help relieve the boredom of sitting in the car for

the last eight hours solid.

Pulling up beside them, Gary unwound his window, and passed the two men four big cheeseburgers he had picked up from the drive-thru. "Anything?" he asked, nodding in the direction of the flat.

Taking the food and praying that Gary couldn't smell the gear they had just smoked, Shay replied: "Still no sign of Jerell, boss. Three older boys came out about ten minutes ago, but that nosey little kid who was eyeing your car up earlier is still inside, we think." Sighing as he spoke, Shay couldn't hide his disappointment that the evening was shaping up to be just as uneventful as the day had been. He unwrapped one of the burgers, unable to wait any longer for his food. The monster-sized breakfast he had consumed this morning felt like it had been days ago.

"Yeah, looks like it might only be the boy in there, boss," Gavin added. "But I'd put money on Jerell being in there too; judging by the comings and goings today, it seems like this could be their main base. Maybe he's keeping a low profile and getting everyone else to do his dirty work for him today, so that he can stay put."

Gary agreed with this assumption. Jerell had to be in there; otherwise their entire day had been a complete waste of time. "I think we should make our move now, Gary," Jamie suggested, sensing that the flat was the quietest it had been that day. For all they knew, there could be fifty boys in there, but they had staked the place out for over eight hours now, and it seemed that most of the kids that had all gone in there throughout the day had come back out again. They knew that the young boy that had come up to the car window earlier was still in there, but he had only looked about eleven or twelve, so as long as he didn't get in the way of business, he was hardly going to be a problem.

"Sit tight, boys, we'll let you know what's happening in a bit," Gary instructed Shay and Gavin, before he drove off back to the other end of the street, aware that two cars sitting side by side blocking the road were more than likely going to draw attention; they could carry on this conversation over the phone when Gary had decided what the next step was. Jamie was right, the flat was probably at its quietest right now, and the chances that Jerell would be showing his ugly mug were slim. They would have to go in: and do it now while they had their chance.

After agreeing on what they needed to do, Jamie rang Shay and told him and Gavin to keep watching the street while they went in. If any kids looked like they were approaching the flat, Gavin and Shay were to distract them.

"What do you mean: distract them? How the hell are we going to do that, Jamie?" Shay didn't like the idea that he and Gavin might have to approach a group of rowdy kids. Having sat here all day and watched the little buggers swarming around the neighbourhood like a bunch of ASBO rejects, he didn't fancy provoking any kind of an argument with any of them. Gavin, on the other hand, would be likely start a fight with the little shits for the pure entertainment value. Shay prayed that for his sake, keeping watch would be all he would have to do.

"Just do whatever you bloody need to do, but you don't let anyone get within twenty feet of that front door, alright?" It pissed Jamie off that Shay was making a big deal about keeping watch, as it was Jamie who was putting his neck on the line by going into the flat to face Jerell; the way that Shay was talking, you would have thought he was sorting out the situation single-handed.

Getting out of the car quickly and taking the guns out of the boot, the three men made their way to the flat; they needed to move fast, as they probably didn't have much time.

Les was lagging behind the other two; he was out of breath trying to keep up. He had strict instructions that once Jamie and Gary had got inside the flat, he was to guard the front door. No-one was to come in or out other than them. They had given him a gun , but Les had been assured it was just for show; it was loaded, but there was no way that he was going to have to actually use it, Jamie and Gary would have the situation under control.

Jamie had imagined the flat to be like Fort Knox, but standing outside the rickety-looking front door he had been surprised to see that it didn't look like it had been reinforced. Giving Gary the eye to check that they were good to go, Jamie kicked his size-eleven boot hard into the middle panel of the door. Luckily, the door flung open, crashing into the wall behind it so fast that it swung back and hit Jamie with its full force as he rushed straight inside, with Gary following closely behind him.

The men bursting into the room startled Jerell. He had been otherwise occupied with the boy kneeling in front of him.

Before the men had come in, Jerell had forced Tyler to take his erect penis in his mouth and pleasure him. Grabbing the boy's hair tightly with his huge fists, and deliberately pulling harder to hurt him, Jerell had thrust his penis so far down Tyler's throat that it had made the boy gag. Jerell hadn't had this kind of pleasure since he had arrived here in England and the boy's warm mouth covering his throbbing dick made him feel like he was ready to explode. Tyler was the type of boy that Jerell liked. All the crying and the choking only made him appear younger and more vulnerable.

Thrusting into the boy's mouth, enjoying the gagging noises, Jerell had been on the brink of coming as the front door crashed open. Pushing the naked boy away abruptly, Jerell pulled up his trousers as he reached over to grab his gun from the table next to the chair.

The men had their guns pointed at Jerell's head. They were stunned by what they saw. Seeing Jerell pulling up his trousers, and a poor sobbing boy trying to conceal his naked body from them as he pulled his jeans on, Jamie felt sickened. Gary scanned the room and noted that it seemed to be only Jerell and the boy in here.

The men's shocked reactions gave Jerell the extra few seconds of thinking time he needed. Limited in his options, he quickly grabbed a now shaking Tyler by his throat, and lifted him up off the chair, almost strangling him, and pressed his gun hard into the boy's forehead.

Jerell hoped that they didn't intended to shoot the kid too or his last-ditch attempt to stop them from shooting him by using Tyler as a shield wouldn't help him.

"What you want coming in here?" Jerell bellowed at the two men.

Gary looked at Jamie; they couldn't shoot the man while he had a gun to the kid's head, chances were that he would end up getting his brains blown out too and neither of them wanted an innocent child's blood on their hands.

Jamie had the gun pointed at Jerell's face; his eyes were locked onto the other man's. "What the fuck is going on?" Jamie had heard stories of Jerell being an animal, but this wasn't the kind of depraved action he had expected to be greeted with. The man before them was a fucking paedophile. Jamie felt his finger graze the trigger, as he tried to control himself. Looking into the petrified boy's eyes, Jamie wanted to stick a few bullets in Jerell's skull for what he had just done to this poor kid, apart from everything else.

"I ask the fucking questions around here." Jerell pressed the barrel of his gun harder into Tyler's temple, showing that he would shoot the kid if he needed to. He figured holding the boy hostage was working, as the men would surely have shot him by now otherwise. "Who the fuck are you? What are you doing thinking you can come to my home?" Jerell was outraged by the audacity of the two men, as he started to feel like he was back in control. These men had broken into his house. They had guns pointed at him.

Outside the room, Les was dripping with sweat, moving from one foot to the other nervously. He was unsure of what he should do; he wasn't very good at making his own decisions. He had been told that he couldn't leave the door unguarded, and hearing the voice that he assumed was Jerell's shouting from inside the flat, Les was starting to feel panicky. Why hadn't they done what they said they were going to do and just shot the bastard? What was taking them so long? As well as hearing all the commotion that was going on inside the flat, he was also trying to keep an eye on Gavin and Shay who were up the other end of the road and now seemed to be in a bit of bother themselves. Les had watched them approach the group of kids that they had obviously recognised from hanging around the flat earlier. They had seen that the kids had been heading towards Jerell's, so they had done what they were told and tried to hold the kids off.

***

Shay hadn't had much time to think about what he was going to say, as he and Gavin speedily crossed the road over to where the group of loud, hyper kids were walking.

"Ha, did you see that look on the guy's face, blood, when he opened the door? He was proper vexed, man." The youngest boy laughed. They had shoved a firework through some bloke's letterbox, while they had hidden in the bushes and pissed themselves laughing as they watched. The panicking man had run out of the house and thrown his front doormat out on to the road and then frantically stamped all over it to put out the flames. He had looked like he was doing a weird tribal dance; the boys had it all on their iPhones, another video to show off to the others.

"That will stop the muggy old cunt from telling the police about us hanging around near his house in future," the oldest boy replied, proud that he had shown the younger ones how to deal with local people that piss you off. The bloke was lucky; a firework would be the least of his troubles if he rang the police again.

As Shay saw the boys getting closer to the flat he had no time to think about what to say to prevent them going any further, and in hindsight wished he hadn't clouded his brain by smoking that gear. Stupidly, the only thing he could think of was to ask for directions to the nearest shops.

"What do we look like: fucking London tour guides or something?" One of the boys said, laughing, as he pushed past Shay, looking him up and down like he was a piece of shit before continuing to walk.

Shay hadn't expected the kids to take the piss, but asking for directions had immediately made them targets for the boys' jibes, now that they knew the two men weren't from around these parts.

"Ah, what's the matter, you two poofters lost, are ya?" The tallest kid tried to push past the two men who were trying to block the path.

Shay looked at Gavin in desperation. They couldn't let the kids get to the flat or all hell would break loose. Gary and Jamie wouldn't stand a chance if Jerell had back-up. Gavin had started to lose his temper with the boys now anyway and fancied teaching one of the little shits a lesson. Grabbing the mouthy older boy by his hood as he tried to push past, Gavin swung him around so that the boy was up close to Gavin's face.

"What did you just call me?" Gavin eyeballed the kid, letting him know that he had chosen the wrong person to piss off.

"You two think you're rude boys, huh?" Shrugging Gavin's hand off his coat, the kid laughed as he looked Gavin and then Shay up and down once again, like they were hot steamy shits; if Gavin had intimidated him the boy certainly wasn't showing it. "You going to get out of my way, or am I going to have to make you?" The boy's threat was loaded, as he lifted his top up and flashed the handle of the blade that was sticking out of his pocket, confident that he could take these two men on if he had to.

Shay looked nervously at the knife, as he silently cursed Gavin's quick temper. The other boys standing around were enjoying the show that was unfolding before them. They loved a good street fight.

***

In the flat, Jerell was slowly moving towards the door, dragging Tyler by his arm as he continued to hold the gun at the boy's head, not once taking his eyes off Jamie and Gary.

Jamie was tempted to shoot; he reckoned if he was fast enough he could take Jerell out without him getting a chance to press his own gun's trigger, and maybe then the boy would be okay. Gary, however, didn't want to take the chance and had shook his head at Jamie warningly, not wanting to get any kid caught up in the cross fire.

But Jerell was almost at the door.

Gary continued pointing his gun in Jerell's direction, but his attention was on Jamie, trying desperately to make sure that he didn't do anything stupid. Seeing the bead of sweat trickle down Jamie's forehead, Gary could almost see his brain whirling away inside his head.

"Let him go, Jamie."

Jamie wanted the pervert to be taught a lesson, but he knew that he couldn't take a risk in case it backfired and the boy took a bullet. He couldn't live with a child's blood on his hands.

"Les: move. Jerell's coming out, and he's got a kid with him," Gary shouted towards the front door, knowing that Les would freak out if he saw a mountain of a man coming towards him, armed and with a kid in tow.

It all happened so fast. Les heard the panic in his boss' voice, as Jerell lurched towards him. Les pointed his gun at Jerell, fighting to control the tremble in his hands. "Put your gun down now," Les ordered; his voice shook and the words didn't come out as loudly as he had wanted them too; he felt so scared he could barely move.

"Don't do nothing stupid, do what your boss man in there tell you. Move outta me way!" Jerell had no time for the fat, sweaty man in the doorway. The man's pistol was aimed at him but he looked incapable of pulling a pint, let alone a trigger. A few more steps and Jerell would be out of there.

"Let him go, Les," Gary called, worried that Les was in danger and knowing how scared he would be.

Panicking, Les moved forward towards Jerell at the same time as Gary shouted at Les to get out of the way.

The shot rang out.

***

Shay and Gavin's fight had barely started. The boy had just flashed the knife as they danced around him in circles trying to avoid getting cut, as the others watched, laughing and jeering.

On hearing the gunshot, the boys forgot about the two jokers that they had been threatening and ran towards the flat where the noise had come from.

Gavin and Shay followed, hoping the gunshot had been Jamie finishing off Jerell; they had been in there longer than planned and Gavin and Shay had no idea what the situation was.

Seeing Jerell running out of the flat and down the street, dragging Tyler, the gang of boys followed. They were unsure why their boss was running, but if he wasn't hanging around, neither would they.

The first thing Shay and Gavin saw when they got to the flat was Jamie, crouched on the floor, blood on his clothes and hands.

"Oh my fucking God, we need an ambulance," Shay said.

"We ain't got time for a fucking ambulance, get Gavin's car here, now." The panic in Jamie's voice was evident. Looking at Les, Jamie ordered: "Pull yourself fucking together, mate, the police are going to be swarming all over here in about five minutes. You need to get a fucking grip."

Les was shaking; a warm trickle of piss ran down his leg, as he went into shock.

Knowing that he wouldn't get any sense out of the bloke, Jamie nodded to Gavin. "Gavin, get Les in the Jag and back to my place. Do it now. I'll call you in a bit. Do not let him out of your sight, you hear me?" Jamie reached into Gary's pocket and rooted around for his car keys; then, trying to think clearly despite the nightmare that had just unfolded before him, he got his own keys out of his back pocket and passed them to Gavin.

Seeing Gavin hold up a shaky Les as he guided him to the Jag, Jamie hoped that Gavin would be able to keep Les under control, the last thing they needed right now was fucking hysterics from him.

Shay screeched up beside the flat in Gavin's car seconds later; Jamie looked back down to Gary who was lying on the floor having taken the bullet that Jerell had meant for Les. Gary's eyes were glazed and he was clearly in a lot of pain.

His hands tightly placed over the hole in Gary's stomach, Jamie tried to stem some of the bleeding. "It's going to be alright, Gary, you're going to be alright," he said, and hoped to God he was right.

Jamie and Shay lifted Gary carefully into the back seat of the Escort. There was no time to wait for an ambulance to arrive; Shay would have to get him to the hospital.

As Shay weaved in and out of the traffic like a racing driver, Jamie's mind was also racing. Jerell was an animal and whatever he had been doing to that poor boy when they had burst in on him was disgusting; it had been the last thing Jamie had expected to see and had shocked him to the core. He hoped that the kid would be okay, but right now his priority was Gary, who was now mumbling incoherently in the back of the car.

"Fucking hell, what are those horrible noises he's making?" Shay glanced behind him. The sight of Jamie and his boss covered in blood made him want to cry. This was bad, very bad.

He pushed his foot to the floor; fuck speed restrictions, the hospital wasn't far but they were running out of time. Gary looked like he was slipping away.

Gary lay across the back seat, his head resting on Jamie's lap. His breathing was raspy; his eyes were opening and closing. Jamie fought to keep him conscious by saying his name and telling him he would be okay. Gary didn't seem able to reply. Jamie did everything in his power to remain in control; he would be strong for his boss, even though he felt like falling apart. Gary couldn't die.

Shay drove like a maniac up Lambeth Palace Road towards the Accident and Emergency unit of St Thomas' Hospital, feeling that they were losing the battle with time. Gary had stopped making the rasping sounds; his breathing was slow, too slow and quiet. He was almost silent.

Chapter 11

Reaching the garage around the corner from the flat, Jerell struggled to catch his breath. He had run so fast, with no idea if the men were chasing him, but he wasn't prepared to stand around waiting for them to catch up. They were tooled up, and there were more of them.

Jerell released his grip on Tyler then yanked up the garage door. He pointed the butt of his pistol at his Beamer. "Get in," he ordered Tyler, nodding at the passenger door. They needed to get out of there and quickly.

Tyler slowly climbed into the front seat. He was numb from the evening's events and scared shitless of what Jerell was capable of doing to him next. He felt totally overwhelmed by everything that had just happened to him and, along with what Jerell had made him do, he couldn't shake the awful image of Jerell shooting the man. Tyler had almost thrown up at the sight of all the blood that spurted out as he had watched the man grab his stomach before slumping to the floor in front of him.

As Jerell opened the driver's door and got into the motor, the boys that had followed them ran up to the entrance of the garage. Jerell quickly unwound his window and leant out.

"Whoa, Jerell, what the hell was that about, man; you showed those jokers, didn't you? Who the fuck was they, man? One of them looks like a goner; think they're all scraping his guts off the pavement now. There's blood everywhere." The oldest boy said. He had caught a good look at the bloodshed as he had run past the group of men all crouching by the front door of the flat. Jerell never failed to impress him with how ruthless he could be. Jerell cut the boy's banter short. It wasn't a laughing matter, Jerell was fuming with himself for reacting the way he had back there, but he had felt cornered, and now he had jeopardised everything he had worked so hard to build up by shooting someone on his own doorstep. He needed to think fast; he needed to keep himself from getting pulled in.

"No-one goes back to the flat, ya hear me?" Jerell spoke as calmly as he could manage, but his heart was pounding. The last thing he wanted was to get sent down for murder, and the way things had gone at the flat, it seemed likely. He was going to have to get off the radar. Staring at the older boy, his dark brown eyes looked so intense they could have almost been jet black. "Rhys," he instructed the older boy, "find Reagan, tell him what's happened. The rest of you, watch the flat. Make sure none of our boys go near it. I don't want any of you connected to that place while all this shit's going on, if dem police start snooping, say nothin', you get me? Keep your heads down and tell all the boys to steer well clear."

Everything had been going so smoothly, and now he had all this shit to deal with. The police wouldn't find anything inside the flat other than a few spliffs, but the blood all over the doorstep was a whole other story; one that he wouldn't be able to talk his way out of. He needed to find somewhere to lay low for a while, until he could find out what happened to the man that he had shot, and he had to hope to God they wouldn't be able to connect the shooting to him. Also, he would have to ditch his gun.

The man must be dead, he thought. There was no way that he could have been shot at close range, right in the gut, and survive. Jerell hadn't meant to shoot him, but he had got in the way. The fat sweaty man had lunged towards him and had unsteadily waved his gun in Jerell's direction. The man had looked shaky and scared but the way he pointed the gun about he seemed capable of shooting him, maybe as a last-ditch attempt at playing the hero.

In that split second, the situation had got out of hand and Jerell had decided to get in there before the fat man had a chance to shoot. Only that other guy, the boss man, had got in between them. He had come from nowhere;

stupidly, he had launched himself from behind Jerell, into the middle of all the drama; the bloke tried to calm the fat man down, and consequently because of all the commotion and intensity of the situation, Jerell had panicked and shot. The boss man had taken the bullet.

"Rhys, tell Reagan he has to go to Louise's. I'll make contact soon. Tell him to stay there till I speak to him. Tell him none of da gear is to be shifted until I give da word. Everything is at a stand-still until I give the say so. We are all in a whole world of shit if 'dem police find anything in the flat and come searching for me." Jerell was thinking fast. Although he had no qualms about shooting, stabbing, fighting or torturing, he was a smart man and gunning someone down on his doorstep had not been a clever move; he regretted his actions. Impulse had taken over, and it was a case of do or die. He had done what came naturally to him and reacted, and in the split second that the fat man had come towards him with the gun, Jerell had acted on instinct and pressed the trigger.

Jerell shooed Rhys and the other boys out the way of his car then pulled out of the garage. Tyler watched the boys run to do Jerell's bidding, wishing that he was with them instead of in this car, with this man. Jerell hadn't spoken a word to the boy since the men had interrupted them, and Tyler felt sick thinking about what he had been forced to do to Jerell, but more than that he was frightened of what Jerell might do next.

Tyler hadn't really understood what Jerell was doing when he had stood in front of him and started to unbuckle his black leather belt; up until then, Tyler had believed that Jerell would have a go at him for making up lies but ultimately he wouldn't be ousted from the group.

Tyler had watched Jerell un-tuck his shirt then undo the big silver buckle on his belt. Tyler was puzzled and had thought that perhaps Jerell would whip him with it, to teach him a lesson for the lie that he had been accused of telling. He remembered the stories Jerell had told about how he had been whipped as a boy back in Jamaica.

But he hadn't whipped him; instead, Jerell had told Tyler to take his penis out of his pants and hold it. Tyler had laughed a nervous laugh, thinking it was a sick joke, or a test maybe; it hadn't been until Jerell had then grabbed him so hard by his hair and tugged it until it felt like he was lifted a foot in the air, a hot pain searing through him, that it finally dawned on Tyler what was happening.

Jerell forced Tyler to put his penis in his mouth and to run his tongue up and down it, which had made Tyler gag. He had been disgusted by the taste, the smell... it was only because he had been petrified beyond belief, that he had managed not to vomit.

If those men hadn't barged in, he didn't know what Jerell would have done next. Tyler knew that it had been the men in that posh motor who had been watching the flat earlier, it was too much of a coincidence, but at this moment in time, holed up in Jerell's car with him looking like the anti-Christ, Tyler wasn't in any hurry to say so.

As Jerell drove, Tyler stared out of the window, tears blurring his vision. He wanted what had happened to have been a story. After all, this was Jerell Morgan; everyone knew he could have his pick of women. But Jerell was into little boys! Tyler guessed that there couldn't be many people other than himself who knew Jerell's dirty little secret. He wondered what lengths Jerell would go to in order to keep his filthy acts concealed.

But no one would believe what Jerell had done to Tyler, especially after all the stories he had told. His lying had been his downfall. Besides, Tyler suspected that if he even breathed a word of what had happened to another soul, Jerell would kill him. Tyler gulped at the thought. His head was swarming with all sorts of feelings; he wanted to get what Jerell had made him do out of his head but it was impossible. Looking down at his hands, he tried to stop them trembling. He may have been scared shitless earlier, but he was just realising that maybe the really scary stuff was yet to come. What was Jerell going to do now?

After a couple of minutes of silence and after Jerell had driven around aimlessly in circles, he punched the steering wheel.

"Fuck's sake," he shouted in frustration, making Tyler jump with fright. Everything was fucked up. The worst-case scenario was that he would be pulled in for this and Jerell had no intention of doing time if he could help it. Prison wasn't for him. If he was lucky enough to get away with this, he would have to avoid the flat until he knew that it was okay to go back there. He and Reagan would have to stop shifting their gear for a while and lie low. Jerell had a feeling that this mess would cost him a small fortune. As he hit the steering wheel, the car swerved. Jerell drove on in anger.

Who the fuck had those men been? He had recognised them but couldn't remember from where. Jerell had many enemies, but until today had been fortunate enough not to be on the receiving end of anybody that he had crossed. He had made a name for himself now, and those fuckers had a nerve if they thought they were a match for him. He had a feeling that perhaps Tyler had in fact been right when he had said that the flat was being watched. It was too much of a coincidence, otherwise. The boy was vigilant, at least.

"Where you live?" Jerell asked the boy sitting so quietly beside him. Tyler looked small and vulnerable huddled up in the passenger seat.

Relieved that Jerell was going to take him home, Tyler told him his address. It was only a few streets away. Tyler had never thought he would see the day that he would want to go home; not that he could tell his mum what had happened to him, but at least he would be safe from this perverted lunatic.

"Who live there with you?" Jerell racked his brain to think of what he could do; where he could go.

Tyler had a bad feeling about where this conversation was going. He said: "Just my mum… but she's a fruit loop, Jerell, if we go back there she'll call the old bill on us, honest she will. She's always threatening to have the pigs come and take me away." Tyler hoped that the thought of his mum involving the police would be enough of a deterrent to stop Jerell from staying there. It wasn't. Jerell knew what sort of a mother Tyler had at home; the same kind that most of the kids that worked for him had. It was Jerell's view that it was no wonder these kids had no goals in their lives other than to run drugs for some big man like himself, when their useless mothers had the morals of alley cats and no care for their children's whereabouts. These kids weren't shown right from wrong; they were dragged up into a life of abuse and neglect. Often they went home to violent fathers or drunken mothers. No wonder England was going down the pan. The way things were in this country was the reason

he had so many boys working for him; it was all in his favour. If Tyler thought

that his mother was going to stop him, he had another think coming. English

people were lazy scum, as far as Jerell was concerned, and Tyler's mother

wouldn't be a match for him. He had heard Tyler go on about his mother to

the others enough to know that she was not exactly what you would call a

decent role model. Tyler was never at school, he was constantly hanging

around Reagan's flat, unbeknown to his mother as she practically lived at her

local pub he recalled. He remembered the conversations that he had

overheard Tyler having with the other boys when they slagged off their

families, trying to out-do each other with stories of the crap they had to put

up with from their parents, each story more shocking than the last. Despite

the fact that the boy was clearly scared of his mother, Jerell had a feeling that

the woman would be putty in his hands. If she was anything like he thought,

money would do the talking and Jerell would be able to persuade her around

to his way of thinking with a little bundle of cash for her 'assistance'. He only

needed a couple of days, maybe a week at the most; he needed somewhere

to stay where no-one would come looking for him. It would drive him mad

sitting around, but if it kept him off the scene for a while, and kept his arse

out of prison, then he would just have to grit his teeth and get on with it.

"We're going to go and pay your mum a visit, boy." Jerell continued to drive in the direction of the boy's flat, as Tyler fought back the urge to cry once more. He had been totally out of his depth before, and now he had been left with no choice but to bring this psychopath into his home. His mum was going to kill him.

***

Tyler took out his key, struggling to turn it in the lock as his hands were still shaking; he was aware of Jerell towering over him. Tyler finally managed to open the door. He prayed that his mum wouldn't be home.

Letting them both into the flat, Tyler was relieved to see that his mother's bag wasn't on the kitchen table where she normally dumped it when she was at home. Thank God she was still out, he thought.

Following Tyler into the kitchenette, Jerell looked around in disgust. What a shithole. He had seen a few hovels, but this place really was rank. There were food and drink stains down the walls and breadcrumbs and butter smears on the worktops. Next to the sink was an overflowing ashtray. A litter tray sat in a corner of the room, confirming that the smell that had hit him on entering the flat had been a combination of fermenting cat shit and piss.

Sitting at a grease-covered table, Jerell despaired; the boy's home was barely a step up from a squat. How people managed to live in such squalor was beyond him. No matter how poor people were, there was no excuse. Jerell felt dirty.

"I think we might have some orange juice somewhere," Tyler said, trying to fill the awkward silence, as he opened the fridge and searched the shelves for something to drink.

He was aware of what Jerell must be thinking. He could see by the way that Jerell was turning his nose up in disgust as he looked around that he was judging him.

Tyler's mother didn't give a shit about the flat; she never had. Most of her life was spent in pubs; drinking was her favourite pastime, and she often didn't come home until she was ready to pass out. She treated the place like a doss house. It was somewhere to lay her head at the end of the night. When she dragged herself from her bed, she would watch a bit of telly while she smoked herself silly and then fuck off out for the rest of the day, leaving Tyler, if he was at home, to fend for himself.

"Do you want a drink?" Tyler managed to locate a carton of juice that had been shoved to the back of the bottom shelf. He felt uncomfortable that they were alone in the quiet flat.

Jerell looked into the sink; a film had formed on the stagnant water in there. Shaking his head, he decided against the juice.

"Where's your mother at?" Jerell asked.

Not wanting Jerell to get the impression that they would be alone for any length of time, Tyler did what he always had done best and lied. His mum was probably at the pub and wouldn't be back until late, closing time, he expected, but he didn't want Jerell to know that. He couldn't risk Jerell getting any ideas about a repeat performance of earlier. Pushing the disgusting visions of Jerell's cock out of his mind, Tyler said: "She's probably over at one of the neighbour's flats; she should be back in a minute." He spoke as convincingly as he could and hoped that Jerell believed him.

As lonely as Tyler had often been in the flat, he preferred that to the times when his mother stayed at home, as all she seemed to do was shout and scream at him. She would also get him to run about fetching her drinks and her lighter. He preferred her absence to her presence.

Tyler had two older sisters, but they had both moved out years ago. He was envious that they had managed to escape this existence as soon as they had had the opportunity. They had found themselves boyfriends and had gone off to start their own lives, as far away as possible. Neither visited, and the only time they phoned was on Christmas morning: even then, they had nothing much to say. Their mother accused them both of abandoning her. Tyler wasn't surprised that they kept away; his mum constantly slagged them off for having the audacity to 'desert' her. She harped on about it so much that Tyler had stopped listening. It wasn't just his sisters: she rarely had a good word to say about anyone.

Jerell drummed his fingers. He was not impressed that he would have to live in this squalor for the foreseeable future, but needs must. He would have to get on with it, it was only a temporary arrangement and lying low here was better than the alternative of chancing capture by the police.

"I want you to do something for me," Jerell said to Tyler, as he indicated to the boy to sit next to him.

Tyler felt sick; if Jerell touched him he would throw up. His legs were jelly, as he crossed the room and took a seat.

"I need you to get rid of my gun, Tyler."

Tyler was relieved that was all he wanted.

Thinking of the old bill had reminded Jerell that he needed to ditch his gun; this one could be linked with the shooting. Jerell didn't want to take any chances of being caught with it in his possession. He figured he wouldn't need a weapon for a while, not while he was here with Tyler and his mother, he would more than be capable of looking after himself. He also had another gun that he kept in a safe at Louise's place.

"You'll take the gun down to the river and get rid of it," Jerell said.

Tyler was happy to do so, getting away from Jerell would be the best thing that could happen.

Taking a T-shirt from the clothes horse beside the kitchen table, Jerell wrapped it tightly around the gun. "You got a rucksack?" he asked the boy.

Tyler went to the cupboard under the stairs where his mum often shoved all their shoes and coats and took out a small rucksack.

Coming back into the room, Tyler handed Jerell the rucksack. He had left his bike at Reagan's, but Tyler didn't mind walking down to the river, it would take longer to get there and back on foot, and the longer he took, the less time he would have to spend here alone with Jerell. Tyler was glad of the chance to get away from the man.

"What if my mum comes back while I'm gone?" Tyler asked, worried that his mum would lose the plot when she came home to find that he had let this man into her home. It was almost eight o'clock, there was a few hours until closing time, but she sometimes came home before then, especially if she had ran out of money and people to ponce drinks off, and if that happened she'd already be in a foul mood.

Tyler had yet to meet anyone who could stand up to his mother's temper or her vicious threats, but he expected Jerell to be more than a match for her. Still, he would be in a whole world of shit with her for bringing this amount of trouble to her door, so either way he was done for.

"If she comes back, she comes back," Jerell said. "You leave her to me. You just make sure no-one sees you ditching the gun, ya get me?"

"I haven't got my bike; I'm going to have to walk." Tyler couldn't wait to get out of the flat, which seemed smaller with Jerell's intimidating presence inside it.

"Don't you be getting any silly ideas, Tyler," Jerell said. "You ditch that gun in the river, and you get your arse straight back here. Any funny business and you'll be in the Thames with it. I'll cut you into tiny pieces and feed you to the fish, ya get me?"

Jerell was glaring with such malice that Tyler felt two inches tall. Jerell had a way of intimidating people, even without his loaded words and evil tone; it was in the cold glare of his eyes. Tyler nodded; his own eyes were wide; Jerell's threat petrified him. He was more than capable of carrying it out, and Tyler knew if he fucked this up, he could be killed. The thought of doing a runner briefly crossed his mind, but he wouldn't be able to get away with it. He wasn't that brave and he had nowhere else to go. And Tyler knew that if he did manage to get away, Jerell would be certain to catch up with him eventually. The man had eyes and ears everywhere; Tyler wouldn't stand a chance.

Chapter 12

Gavin, his hand on Les' shoulder, gently helped him onto Jamie's black leather sofa and went across the room to switch on the TV; anything to stop the looming silence. The plasma was plush, the thing must be at least sixty inches, he thought, and it must have cost a bomb. Jamie had expensive taste.

What a nice pad, Gavin thought, as he looked around the apartment. When he had first come through the door, he had whistled in awe. Jamie had obviously invested his earnings wisely, unlike himself and Shay who had a tendency to piss most of their money up the wall with heavy drinking sessions, pulling birds was the ultimate objective of such evenings. Clearly he was missing a trick, though; glancing around Jamie's chic bachelor pad, Gavin saw what he could have if he chose to stop spunking his cash on good times.

Gavin had wondered many times over the past couple of years what Jamie's place was like. The flat Gavin shared with Shay looked like a squat in comparison. They often struggled to meet the bills, preferring to spend their money on gear and strip clubs, and as for their bulky old fashioned telly, it had an arse bigger than J-Lo's, it was nothing like the slim-line model that Jamie had gone for. Feeling a bit jealous, Gavin reasoned that Jamie must lead a very dull life, and probably spent most of his time dusting and cleaning and fluffing up his fancy cushions. He reasoned that actually given the choice, he would rather have a big pair of titties grinding in his face on a Friday night at one of the clubs, than sit here on his tod, in a bare room, watching a fancy telly. He would like to live in a spotless apartment like this one, though: there was no dirt or mess anywhere.

Jamie was a very private man who didn't give anything about himself away. His home was just like Jamie, Gavin reflected, immaculate and bare. It had no personality, giving away no clues as to who lived in it, of who was really inside. The apartment could have belonged to anyone: a middle-aged school teacher or a highly paid corporate lawyer; it was a blank canvas.

Gavin found it strange that in the two years he had worked alongside Jamie, this was the first time he had been inside his gaff; in fact, Gavin couldn't remember a time when any of them from the garage had been invited over. Jamie was all about work, Gavin knew that. Jamie took his job extremely seriously and was a control freak. Gavin had no clue what he was like outside of work. His guard was always up. Jamie never spoke about girlfriends or family, and it was as if his social life didn't exist. Gavin couldn't quite work him out, he was a bloody good-looking fella with all that jet-black hair and that chiselled look about him that women normally couldn't get enough of, and he must have a nice amount of cash tucked away. Still, he reasoned it was none of his business, each to their own as they said. If Jamie was happy to live like a recluse, he could get on with it.

Walking across the shining wooden floor to the dresser on which bottles of spirits were displayed like carefully placed ornaments, he thought Jamie must have a severe case of OCD: either that or a bloody good cleaning lady. Gavin unscrewed one of the already-open bottles of Scotch and poured a drink for Les who was now slumped on the sofa, staring into space, his mouth hanging open. Gavin had to stifle a chuckle. He was a sight, poor old Les, the bloke's expression made him look like a proper mong.

Gavin had never been good at comforting people; such situations were his worst nightmare. He didn't have a clue what to say to Les. He was better at telling crass jokes to make people laugh or if he really struggled to make a connection with people he used the opposite tactic and wound them up to get a reaction, which usually did the trick and got a bit of banter going. Gavin could rib people all day long, but reassurance was something that didn't come naturally to him and, given the sensitivity of the situation right now, Gavin felt way out of his depth. He wished that Jamie had let him drive to the hospital instead and that Shay was here with Les. Shay would be better in this situation. He was a right soppy sod, sometimes a few sandwiches short of a picnic, but he meant well. He would do a much better job of looking after Les.

Gavin had no idea what he could say to Les to make him feel better. He didn't

know if Gary would pull through himself, so how he was supposed to comfort

Les he had no idea.

Visualising Gary bleeding and almost unconscious, Gavin hoped that Jamie

and Shay made it to the hospital in time. Having filled Les' glass to the brim,

he poured himself a large Scotch too; they could both do with a stiff drink.

Gavin handed Les the drink, encouraging him to sit up.

Les continued to gawp into space. On the TV, a game show was on;

exhausted, Gavin sat down at the opposite end of the sofa to Les.

"Get that down ya, Les, eh?" Gavin took a gulp of his own drink, and savoured

it as the heat trickled down his throat. He looked over and noticed the urine

stains on Les' trousers, and he wondered if he had even realised that he had

pissed himself.

Les was a drama queen at the best of times, they all knew that. Gavin just

hoped that a strong drink would help Les clear his head or at least take the

edge off his shot-to-pieces nerves.

"Drink up mate, it will do ya good," Gavin encouraged; he had finished his

drink in two slurps. He watched as Les' hands trembled and his untouched

Scotch spilled over the glass, forming a small puddle of liquid on the expensive-looking flooring.

"I knew." Les spoke quietly, still staring into space and seemingly talking to the room in general rather than Gavin. Les then hung his head and stared at the floor. "I knew this would happen, I dreamt this last night. We shouldn't have gone. Now Gary's going to die and it will be our fault, that bullet was meant for me, he jumped in the way." Les sobbed loudly. A long string of snot was hanging out of his nose, as his body shuddered with every cry. It should have been him, it could have been him. The tears kept coming.

Shifting closer to Les, Gavin lifted the man's drink. "Drink," he ordered, "you need it mate, you're in shock. It's nobody's fault. We all knew what that cunt was capable of. And we all went in with our eyes wide open, Gary included."

Gavin sounded so matter-of-fact that Les felt embarrassed that he wasn't as good at holding it together as his younger colleague; it was another fault he could add to his long list. Doing as he was told, Les placed the drink to his lips and took a big gulp. Choking as the liquid bounced off the back of his throat, Les coughed noisily. Gavin shook his head at the sight of a spluttering Les, Scotch running down his chin as he winced at the strength of the drink.

"What are we going to do with you, eh?" Gavin smiled, feeling sorry for Les; after all, he supposed, Les had known Gary a lot longer than he had, they went back years. They were good friends, and it was not surprising that Les was distraught. Gavin couldn't imagine what the man must be feeling. If it had been Shay who had taken the bullet today, Gavin would have been the same, if not worse, and aside from that, Gary had taken a bullet for him, it was no wonder Les was shaken up.

Gavin wanted to get Les sorted out; it would hopefully keep his mind off the day's events. He went to have a nosey in Jamie's bedroom. Jamie was much smaller than Les, but Gavin hoped that he would be able to find something amongst Jamie's clothing that Les could change into: anything, as long as it was clean, would do.

The fact that Les was sitting there with piss dribbling down his leg at his age was a sight that even in this extreme situation Gavin was having problems stomaching. Les may be distraught, but he also looked a state right now.

After a few minutes of rooting through Jamie's walk-in wardrobe, Gavin came back into the room holding a large navy dressing gown. It was probably big enough to cover Les' heavy frame, while Gavin sorted out his trousers.

"Come on, Les, Jamie's got some sort of high-powered futuristic shower in his bathroom, why don't you go and get yourself cleaned up, use up all of his lotions and potions, he won't mind, and then whack this on."

Gavin passed Les the dressing gown. A shame-faced Les looked down at himself; seeing the dark stains, his face flushed at the realisation that he had wet himself. "Drop your kecks outside the bathroom door, and I'll try and figure out how to use the washing machine." Gavin paused, wanting to lighten the mood and help Les to forget his embarrassment. "Me washing your kecks... who'd have thought, huh? You're fucking privileged, man. I don't even do my own washing, I take a sack of my stuff over to my old dear's every weekend, bless her."

Les did as he was told and trudged off to the bathroom, grateful for something to do.

Glad that he was helping to keep Les occupied for at least a few minutes, Gavin made his way to the kitchen to see if he could work out how to use Jamie's washing machine.

By the time the sun had risen, Gavin had washed and dried Les' clothes. Les was sprawled out on the sofa, snoring, Jamie's dressing gown draped over him, barely covering his thighs.

Gavin was sitting on a chair in the lounge, flicking through the TV channels as he waited for news from Jamie; although his mind was too busy to notice what was on the screen, he found the background hum, and Les' snores, comforting. There was nothing good on at such an early hour. Gavin changed from one channel to the next, irritated with the lack of choice. They put the most bizarre shit on TV at this time; who the fuck in their right mind watched it, he thought, as he settled on an old film that he had seen at least ten times.

Gavin liked to be around people: their noise... their drama... he loved it. As impressive as Jamie's apartment had first seemed hours ago when he had arrived, the walls were now closing in on him. The place was too clean and sterile, and if it wasn't for the sound of the telly and Les' snores, Gavin would have felt like he was going mad.

He had helped himself to another Scotch and had made sandwiches for him and Les earlier. Les had seemed much calmer after he had showered and eaten. He had insisted that he was too worried to sleep, but as soon as his head had rested on the arm of the sofa, he had immediately conked out, exhausted from the stress of it all. It had been one hell of a day.

Hearing a key turn in the door, Gavin sat bolt upright; he quickly muted the sound on the television and prepared himself for news.

Jamie walked into the room first, with Shay closely behind him. Gavin noticed that their body language looked defeated. Shay had his head bowed, and looking at their pale worried faces, Gavin saw that emotions were running high. He raised his eyebrows at Jamie.

Looking at Les to make sure he was asleep, Jamie shook his head.

Chapter 13

The sky was dark grey, with a hard rain and a vicious wind. Reagan zipped up his jacket as he walked. The day may have been shitty, but he was in a good mood. He could finally give Jerell some positive news, which would hopefully stop the man from completely flipping out. It had been two weeks since the shooting and things had seemingly cooled down, so they could start to think about their next step. They needed to get back into the game, start getting their gear back out onto the streets before some other little scroats muscled in on their territory.

These past couple of weeks that Jerell had been hiding out, he had been doing Reagan's head in by bombarding him with text messages and phone calls telling him what to do and what not to do. Lying low wasn't really Jerell's thing, it had turned out, and the bloke had obviously been going stir-crazy: he had almost sent Reagan mental too in the process.

Reagan had continued to help Louise grow their crop of weed, and because he had been given strict orders not to sell it, there was enough gear to get half of London stoned. Reagan had failed to persuade Jerell that he was capable of shifting the gear for him, eager for a chance to hold the fort while all this heavy shit was going on with the police, but Jerell had been adamant that everyone must stick to his rules. The boys had been told to stay well away, and they had unwillingly done as they were told. There hadn't been much else for Reagan to do; he had just kept his ears open for news about the man that Jerell had shot and now he had it.

A car whizzed past Reagan, so near the kerb that its wheels skimmed it, making a puddle rise up and soak the bottoms of his expensive new trainers and favourite chinos.

"Fucking great," Reagan yelled at the car. He bet the arsehole that was driving the car had soaked him on purpose. Still, not even wet clothes could wipe his smile from his face today. He trudged on.

Reagan had been fuming when he found out what Jerell had done. He was sure that it would fuck things up. He should have guessed that something like this would happen, though; Jerell had anger issues and needed to get a handle on his temper. Reagan had been shit-scared that the old bill would come knocking and they would get found out for what they had been up to. The idea of being in prison with a load of nonces terrified him. He imagined his flat

being upended by some jobsworth police officer snooping through all his

personal stuff. He was glad now that he had always listened to Jerell and that

they had never kept anything of importance in the flat. Jerell's passport and

fake IDs was in the safe at Louise's house, along with his guns and most of

their cash. The only drugs they ever had in Reagan's flat were a couple of

spliffs; Jerell had remained strict about that so the police wouldn't find

anything there.

Reagan had been staying with Louise. This was another thing Jerell had

insisted upon. This, as it turned out, hadn't been such a bad thing; Louise was

a good girl, and the fucked-up situation that Jerell had caused had worked in

Reagan's favour. As Reagan neared the cafe where he had arranged to meet

Jerell, he had to use his willpower to stop himself from getting a boner from

his memories of last night's bedroom antics. Louise was something else, and

from the very first time they had slept together, they had been at it morning,

noon and night. Reagan couldn't think of a better way to spend the time that

he now had on his hands. Thinking back to the first night that they had spent

together, when Louise had allowed Reagan into her bed, he smiled at how

lucky he was. She had said: "You can share my bed, but don't get any ideas.

It's just somewhere to sleep, yeah? Save you kipping on the floor." She had insisted if he couldn't keep his hands to himself, she didn't care how uncomfortable the floor was he'd be hitting it. Reagan had laid there for what seemed like hours, listening to the sound of Louise's soft breathing. He hadn't expected that lying in bed with the girl and not doing anything would be a problem, seeing as he had never even slept with a girl before.

Reagan's only sexual experience had been the abuse he had suffered at the children's home, which had been enough to make him want to avoid any type of sexual experience like the plague. He had never breathed a word about what the care home manager, Mr Bell, had done to him night after night. After the encounters that had been forced upon him back then, Reagan had often wondered when he was much younger, if doing 'those things' to Mr Bell made him gay. He had been so confused for so long that it had been easier just make sure that he never let himself get physical with anyone; sex became a taboo for him.

As Reagan had got older, he was pleased to find that he did find girls attractive, but he had always remained too scared to do anything sexually, as it only stirred up the buried emotions inside him that he wasn't capable of dealing with.

Lying in the bed next to Louise that first night, though, something inside him had stirred. It had shocked him that he was able to feel such strong, intense feelings.

Hearing her soft breathing, just inches from him, and smelling her delicate musky scent, he had been shocked by his thoughts, as he wondered what she would be like to touch and to taste. He felt himself get aroused, to the point he had been unable to sleep. Lying there frustrated, his feelings tormented him.

After what seemed like ages, he must have drifted off. His dreams were erotic, and in his sleep he continued to feel aroused, envisaging Louise's hot skin all over him as she straddled him and pressed her small pert breasts against his naked chest; he could smell her hair as it fell around him and again, even in his sleep, he felt his cock stiffen.

Opening his eyes, still half-asleep, Reagan woke to find that he wasn't dreaming; Louise was wide awake and draped over him.

Feeling his cock throb for her, Louise had taken her time to drive him wild. Her mouth pressed gently against his skin, grazing his stomach, as it moved lower down his body. She teased him with her mouth until he couldn't control himself any longer, any thoughts of being scared about sex disappearing. He wanted her. After she had worked him into a frenzied state, he pulled her up towards him and rolled over on top of her, taking her quickly with a force that he hadn't known he possessed.

Afterwards, as she lay next to him in silence, Reagan had been worried that he had hurt her or done it wrong. It had felt amazing to him, but then he didn't have anything to compare it to. Louise had reassured him that it had been perfect, and within minutes they were all over each other again, the second time slower and more intense.

Reagan hadn't been able to get enough of Louise after that, and she had said that she felt the same about him. She had taken his virginity, although this was something that he would keep quiet about. He had a reputation to uphold. Nor did he want anyone finding out what had happened to him in the past.

Now that Reagan had heard the news about the guy whom Jerell had shot, he knew that it wouldn't be long until the two of them were back doing their thing, and life could get back to normal again, but this time he would have Louise. All in all, things were looking good.

Reaching the cafe, Reagan pushed open the door. Jerell was already seated at a table in the far corner, a very pale Tyler next to him.

Reagan had tried to erase any thoughts of what Jerell might have done to the boy on the evening that he had left them together. He knew that it hadn't been long after that that the shooting had taken place, so Jerell couldn't have had much time alone with Tyler. Maybe nothing had happened. Reagan hoped that his suspicions were paranoia after everything he had been through.

As well as his pallor, Tyler had grey shadows under his eyes and a vacant expression on his face. Reagan guessed that having Jerell staying with him was difficult for the poor kid. Reagan knew that Jerell was bored of waiting around for things to cool down, and he was a nuisance when he was bored and agitated at the best of times. The boy was probably just sick to death of his company.

"What you want to drink, Reagan? Tyler will get it." Jerell kicked the chair out opposite him, indicating to Reagan to sit down.

"I'll just have a coke, Tyler," Reagan said.

"Make it two, Tyler, and get yourself another one." Jerell placed a note on the table and turned his attention to Reagan. "So what's dis news? Why you not tell me over the phone? Why you make me sit here and wait, huh, I'm going stir crazy." Jerell was annoyed that Reagan had insisted they meet. Jerell wasn't sure if the news would be good or bad, but he had figured maybe it was bad as Reagan hadn't just come out with it.

"I wanted to tell you in person, Jerell." Seeing how tense Jerell was, Reagan realised he had added to the man's anxieties. "The police were looking for me. The council have my name on the tenancy, it didn't take the coppers long to find out who lived there. Anyway, this is it. The guy you shot, his name's Gary West. He owns West's Garage, off the High Street."

Jerell raised his eyebrows. He remembered the dodgy motors with which he had shafted the man with a few months back; he had done the same to a few firms around the borough.

"Well, he's alive, Jerell. That's the main thing." Reagan watched the relief spread across Jerell's face. "He came up a blinder for us an' all... told the police he was in the wrong place at the wrong time. He made up some story about seeing someone trying to break into the flat. He told the coppers he tried to stop some burglar and was shot at close range before the guy did a runner empty-handed."

Jerell was glad that the man was okay; it would keep the heat off him. His thoughts of getting sent to prison could be put to bed. He couldn't believe the man had survived that bullet, though, God only knew how he had done.

"The fucking funniest thing ever though..." Reagan laughed, still as chuffed at this last bit as when he had first heard it. "This Gary bloke threw them off your scent. He only bloody told the coppers that the gunman was about five foot tall, oh and this will tickle ya..." Reagan paused for effect, enjoying leaving Jerell hanging, even if it was only for a few seconds. "He only went and told 'em the gunman was Chinese. A fucking Chinese midget the pigs are looking for, how fucking funny is that, huh?" Reagan waited for Jerell to join in his laughter, but Jerell was staring into space.

Jerell didn't know why Gary West would have thrown the police off his scent. He remembered meeting him. Jerell had put the guy well and truly in his place with shit cars, it was a move that had enabled Jerell to then take over the big contract that West had with the Ugandans. Jerell had a few of his boys pick up some nice luxury motors at almost thirty percent cheaper than West's price.

The bloke could have served Jerell up to the police on a platter with fucking garnish if he had wanted. So why hadn't he; what was the man up to? He was probably trying to keep himself and his own men out of the firing line. Gary wouldn't want the police snooping around his yard any more than Jerell would, he guessed; everyone had dodgy shit to conceal. Jerell must have an army of enemies out there by now; he had stepped on more than a few toes to get where he was today. He would have to step his security up when all this was dealt with, you couldn't start fires in this game without occasionally getting your fingers burnt. Next time he wouldn't be such an easy target.

Tyler came back with a tray of drinks and sat at the end of the table. Reagan noticed that the boy looked like he was carrying the weight of the world on his small shoulders, and that his eyes were full of pain. He hung his head as he drank his coke through a straw. Tyler was normally the most cheerful kid Reagan knew, and usually he was so busy spouting his exaggerated stories that short of gagging him you had no chance of shutting him up. Tyler seemed like a shadow of his former self, but he hoped the boy was just growing up.

Jerell was glad that Reagan had come up trumps and found out the information, but the boy could have told him the news over the phone. Instead, he had made Jerell sweat. It irritated him that Reagan kept acting like they were a team, when it was Jerell who was in charge; the boy should remember that.

"So what happen when you spoke to the police, you allowed back to the flat?" Jerell asked.

"Yeah, I went to the station after I heard that West had kept us out of it. Told 'em I'd been away, seeing my bird; made out I didn't have a fucking clue what was going on. They believed me on the spot, it was quite funny, they took me into the side room and broke it to me gently that I had been a victim of an attempted burglary." Reagan laughed again, this time mockingly. "Just goes to show, those pigs don't know their arses from their fucking elbows."

As Reagan spoke, Jerell's mind was whirling. He needed to get back to supplying the gear and, if the police weren't looking for him, he could start getting things sorted. You couldn't keep off the streets for too long, the druggies would find somewhere else to get their gear.

"Okay, this is what we gunna do," Jerell decided. "We find a new flat; even better a house. We got more than enough money coming in. We ain't going back to your place, Reagan; there's too much heat there. You go and get your shit together and see whoever it is you need to, and make sure that you get rid of the flat. I'm sure the council have enough pregnant schoolgirls that need housing that they won't bat an eyelid at you giving your place up."

This was an unexpected blow from Jerell; Reagan hadn't thought he would have to give up his flat. He had never owned anything before.

"Yeah, I want a big house, we need more room." Jerell would take no prisoners. There was serious money to be made and soon everything would be back in place to do it. "It'll be somewhere more private. We gunna get back out there and make some money."

Reagan left the café with a list longer than his arm of things to sort out within seven days. Jerell would continue to stay at Tyler's place until Reagan had found the new house.

Chapter 14

"Fancy some breakfast, Gary: eggs and bacon alright?" Jamie popped his head around Gary's bedroom door.

Gary was sitting up in bed. He had already read a newspaper from cover to cover and boredom was setting in at the thought of another day sitting around and twiddling his thumbs. The only good thing was that his appetite was gradually starting to come back, and the offer of another of Jamie's perfect fry-ups made his mouth water; he was famished. Slowly but surely Gary was improving; he had been told to have lots of rest, and on the condition that he would have someone to help look after him twenty-four-seven, he had been discharged from the hospital.

"Oh, go on then." Gary smiled, pretending he had had his arm twisted. He was so grateful to have Jamie staying with him. His body was still weak, even after a fortnight of resting, but he was recovering well. He still needed help walking, though, and hadn't even been able to make it to the bathroom for the first few days that he was at home without Jamie supporting him. "But I want to come out to the kitchen this morning, Jamie, and eat at the table with you.

Staring at these four bleeding walls is sending me bloody bonkers," Gary insisted, needing to get out of his bedroom if only for an hour. It may only be to another room, but it was still a much needed change of scenery as far as Gary was concerned.

"Okay," Jamie agreed, "but this is your last cooked brekkie, so you'd better make the most of it, okay? The doctors will string me up by my bits if they find out that I've been filling you up on this greasy slop every morning. As of tomorrow, it's going to be fruit smoothies, and if you're lucky, I'll throw in a bit of muesli. Doctor's orders, so no arguing!" Jamie had been spoiling Gary by cooking him a fry up, each morning, knowing that he couldn't resist a full-on English breakfast, and his plan had worked: Gary had started to regain his appetite.

Jamie couldn't praise the doctors at St Thomas' Hospital enough. They had whisked Gary off into an operating theatre on arrival at the hospital and had operated into the early hours of the morning, desperately fighting to save his life. That night had been the scariest of Jamie's life. He had paced the corridor outside the theatre, not knowing what to do with himself, until the doctors had finally told him that the bullet had missed Gary's vital organs and they had stopped his blood loss. Gary was a lucky man. Under the doctor's orders Gary was to take it easy for a while and build his strength back up.

It had been just over two weeks since the shooting and Jamie was just thankful that Gary had, against the odds, pulled through. The thought of losing his friend had been too much for him to bear.

"Right you are, then," Jamie agreed, helping Gary to sit up and twist his legs around to face the edge of the bed; seeing him grimace, Jamie was aware that Gary was still in a lot of pain.

Jamie figured that it would do Gary no harm to come and eat in the kitchen. The doctors had encouraged him to gradually introduce Gary to slow movements, such as walking short distances, as it would help Gary to build up his core muscles, and Jamie thought that while Gary ate he would also get the chance to get into his bedroom and strip all the bedding off and put some clean sheets on. Gary hated him faffing about, but Jamie wanted Gary to be as clean and comfortable as he could make him.

Matching Gary's slow pace and keeping him steady as they walked to the kitchen, Jamie helped him to sit in a chair.

Gary tried to stifle a groan, as pain seared through his stomach, but he hadn't managed to keep it from Jamie, who was looking at him worriedly.

"Don't you go stressing yourself out about my little aches and pains, Jamie lad." Gary shook his head dismissively at Jamie's concerned glance. "I was creakier than a barn door even before this happened."

Gary had a habit of shrugging things off, and Jamie knew a man in pain when he saw one. Realising that Gary wouldn't appreciate him making a fuss he got on with preparing a feast.

"Scrambled eggs; bacon; hash browns; tomatoes; mushrooms: how does that grab ya?" Jamie whisked the eggs as Gary watched him, smiling.

"You know, Jamie, you're a star doing all of this for me." Gary was truly grateful for all Jamie's help the past two weeks; the boy had been constantly at his side, fetching his painkillers, even helping bathe and dress him. Gary would have been lost without him.

"It's only bloody bacon and eggs, Gary, hardly à la carte, it's no trouble at all, mate." Jamie chuckled. He enjoyed looking after Gary, and knowing that his help was appreciated and that he was genuinely needed made it more than worth his while, and he had really got used to having a bit of company himself for a change.

"Nah, you wally. I'm not talking about the breakfast, although you do make a mean fry-up. I mean this – all of it. You've really helped me get back on my feet, you know, son."

Jamie felt a swell of pride at the word 'son'. Gary had called him it for years, and Jamie had accepted it as a term of endearment, as they had been close for a long time. But when Gary said it lately, it had more meaning. Jamie was aware that their bond had become even stronger because of what had happened, and he had been surprised at the secure feeling Gary gave him. Jamie had always thought it was a bit of a cliché that bad things brought people closer, but it was true in this case. Jamie couldn't begin to think about what would have happened if Gary hadn't made it.

Seeing his boss go all teary-eyed and sentimental, Jamie shrugged it off. "Don't be soft, mate. Honest Gary, it was nothing, you'd do the same for me, and you know you would! Anyway, if it weren't for me insisting that we go in there all guns blazing to sort that Jerell out, you wouldn't be in this sorry state right now."

Jamie busied himself making tea and buttering toast. The last thing Gary needed right now was him getting all het up about Jerell.

Gary watched him. Jamie was a good boy, a bloody diamond. He had always known that, and now he loved him like the son he had never had. Gary didn't have any family. The only thing he had loved in the past was his business. From day one, it had been his baby. Years ago, when he had first started up, his garage had meant everything to him, and he had never met a woman who measured up to it. Gary knew there wasn't a woman on this Earth that would be happy playing second fiddle to his work. His hours were long, and there was too much at stake with the people he dealt with to have a woman hanging around.

Sitting here now, watching Jamie whistle to himself as he cooked, made Gary realise what he could have had. He deeply regretted his priorities then.

As he sat and watched Jamie prance around the kitchen, acting out an exaggerated Jamie Oliver impersonation, Gary laughed, but the tears creeping out of his eyes, which he hastily wiped away, were not ones of mirth. Ever since he had turned fifty, he had started to think about never settling down and having a family and the shooting had put things into perspective. He was past having kids now, he knew that. Jamie was the nearest to a son he would ever have.

As Jamie was plating up the bacon, the doorbell rang. The two men looked at each other. "Les!" they chimed in chorus. Les had turned up at the house at the crack of dawn every day since Gary had come home. The first few days Jamie had hinted to Les that he should go home and get some sleep just to get rid of the annoying bugger, as he had turned up on the day that Gary had got back from hospital and stayed for almost twelve hours, but Jamie knew, as irritating at Les was, he meant well. He cared about Gary as much as Jamie did, and Jamie knew that he wanted to be there for him too.

Jamie grinned, as he put an extra placemat on the table. "Why do you think I cooked extra bacon, huh? I swear that bloke only comes round this early so he can get fed some proper grub."

Jamie opened the door. "You alright, Les?" he asked, as Les stepped into the house.

"Just thought I'd pop in and see how the patient's doing," Les said, as he followed Jamie through to the kitchen.

Les wasn't happy that Jamie was the one looking after Gary; it had put his nose out of joint. As Jamie had taken on the role of Gary's carer without consulting him, Les had taken it upon himself to do the next best thing and spend as much time as possible visiting the patient.

"Fancy some brekkie, Les?" Gary winked at Jamie.

Seeing his boss sitting in the kitchen, able to eat at the table with them, Les perked up, chuffed to see Gary with a bit of colour in his cheeks once more.

"Only if there's some going spare, I don't want to put you out or anything," Les said, as he sat at the table. He noted that Jamie had already set a place for him next to Gary, and again felt irked that Jamie was forever one step ahead of him. "I was just going to grab something later, you know, but if you're sure that there's enough to go around?" Les added, seeing the two men exchange amused glances.

Jamie rolled his eyes, and Gary let out the chuckle that he had tried to conceal.

"What?" Les felt he was missing out on a joke.

"Nothing, Les," Jamie put a plate of food in front of Les and said: "Get that down ya."

Having fed the others, Jamie tucked into his own breakfast. He had been eating better since he had been staying with Gary; he guessed that was because he was making proper meals to help Gary build his strength back up and so had started eating properly himself. If he had been at home, he might cook pasta or something, but it barely seemed worth the effort of cooking a big meal if it was just him that was eating.

"You alright keeping an eye on Gary this morning, Les, if I just nip out in a bit and see how the boys are doing down at the garage?" Jamie finished his last mouthful, his stomach full now. Les could keep Gary company while Jamie changed the bed sheets, then he needed to go out. He wanted to pop in and see how Gavin and Shay were getting on down at the garage. Jamie didn't want to leave everything down to them. They were more than capable of doing all the day-to-day stuff, and they had been able to keep the orders in check while Gary had been out of action, but Jamie always liked to be the one in control, so he wanted to get down there and make sure everything was running smoothly; the less Gary had to think about at the moment the better.

"Of course I can, I was going to pop in later myself. Maybe now you're looking a bit better, Gary, I should get back to work." Les looked at Gary to see what he thought. They were all well aware that there wasn't enough work for them all now that they had lost the main contract. Shay and Gavin had only been in there doing legit MOTs and a few services this week. They had just been keeping the diary in order so at least there wouldn't be a backlog to deal with; if they didn't stay on top of things, they would lose the little trade that they had coming in.

As Gary was looking perkier today, Les felt that he could he could finally broach the subject of work. He didn't want to stress the man out after all he had been through, but he was worried that he might end up out of a job.

"I think that's a good idea, Les, you get yourself back down there and hopefully in a week or two I'll be feeling like me old self again." Gary smiled, optimistic for the first time since the shooting that he was going to be alright. He was still in pain, but it was milder than it had been. "And Jamie, while we're talking about the garage, I think it would be a good idea if you take over for a bit for me."

Jamie couldn't mask his surprise at Gary's words. He could sense Les' hackles rise.

"It's going to take a while for me to get myself back to a hundred percent; I'm going to have to take it easy for quite a while," Gary explained, "and when I am better, I want to take a step back from it all, anyway. It's time for me to think about handing over the reins. Just for a while, and see how it goes, eh?"

Jamie had assumed that Gary would be back in the garage before he knew it; the thought of running the place himself had never entered his head. Trying not to sound as overwhelmed as he felt, he said: "Of course I'll look after the garage for you, Gary; it'll be a pleasure. You know I'll do a good job. I learnt from the best, after all."

Knowing that Les was seething, Gary turned to address him, hoping that he would understand. He had wanted to say his bit in front of him, so that he didn't feel excluded. "Is that alright with you, Les?"

Les felt sick. First Jamie had moved in with Gary to look after him, now he had been given the garage. Gary clearly had no use for him anymore.

"You know this is the right thing to do, Les," Gary said. Les was prone to hissy fits, and Gary wanted to get how he was feeling out in the open in the hope that Les would then just get on with it. "Jamie is younger and stronger than us both; you and I know that. There'll always be a place there for you, Les, as long as you want it, yeah?"

Reluctantly, Les nodded. He was miffed that Jamie was being handed the responsibility of the garage after all the years that Les had put in, but he really did hope that Gary meant it, and that all his hard work hadn't been in vain.

"Well, Jamie can't do it all on his own, can he? He's going to need your help, just like I always have. I want the pair of you to put your differences aside and start bloody getting along." Gary's voice was stern. He was more than aware

of the constant rivalry between the two men, even if it was often from Les'
side.

Trying to avoid looking at Jamie, Les said that he would do what Gary asked,
for his sake and for the garage's. But there was no way in hell he was going to
get along with Jamie Finch: that was never going to happen.

"Whatever you say, mate. You just get yourself better, and me and Jamie will
look after everything."

Chapter 15

Gavin was laughing so hard, tears were streaming down his cheeks. Shay was a legend.

They were in the office; Gavin was slouched in Gary's comfortable leather chair, his long legs stretched out on the desk, Shay opposite him, tipping back and forth on a chair. They had only had two cars booked in for that day and had sorted them out by ten thirty. Other than the cleaning up, they had nothing to do and so had decided while it was quiet that they would have a joint and a chat.

"And then she said... 'What sort of girl do you bloody take me for, Shay?' and got all stroppy, started stomping around the bedroom gathering all her clothes up, you know what women are like when they're bloody on one. So I just told her, 'That wasn't what you said last night when I had my cock up your arse.'"

Gavin was roaring with laughter. "She never let you give it to her up the arse?"

This latest bird of Shay's sounded like a nightmare. Gavin had met the girl on a few occasions when they had passed in the hallway at the flat, and she had seemed like a right snotty cow. She was way too up stuck up for the likes of

Shay, Gavin had thought, and he was finding it hilarious that Shay had

managed to ditch her, in the true Shay style that his friend was fast becoming

notorious for.

"No, she didn't." Shay grinned. "Chance would have been a fine thing. But she

was so drunk last night, we both were, and after her getting all mardy with

me, the look on her face when I made out that she had was bloody priceless.

She probably went home to check her arsehole was still intact."

Gavin shook his head in wonder, trying to picture Shay wiping the hoity-toity

look off the poor girl's face; he almost felt sorry for her.

Shay was terrible when it came to relationships; the only time that he didn't

have a bird on the go was when he was in hiding, avoiding one. Gavin was

always amazed at the amount of girls Shay attracted, and even more baffling

was how many of them turned into stalkers once they were with him. The

phrase 'treat 'em mean, keep 'em keen' clearly worked a treat; they must see

Shay as the ultimate challenge. Gavin himself had had the misfortune of

having to deal with countless teary phone calls to the flat, often while Shay

was sitting next to him, encouraging Gavin to say whatever it took to stop the

girl from calling him again.

"So you're officially a free man again then, huh?" Gavin was glad that he would have his pulling partner back in time for the weekend. He fancied going out and seeing if he could meet a nice bird and get laid himself. He didn't manage to get the girls as easily as Shay. Shay had a cheeky schoolboy charm about him; girls just couldn't get enough of his 'little boy lost' routine. Gavin didn't have the patience for that kind of thing. If girls didn't like him the way he was, that was their loss. He didn't put on airs and graces for anyone.

"Mate, I'm officially single. Think I'm going to keep it that way for a while." Shay breathed out a plume of smoke. "Women are more trouble than they're blimmin' worth. Here, I've got a good one for ya. How do ya turn a fox into an elephant?"

Gavin shook his head. "I dunno, Shay, how do you turn a fox into an elephant?"

"Marry her!" Shay slapped his leg, laughing, as Gavin rolled his eyes. "Yeah, I'm done with birds for a bit."

Gavin grinned knowingly. Shay without a bird wouldn't happen; the bloke's sole purpose in life was sex. Gavin would give him an hour of them being in a club on Friday night before Shay found himself another deluded girl who wanted to try her luck with him, Gavin would put money on it.

"Hello?" Jamie's voice rang out from the workshop, interrupting the conversation. "Are you two grease monkeys hiding in here?" Jamie was pleased to see that the cars that had been booked in were ready for collection, the signed-off paperwork for the customer neatly tucked behind each windscreen wiper.

Stubbing out the joint and getting out of Gary's chair, Gavin called out: "We're out the back, Jamie, having a five-minute break after finishing this morning's jobs; you fancy a coffee?"

"Arse-licker!" Shay grinned at Gavin and fanned the air to disperse the smoke. He knew why Gavin was trying to keep Jamie sweet, though; if he had walked in and found Gavin sitting at Gary's desk, looking like he owned the place, Jamie would have had a pop. He had been strange lately, acting like he was Gary's personal bodyguard. It was understandable, they guessed, especially after all Gary had been through, but Jamie had just been a bit unpredictable in his moods lately.

Jamie walked into the back office. He saw the dog ends in the ashtray and recognised the smell of weed. He wasn't stupid, he knew what Shay and Gavin had been doing, and they both knew that weren't to smoke full stop on the premises, let alone gear. He decided that he would let it slide just this once, as to be fair the boys had been pretty much left to it this past week, and they had both done a blinding job and just got on with everything that had needed to get done. He knew they had a smoke sometimes, they were fools if they thought that Jamie hadn't cottoned on to them doing it on the sly; he could always smell it on them.

"Open the window, Shay, it fucking reeks in here," Jamie said, so that they were under no illusions about pulling the wool over his eyes. Taking a seat in Gary's chair, he opened the diary. Without looking up, he said: "Go on then, Gavin, stick a coffee on. We can have a little chat while I'm here."

Jamie looked serious; Shay and Gavin wondered what was happening.

Gavin came back a few minutes later and put a mug of coffee on the table for Jamie, before taking a seat opposite him, next to Shay. "It's nothing bad, boys, don't worry." Jamie noted their worried expressions. "It's just that me and Gary had a little chat this morning," Jamie continued with the boys' blank faces staring back at him.

"How's he doing today?" Shay had meant to go round to Gary's house last night but had been too occupied with the girl. He and Gavin were going to go when they finished work.

"He's good, Shay, really good: I left him with Les chewing his ear off over some football results. I think he'll be properly back on his feet in no time now, he's really starting to make progress. That's what I wanted to talk to you about, actually." Jamie took a sip of the coffee and tried not to grimace at the strength of it; Gavin made bad coffee. "Fuck me, Gavin, have the cows gone on strike, mate?" Jamie put the mug down, deciding to give it a miss. "Gary had a chat with me and Les this morning. Gary's decided that he wants me to take over here, just for the time being, until he's his old self again."

Shay and Gavin nodded. They were both relieved that it wasn't anything more serious. It had been so quiet lately that they had wondered if Jamie were going to tell them he was shutting the doors for good. Jamie taking over wasn't really surprising. He had been running the show for a while now, even if it had been unofficially. He was more than capable of doing the job, and Gavin and Shay had mainly taken their orders directly from him recently.

"And what's Les got to say about it?" Gavin asked. Les was sure to be fuming over the situation, especially as he already seemed to have a problem with everything that Jamie said or did.

"You know Les." Jamie rolled his eyes. "He was fine about it; at least he said he was. Anyway, it's tough shit if he's not. It's Gary's decision; Les is just going to have to get on with it."

"So when's Gary coming back, then?" Shay was wondering when they were going to start taking on some new car deals, the endless MOTs had been mind-numbing. He wanted to get his hands on a few nice motors; he had started to become hooked on the adrenaline rush when they got sent out on a job.

Jamie knew what Shay was getting at and totally agreed that they needed to regain a bit of control and get something big off the ground again. The Ugandan contract was gone, and Gary wanted them to all steer well clear of Jerell after everything that had happened. There were more than enough contacts to go around, and Jamie was trying to sort out another avenue of income for them. He had his own buyer of luxury motors already waiting. It wasn't the scale of contract that they had been dealing with originally, but it was a nice little earner, and would more than keep them all going. Now that Jamie was in control of the garage, he was going to start making a few changes for the better. He wanted to show Gary that he was more than competent at doing the job, seeing as Gary had been so keen to give him the opportunity.

"Gary is going to need another few weeks away, at least," Jamie answered. Shay and Gavin looked miffed; they dreaded the thought of more quiet days. "But we ain't waiting for him to come back so that we can get moving. We're getting started today. I want the diary cleared. You two need to get the bookings done and don't take on anymore until I tell you. We've got a massive contract lined up. We're going to have top-end motors coming out of our fucking ears soon."

The boys were happy to hear it. Once you started getting used to earning a certain amount of money, you wanted to maintain your standards. If they were busy, then that meant more readies coming in.

Before he left the garage, Jamie ran through everything he wanted the boys to get sorted. He had told them to clear the diary and get anyone that they could move, booked in for today and tomorrow and to cancel anything else. Jamie respected Gary's decision to leave Jerell Morgan alone, and begrudgingly he would go along with it for Gary's sake, but there was no way that he would see this garage go under while he was in control. There were going to be changes around here.

Leaving Shay and Gavin buzzing about the place filled with a newfound optimism, Jamie made his way over to Tulse Hill Tesco Express, to pick up a few bits for Gary. He was glad that he had his appetite back, but the man had been eating food quicker than Jamie was capable of cooking it these past two days, and he knew that Gary needed to stop eating all the greasy fry-ups that he had been making for him, he needed to eat more healthily if he wanted to make a speedy recovery.

After wandering around the shop and filling up his basket with as much fruit and vegetables as he could fit in it, he was just getting back into his car, when he glanced over and saw a group of kids that he thought he recognised walking down the road. They all wore the same dark hoodies and baseball caps, but the glimpse Jamie had of the smallest kid in the group, left him feeling almost sure that it was the boy who had been with Jerell in the flat.

Despite knowing that Gary would kill him if he found out, Jamie couldn't let things lie, he wanted to see where the kid was heading. Maybe it would lead him to Jerell. Jamie decided it would do no harm to follow him, check out where he lived. Knowledge was power, after all.

Jamie took his time driving out of the garage car park. He waited until the kids were further down the road then slowly pulled out onto the main road and started to follow them. The kids turned into a side road. Waiting at the top of the road for a minute, he wanted to give them a chance to get to wherever they were heading without them spotting him.

***

Tyler was pissed off. Rhys and the others had spotted him walking back from his meeting with Reagan, and they were pestering him as he made his way home.

"So where's he holed up then Ty?" Rhys asked for the fifth time, frustrated that Tyler was giving nothing away.

"If Jerell wants you to know where he's staying, then he'll tell ya himself, man," Tyler repeated for the fifth time.

"What makes you so special, Ty? You think only you can know where he is?" Rhys scoffed at the kid. Tyler making out like he was Jerell's main man was annoying Rhys. He wanted to know if Jerell was hiding out somewhere; how come it was only Reagan and Tyler who were allowed to know where he was? The Larkhall Boys had a pecking order, and this little shit was far down in it. Everyone knew that Tyler was a liar, the kid did nothing but spout Jackanory to anyone who would listen. The kid had hinted that he knew where Jerell was, until Rhys had called him on it and insisted that Tyler tell them; now Tyler was backtracking and telling Rhys it was none of his business.

"Look, Rhys, just leave it will ya." Tyler was worried that the boys were going to follow him home; Jerell would go mental if he thought Tyler was telling people his whereabouts.

"You're just a fucking batty boy, Tyler. Think you're all that? You're just some stupid fucking kid. Jerell wouldn't tell you shit, man, you're a fucking liability." Rhys looked pleased with himself as the others laughed at his diss. He hadn't wanted to lose face in front of them because he couldn't get information out of Tyler.

"What's in your bag?" Rhys added noticing how tightly Tyler was clutching it.

"Nothing."

"Tell me what's in your bag." Rhys could see the boy was hiding something.

"No." Tyler tried to turn away as Rhys grabbed the rucksack from his shoulders. Tyler immediately protested and tried to take it back.

"Give it back, Rhys, it's shit for Jerell... just leave it, will ya?"

Rhys took a look in the bag. Seeing paperwork in there, presumably for the new place that Reagan had mentioned, he realised perhaps Tyler did know where Jerell was. All this stuff must be from Reagan. If Jerell got wind that Rhys was giving Tyler grief while he was on a job for him, Rhys would get his arse kicked.

Zipping up the bag, Rhys threw it at Tyler with force. "You best fuck off, Ty."

Tyler placed the straps of the bag over his shoulders, and crossed the road, happy to get away from the boys. He carried on walking towards the flat.

* * *

Jamie had sat and watched as the boy had broken away from the group of kids and crossed the road. Seeing the kid go down an alleyway alone, Jamie pulled into a parking space and followed on foot.

Walking slowly, so that he could stay undetected, Jamie watched the kid go into an eight-storey-high block of flats. Jamie started to feel uneasy; he knew this area well and couldn't stand it. Although the last time he had been here seemed a lifetime ago.

Pulling his hood over his head, so that no-one would recognise him, Jamie followed the boy up the concrete steps to the second floor of the tower block. The second floor: what were the chances? Jamie held his breath as he waited. Leaning up against the depressing grey walls, the familiar stench of urine in the stairwell drifted up his nostrils and burned the back of his throat; some things never changed.

Slowing down, Jamie waited before looking around the corner. Further down the balcony, he could see the boy unlocking the door to a flat.

Jamie staggered back into the stairwell. He leant over and threw up the bile that had burned his throat; it splattered the floor and splashed the grey walls.

Rushing back down the steps, Jamie ran through the alleyway and into his car. Getting a tissue from the glove box, he wiped his mouth. He felt like the car was closing in on him, an unfamiliar feeling of panic writhing through him as he desperately tried to make sense of what he had seen. It couldn't be true. But it had to be.

Driving away, he tried to digest what he had seen. He had just realised that things were a lot worse than he could have anticipated.

Chapter 16

"I'm back," Tyler called, as he let himself into the flat.

Hearing Jerell talking on his phone in the lounge, Tyler dropped his bag onto the kitchen floor before pouring a large glass of coke and helping himself to a handful of chocolate biscuits. The cupboards had lots of food inside them, for a change, and Tyler intended on making the most of it. Filling up the cupboards had been one of his mother's conditions for letting Jerell stay. Jerell had offered her cash to tide her over and said that he would fill up the cupboards with food, he was a big man and could eat for England and Jamaica rolled into one, and in return she would give him a roof over his head and make sure no-one was any the wiser about him being here.

Tyler gulped his drink, savouring the sweetness. It sounded as though Jerell was on the phone to Reagan, getting him to sort out a few last-minute things before they moved into the new place. Jerell had also had Tyler running about all over the place, which he didn't mind. If he was out doing jobs, it meant that he wasn't alone with the man.

However, Tyler anticipated a long evening ahead of him; he felt like a prisoner in his own home; Jerell was watching him constantly.

Tyler's mum had left just before him this morning, wanting to get to the pub as soon as it opened, and Tyler knew that she wouldn't be back until much later on tonight. Now she had money in her pocket, she was worse than ever; she got paralytic every night, spunking the money away.

"The locals treat me like a celebrity," she had boasted to Tyler as he was eating his dinner, a cheese sandwich, the night before. "I'm frigging royalty."

Tyler hadn't wanted to tell his slurring mother that maybe they were taking a leaf out of her book and keeping her sweet while they ponced back some of their money. He decided to keep his mouth shut and had taken a big bite out of the sandwich so that he wouldn't be able to reply. They were all just probably dying to find out how she had landed herself with a bit of cash for a change, none of them gave a shit about her. She was a bloody handful when she was out, always sticking her oar in where it wasn't wanted and causing dramas. She had been so busy boasting to Tyler about how she had become flavour of the month that she hadn't even given the fact that he had to stay in the flat all day with Jerell a second thought. Tyler had finished his sandwich in silence; his mother had staggered past him and up the stairs to bed without so much as even saying goodnight to him.

Tyler hadn't made it home in time on the night that his mother had come back to find Jerell in her house, so he couldn't be sure of her initial reaction. He imagined that she had got the shock of her life when she had been faced with a big black man sitting at her kitchen table waiting for her. Tyler had hurried to the river where Jerell had instructed him to dump his gun. He had walked so fast he had given himself a stitch. Tyler had held his side as the hot pain had torn through him, wanting to get back home before his mum returned.

Tyler had been too late. When he walked in, she was sitting opposite Jerell at the kitchen table. Neither of them was speaking, and Tyler's mother's face resembled a slapped arse.

Tyler had stood in the doorway, trying to gauge what had been said, while his mum glared at him. Jerell had obviously laid down the law. She looked as if she were shitting herself, like someone who didn't know how to play out the situation that had presented itself. Tyler could understand that feeling; Jerell could intimidate most people. He had an air about him of someone who was not quite the full ticket.

"I've agreed that Jerell can stay," his mother had said, at last. Tyler suspected that she hadn't been given any choice; the way his mum had spat the word 'agreed' confirmed his thoughts. Jerell could take the sofa, as long as he agreed to her terms. "There are a few conditions, though," she continued, trying to save face and pretend that she had a say in the matter.

Tyler was stunned. In all his young life, Tyler had never seen his mother look so browbeaten. She looked small and pathetic as she sat there, clearly trying to suppress her anger. Tyler wondered how she felt about being on the receiving end of bullying. He couldn't help thinking that it was revenge at its sweetest. No matter how trappy his mother could be, she didn't stand a chance against Jerell. It was karma.

The two weeks since Jerell had moved in had followed the pattern of his first day. Watching him manipulate Tyler's mum was fascinating. Tyler enjoyed watching her squirm. He had never seen her act in an obedient manner. She complied with everything that Jerell insisted on, without a murmur.

Jerell had given her a large wad of rolled-up notes as payment for her 'letting' him stay; he knew that it would keep her sweet, and he was also aware that if he lined her pockets with cash she would make herself scarce at the pub. It would be money well spent.

"Ya get them?" Jerell had come quietly into the kitchen, making Tyler jump when he heard him speak. He dropped his glass, which rolled across the table, the last few drops of coke spilling. Tyler grabbed the paperwork that he had left on the table, next to his bag, before it could be stained. He passed it to Jerell.

Jerell hadn't touched Tyler since the day of the shooting. However, he watched him, staring intensely. Tyler had a feeling that it would only be a matter of time before he did something again. Tyler had his suspicions that Jerell hadn't done anything because he didn't want any drama while he stayed at the house, in case Tyler's mum found out. He was playing it safe. He hated Jerell for what he had made him do, even the thought of it made him want to puke. The sooner Jerell was out of the flat the better, Tyler thought, as he grabbed a cloth from the worktop and started mopping up the spilt drink, as Jerell looked over the papers.

"Everything's in place." Jerell had a rare smile on his face as he folded the papers and threw them down on the now clean table. Reagan couldn't have picked a better house from the description he had read. Jerell was happy that he would soon be back in his own place, doing his own thing.

"Reagan's picking the keys up first thing tomorrow morning. So I want you to get your backside over to Louise's now, so that you can give Reagan a hand to get everything packed up, and then you can take it all straight over to the new place in the morning. I'm gunna meet you there at lunchtime."

Tyler was knackered from walking back from Louise's with the documents, and the thought of heading straight back out again was the last thing he wanted to do, but he knew he didn't have a choice, and once again he couldn't help thinking that anything was better than staying at home with Jerell. The sooner Tyler helped Jerell to get himself organised, the sooner Jerell would be leaving, and Tyler would have his life back again, so he happily obliged.

"Pack your things before you go, Tyler."

"My stuff?" Tyler wondered why he would need to pack?

Jerell smiled at the confusion that had spread across the boy's face.

"You heard me right, boy. Pack your things. You're coming to live in the house, too. It ain't like you gotta leave much behind. This ain't no home, this is a fucking shithole." Jerell looked around at the mess and dirt; the flat was a dive. In the two weeks that he had been staying, Tyler's mum had been drunk every day. She only came home late at night to sleep, and got out of bed when the pubs opened at eleven. She was the epitome of what Jerell detested in English women. They had no self-respect. Woman like her were the reason that Jerell had so many boys like Tyler working for him. "Your mum doesn't give two shits about you, Tyler. The only thing she cares about is where her next drink is coming from. You don't get no schooling. What chance do you stand out there in the world? So you may as well come with me." Jerell shrugged, as if it were the obvious solution. "Besides, I got plans for you."

Dread filled Tyler's stomach on hearing Jerell's final words. He had an awful feeling that he knew exactly what Jerell's plans were. Jerell wasn't doing a Dr Barnardo and whisking Tyler away from his dismal life with his mother for a better one. Jerell was thinking of himself.

Tyler nodded dumbly. He felt petrified. If he moved in with Jerell, he would never be able to get away; Jerell would do what he liked. As Jerell looked at him, Tyler had never felt so scared.

Chapter 17

Jerell sat bolt upright, unable to relax. He plucked the bobbles of thread that were sticking out of the cheap fabric of the worn sofa; his impatience was getting the better of him.

Today was the day that he would be leaving this dump and moving into his own place with Reagan and the boys, and he couldn't wait to get going. Reagan and Tyler would be over at the new house now, and Jerell was eager to join them, but there was one last thing he had to do before he left, and he was going to get pleasure from doing it.

Jerell had been up for hours. He didn't have much to pack, just a small bag of clothes. Reagan would take care of the rest. Jerell couldn't wait to have his own space again, especially as the house they were moving into was a palace in comparison to this dive.

Jerell looked at the clock once more. The lazy cow would probably be in her bed for at least another hour, sleeping off the copious amounts of alcohol she had drunk last night. He had heard her come in just after one in the morning, crashing around downstairs like a fucking bull in a china shop. She wasn't exactly light on her feet at the best of times, but when she was half-cut she was like a bloody dancing rhinoceros.

Jerell wasn't prepared to wait any longer for her to finally grace him with her presence.

He was feeling twitchy and decided he would go to her. He climbed the stairs two at a time, his patience well and truly gone and his temper building as he burst open the door and stormed into the bedroom.

The stench of the stagnant room, sour body odour mixed with the overpowering smell of alcohol, filled his nostrils, making him retch. If the smell alone wasn't bad enough, the sight before him was worse. He could just about make out, as the curtains were still drawn and the room was in almost total darkness, her silhouette on the bed. She was face down, sprawled like a starfish across the bed sheets, wearing nothing but her knickers, dirty and hung-over.

"Get up," Jerell ordered, waking her instantly. He wondered if she even knew that her son had packed up his things and left last night, while she was out getting off her face. She was a poor excuse of a woman, and the longer he stood here looking at the state of her the more he wanted to kick the living shit out of her. He had so much pent up anger and frustration from just sitting around the past few weeks that he could have kicked her from here to Brighton.

"What the fuck's going on?" Tyler's mum was startled by her rude awakening. Jerell loomed at the foot of the bed, she could just about make out his forehead, wrinkled with anger, as he stared back at her. Her head pounded from the shots she had downed last night at the pub. She tried to get herself together but confusion made her head bang even louder. She wanted to sort whatever it was out as quickly as possible, so that she could get some more shut eye.

"I said, get up," Jerell's voice was quieter, more controlled, than before. But his tone spoke volumes, his calmness unnerving.

Even putting one foot in front of the other this morning would be a challenge, she thought, as she struggled to sit up, feeling queasier with every movement. As she moved her legs slowly over the side of the bed, and tried to fight back the urge to vomit as the room started swaying, she thought that she couldn't be arsed with this crap; if Jerell hadn't woken her up, she could have happily stayed in bed for at least another few hours.

But Jerell had no tolerance left. As he watched her pathetic attempts to gain

his sympathy he shook his head at the woman, disgusted with the state that

she allowed herself to get into. Unable to contain himself any longer he

launched himself at her, grabbing a fistful of her greasy hair as he pulled her

out of the room, towards the stairway.

"What the fuck are you doing, Jerell?" she screamed, she winced in pain as

she felt a massive chunk of hair being torn from her scalp.

"I'm doing what I've wanted to do since the first minute I set eyes on you."

Jerell released his grip from her hair, giving her a few seconds of relief from

the pain, before he kicked her in the stomach. Losing her balance, she toppled

down the stairs, her plump body bouncing off each step as she desperately

tried to grab hold of the banister, hoping that it would break her fall. As she

landed in a heap on the floor at the bottom of the stairway, her head was

throbbing in pain and her vision was fuzzy. She tried to get up. That kick had

been hard, and she felt like she had had the wind knocked out of her. Even

with her blurred vision, she could just about make out Jerell's dark towering

figure coming towards her as he made his way slowly down the stairs. She

groaned in pain, as he grabbed her by her arm and dragged her into the

lounge. Using all his strength, as she went limp with fear, he threw her across

the room, where she landed against the coffee table.

A sharp pain seared through her right foot, which was twisted at a funny angle, and she knew straight away that it was broken. The pain was excruciating.

Jerell prodded her stomach with his boot, enjoying the scared expression that flashed across her face as she wondered what he was going to do to her next. He looked down at her; if she wasn't such a horrible cunt she would be pitiful, he thought. Her pleading looks and the pathetic whimpering were doing nothing but agitating him even more.

"You women are all the same. Why you choose to have a child if you can't be bothered to look after it?" Jerell shook his head in anger at the woman in front of him, as she shook with fear. She was wearing nothing but grimy-looking knickers, and the rolls of fat that rippled around her stomach and her thighs wobbled as she trembled. She didn't try to cover up her large saggy breasts as she lay there like a lump of lard. The sight of her was making him feel sick. This woman wasn't capable of looking after herself, let alone a kid. Jerell's own mother had upped and left him when he was born; she had walked out on him and never contacted him since. Even though he had been happy enough being raised by his grandma, he had grown to despise women because of what his mum had done. Especially those that thought that they could just pop kids out and let someone else clean up their mess.

"Please, Jerell; I don't know what I've supposed to have done. If you can just tell me, then maybe we can sort out whatever this is about." She spoke quickly, hoping that her words would be enough to resolve whatever the issue was that had caused him to react this way. There had to have been some kind of a misunderstanding, she thought, as she had done absolutely nothing wrong. Quite the opposite, in fact, she had gone out of her way for him and had given him a roof over his head, and now here he was acting like a fucking animal towards her, and she couldn't for the life of her fathom out why.

"Is it Tyler? Cos if he's done anything wrong, I'll kick his scrawny little arse, I promise you, Jerell. That kid can be a right little shit sometimes, trust me I bloody know."

Jerell sat in a chair, watching her hoist herself into a sitting position, positioning herself so that she was now leaning her back against the front of the sofa.

His silence, as he looked at her, was more unnerving to her than his violent outburst.

Finally, he spoke. "Oh, Tyler is a little shit alright," he said, nodding in agreement. "All dat boy do is run his mouth around the place telling stories; he tell so many lies I don't know if he is coming or going. Shit, I don't tink he know himself if he is coming or going." Jerell continued to speak quietly, as the woman sat with blood trickling down her forehead, from the cut above her eye that was the result of her crashing against the coffee table. Jerell continued: "He steals, he lies, he don't get no schooling."

Jerell was telling her what she herself, knew better than anyone, and she wondered what the kid had said or done to cause this amount of trouble for her; when she got her hands on him she was going to teach him some fucking respect.

"He don't wash, you know? He go round da place stinking, he smell so bad the other kids don't want to sit next to him, you know dat?" As Jerell reeled off a long list of Tyler's bad traits, his anger gathered speed with each word. "You hear what I saying?" Jerell asked, his calmness fading as he spoke, his voice getting louder.

Tyler's mum nodded in agreement, even though she barely comprehended his words; she was just gauging his expression and hearing his angry tone. She was terrified about what else he would do to her. Whatever Tyler had done, the boy was going to get a slap when she got hold of him. Jerell could say what he wanted about the boy: it was all true, every word of it. Tyler was a little shit, she could vouch for that, but she still didn't know what this was about.

"The boy is screwed, you know? He ain't got no life that he can look forward to. He gunna end up festering in this grimy flat for the rest of his days, another down and out. And you know why that is?" Jerell demanded.

She thought about it, praying for the right answer, not wanting to anger him even more. "He's lazy?" she ventured, the first thing that came to mind. Seeing Jerell smile, she felt relieved.

"He's lazy." Jerell laughed. She realised he was mocking her: she had got it wrong.

"No. It's not because he's lazy." Jerell stood up. "Guess again."

Tyler's mum felt she was going to wet herself. She had never seen a man look so angry: he looked demonic.

"I don't know," she whimpered. She guessed that whatever she said next wasn't going to help, he was furious, and she didn't have a clue why.

"He ain't got a chance in life because he's been lumbered with a lazy cunt of a mother like you." Jerell was seething at the bare-faced cheek of the woman. She wasn't bringing her kid up properly, she was dragging him up. She seemed oblivious to what a shit job she was doing of it, as well, she clearly didn't realise that she was even doing anything wrong by the boy. She was the reason the boy didn't stand a chance.

"I'm going today, and I'm taking Tyler with me. You're going to let the boy leave." Jerell had uses for Tyler, which he had no intention of sharing with the boy's mother, and she wasn't going to stand in his way. Jerell hadn't touched Tyler while he had been staying at the flat and, with the countless times that they had been alone together, it had been a hard task. If Tyler came with him to the new house, and his lazy bitch of a mother didn't interfere, he could do what he liked and no-one would be able to stop him.

"How much will you give me?" Tyler's mum's mind was instantly on the money she could fleece from this man who seemed so intent on taking Tyler with him. She may as well get something for herself out of it, as Jerell seemed to think he could do whatever he liked. It wouldn't be long until Tyler fucked off, anyway, her other kids had left her as soon as they had the opportunity, and with him gone too it would be one less thing to worry about.

"How much?" Jerell was, briefly, confused. Then he realised what she meant. He hadn't thought her capable of sinking any lower, but this was something else. "I have lived in your house for over two weeks. You haven't cooked one single meal, done one bit of washing. Your house is a dump and your kid looks like a two-bit tramp." Jerell grabbed her chin, forcing her up from the chair; once again the pain from her foot shot through her, as she put the pressure of her weight onto it, having no choice but to stand.

"And now you have the fucking audacity to ask me for money for him. You're willing to sell your own child? You fucking disgust me," Jerell continued.

She realised that she had once again read the situation wrong. But she had laid her cards on the table; she wanted to gain something from him taking Tyler, and she no longer cared what Jerell thought. He had been happy enough to give her money to stay at her flat for the past two weeks, so he was clearly good for it. She was beyond putting on an act for the man now; he knew exactly what she was. If he was going to beat the shit out of her, then so be it but if he wanted to take Tyler, he could make it worth her while.

She looked at him defiantly. She wasn't letting the boy go for nothing.

"How much you want?" he asked her, wondering what price the woman would put on her child's head.

"I want three grand." As soon as the words had passed her lips, she thought she should have asked for four.

Jerell had seen a lot in his life, but scumbags like this woman never failed to surprise him. She was willing to sell her boy for three grand. He owned watches that were worth more. He thought of his own mother leaving him when he was an innocent, tiny baby. He had no memory of her, but he had often wondered whether things would have been different if she had stayed: whether he would have been different. Women, except for his grandma, had made him angry ever since.

"Three grand and he can go," Tyler's mum said; those were her terms, and he could take them or leave them.

She didn't get an answer.

Instead, Jerell started to rain heavy blows onto her, taking out all his hate and anger on her like she was a punch bag. She curled into a ball, her arms over her head, her body was on fire with the pain. The blows kept coming, harder and faster. Until her body went limp.

She lay there, seemingly lifeless, as Jerell Morgan pictured his own mother's face, which he had only seen in the photos his grandma had kept, as he lost all control.

Chapter 18

"Told ya this place was the dog's bollocks, didn't I?" Reagan said proudly, as Rhys parked on the driveway outside the large detached house.

Tyler stared out of the window, his mouth open. "Wow," he murmured. The house looked like it belonged on a Hollywood film set. Reagan had told him that it was amazing, but he had played it down.

Seeing the boy's expression, Reagan felt smug. Judging by the boys' reactions, he had come up trumps and he hoped that Jerell would be as impressed with it as they both were.

"This ain't nothing, boys; just wait till you get inside." Reagan smiled.

He had forgotten how big the place was. He had only seen it once, with Louise; they had been lucky, as it had just come on to the market for leasing and they had been the first people to have been offered a viewing. Reagan had only been inside for a few minutes when, completely taken by the place, he had told the estate agent they had to have it.

They were only a few minutes away from the old estate, but the grey depressing concrete flats they had left behind couldn't have compared more starkly to the lush houses that were around here. This neighbourhood was stunning.

Turning down the loud garage music blaring out from the speakers, and getting out of the car, following Reagan, Rhys couldn't help feeling like they stuck out like sore thumbs.

Rhys loved his car. It had been a wreck when he had bought it. It was almost fifteen years old, a couple of years younger than him, and there was more mileage on the clock than if Lewis Hamilton had owned it, but it was Rhys' baby.

He had worked hard, doing whatever Reagan and Jerell had asked him to do; there had been no job too big or too small. He saved almost every penny that he earned, and as soon as he had enough money he took his car to have its bodywork sprayed neon-yellow. It may be an old banger underneath the paintwork, but Rhys had made it his mission to soup-up the little car, and it was his pride and joy. He was so proud that, at seventeen years of age, he actually had his own motor and had passed his driving test and had done it all off his own back. His old man did nothing but put him down, and Rhys' sole reason for wanting to pass his test had been so that he could show his dad that he wasn't 'thick as shit' like he was constantly made out to be. Rhys hadn't even been given a smile when he had come home from that day, showing the certificate off proudly. He didn't let his dad's dirty look, or lack of praise, bring him down though; he just set about working to buy himself a car.

It was rare on the estate that someone his age had the opportunity to take their driving test and get a car, no one owned shit, and Rhys had impressed the boys that he knocked about with; as far as he was concerned that trumped whatever his dad did or didn't think about him passing his test.

Seeing his bright-yellow car sitting here now, though, Rhys compared it unfavourably to all the other classy motors that were dotted about the close, its bright colour looked a bit brash in comparison. The cars around here were high end; the sort of wheels he and the boys went out nicking for Jerell.

As Rhys helped Reagan to unload the car, he could see curtains twitching in the neighbouring houses. He could see a couple of old gits across the road standing at the end of their driveways staring in his direction and shaking their heads disapprovingly, blatantly slagging him off, he thought, copping the hump. Who did they think they were? Unable to contain himself, he took great pleasure in telling the snooping bastards in no uncertain terms to fuck off.

Tyler laughed, as Rhys lost his cool with the old men over the road. They looked

flustered as he hurled a mouthful of abuse, and they both scarpered within

minutes, probably to avoid the situation getting more out of hand. When Rhys

got riled up, his face went bright red, and he had spittle round the corners of

his mouth. He made Tyler think of an angry Rottweiler. Rhys had major anger

issues; he carried a chip on his shoulder about stuff. There was little you could

say to him that wouldn't piss him off. He wasn't all bad, there were times when

you could have a laugh and a joke with him, but sometimes you only had to

look at him in the wrong way, or say the wrong word, and he would be gunning

for you.

Although Rhys was holding a box, he kicked Tyler on the shin with a sharp punt,

causing the boy to let out a yelp that instantly stopped his chuckling.

"Shut it you!" Rhys warned, fucked off that not only had the neighbours been

gawping at them, but now Tyler thought that him losing his temper was

amusing too, he hated people looking down their noses at him, or even worse

laughing at him, he had enough of that from his old man.

"Cool it, yeah," Reagan called, as he opened the front door, so that he could

get Rhys and Tyler inside before Rhys really pissed someone off. They had only

been in the street for a few minutes and Rhys had already caused a scene.

Jerell would not be happy if he found out that the boy had started a war with the neighbours before they had even managed to get their stuff moved into the place. Jerell had said that he wanted to move in without a fuss. As long as the bills were paid, and they didn't bring any dodgy shit to the house, there was nothing that the disgruntled neighbours or the police could do. Their money was as good as anyone else's. Jerell had instructed them that when they moved their gear in, that they were not to draw attention to themselves. Now they were here, amongst these pristine houses, Reagan thought what an almost impossible task that was going to be. There was no way they were going to fit in around here. Neighbourhood Watch had probably already called an emergency meeting on seeing them arrive in Rhys' florescent boy-racer car.

"It's a bit posh round here, ain't it, you sure we've got the right place?" Rhys said, as they stepped inside the large arched doorway, lugging the heavy box.

Inside, the place sparkled. Everything looked immaculate; from the thick cream carpets that covered the entire downstairs, to the large modern kitchen that was so clean it could have passed itself off as being newly fitted.

"Told ya, didn't I? Millionaires would be happy to live here. You know that programme, you know the one... what's it called, the one on MTV? *Cribs*, that's it. That's us now, innit, living the fucking dream," Reagan said, as he looked around at the gadget-filled kitchen, taking it all in, impressed with himself once again at his choice of house.

"Check out this bad boy, then." Rhys couldn't contain his excitement as he put his hand under the compartment of the huge American-style fridge and caught a large handful of ice cubes that shot out as he pressed the button. "That is proper sick, man!" He laughed, he had only seen stuff like this on TV, and now they were going to be hanging out in a pad like this, living like celebrities, as Reagan had said, it was a crazy thought.

Reagan shook his head despairingly, as Rhys shoved Tyler's hand under the ice dispenser, only this time he pressed 'crushed' and slushy ice poured out of Tyler's hand. Rhys roared with laughter as Tyler winced at the coldness, before he shrugged his shoulders at Rhys' joke and then good-naturedly started to eat the remaining ice. The laughter from the two boys was contagious and Reagan laughed too as he watched them, suddenly feeling swept away with all the excitement.

The three of them wandered about the place, giving it a once over. It was like a show home. Jerell was going to be over the fucking moon when he turned up, Reagan thought happily, wanting once again to show that him that he had done a good job, and could be trusted when he was asked to do something.

"Let's sort all this shit out," Reagan instructed Rhys and Tyler. It was almost midday and Reagan wanted to get everything in order before Jerell turned up, which would be any minute. He pointed at the boxes and bags that they had brought in from the car. Luckily the place was fully furnished, all they had had to bring along with them was a few bags of clothes, some bedding and a large box that was filled with all their personal stuff, such as toiletries and some CDs.

"Reagan, which bedroom are you having?" Rhys called from the top of the stairs. There were four bedrooms. Reagan knew that it was only right to leave the master bedroom at the front for Jerell, who was, after all, the boss and would expect nothing less.

"Just stick my gear in the back one, Rhys; it's the grey one with the en-suite," Reagan shouted, thinking that the bedroom he had picked would be perfect for when he had Louise staying for the odd night. Things had happened so quickly between them both, and Reagan had developed strong feelings for her, in such a short space of time. Having that back room would work out very well for him, as it would mean they could have their own bathroom, and more importantly their own privacy.

"Oi, Reagan," again Rhys shouted down the stairs, "just a thought, mate, but maybe we should invest in some walkie-talkies; this place is so big it's got its own fucking echo."

Laughing, Reagan opened the kitchen cupboards. The landlord had left a range of stuff in the cupboards for them to use up. None of it was the sort of food that he and the boys would have chosen. One entire cupboard was full of flour, dried herbs and spices. The landlord obviously didn't have a clue what type of people he was leasing the house to.

Reagan and Louise had gone to the estate agent's office to sign the paperwork and pay the deposit. They had had a right old laugh, dressing up all posh. Reagan had had to force himself not to laugh when Louise had put on a fake voice, it was hilarious to listen to, but all credit to her, she had pulled it off. Louise was an amazing actress, and it had been her that had helped him to seal the deal; she had batted her eyelids, giggled and flirted with the agent just as Reagan had told her, leaving the man so flustered and embarrassed that he had signed the house over in minutes, too distracted by her beauty to keep his mind on the task of checking out the paperwork.

Reagan had needed to produce bank statements and proof of earnings for the estate agent. Thankfully, Jerell knew a guy who could make forgeries of any documentation so realistic that it was a shame the man's craft was illegal, the guy was clearly gifted when it came to creating paperwork, and Reagan suspected that even the pigs would have been fooled by the papers that he had managed to produce for them.

And now the place was theirs for the next year, at least, as long as they didn't give the landlord any reason to kick them out for breach of the tenancy agreement, which Reagan would ensure didn't happen. He reminded himself that he would have to sit the boys down later and lay down ground rules. Rule number one, after seeing Rhys' little outburst earlier, would be not to fuck off the neighbours.

"You did good, Reagan boy; this is nice... very nice." Jerell's voice came from behind him and made Reagan jump. He leapt up, forgetting there was a cabinet door open above him and whacking his head on the corner of it.

"Shit, Jerell, you scared the fucking life out of me, man," Reagan said, clutching his head.

"You left the front door open," Jerell told him, as he looked around the large kitchen. He whistled, seemingly as impressed with their home as the others had been.

"I've got all your stuff here; it's in your room." Reagan was pleased by Jerell's reaction and couldn't wait to show him around. He closed the cupboard doors and led Jerell to the stairs so that he could give him a tour of the place.

Upstairs, Jerell and Reagan stopped outside the smallest of the four bedrooms, where Rhys and Tyler had their faces stuck up against the window, their noses pushing against the glass, as they nosily gave the neighbourhood a proper once over.

Oblivious to Jerell standing in the doorway, they too jumped at the sound of his voice: "What you boys think den?" Jerell asked, knowing that the boys must be impressed.

"It's a fucking palace, Jerell." Rhys was beaming. He was thrilled that Reagan had asked him to move in as it meant that he was climbing up in the ranks of the group, and he could see himself living in a house like this. It was hardly going to be a sacrifice leaving his miserable cunt of an old man's place to live somewhere like this.

"Yeah, it's great," Tyler added, not turning around to meet Jerell's eyes; his voice was quieter and less enthusiastic than Rhys' had been.

Reagan could see the change in Tyler's body language since Jerell had arrived, and he recognised fear in the boy's voice. He knew that the boy could be a little shit, making up lies and stories to stir things up, but this quiet, scared version of Tyler was worrying. Once again, Reagan wondered if he should talk to him; maybe he could get the boy on his own.

Tyler was thinking that with Jerell standing in the doorway, the room felt as if it had shrunk to the size of a prison cell. He shuffled his feet and continued to look out of the window. Jerell had told Tyler he may as well move into the house, as he was left at home so much on his own anyway. Jerell had said to

Reagan that once they were up and running again in this new place, they would

be so busy it made sense to have others living with them. Reagan had

suggested Rhys, as the boy seemed dedicated to doing a good job, and Jerell

had chosen Tyler. Tyler had been dreading it. The last thing he wanted to do

was spend any more time living with Jerell. The man gave him the creeps; the

thought of Jerell trying to do that disgusting thing again made him want to

throw up.

Tyler had practically been counting the minutes until Jerell was finally moving

out of his mum's place and he had been horrified when Jerell had dropped the

bombshell last night that he would be leaving with him. Jerell had told Tyler not

to mention it to his mother, he had said that he would square everything with

her, and Tyler had been too terrified to do anything but nod his head in

agreement. Tyler knew that there was nothing that he could do; he was too

scared to tell Jerell that he didn't want to come, as he would have just forced

him to; Tyler knew that he didn't have any say in the matter.

"This is your room, Ty; I've got dibs on the bigger room as I'm older." Rhys

ruffled Tyler's hair as he walked past him, out of the smallest room, to go and

make claims on his new bedroom. Tyler guessed, as volatile that Rhys could be,

at least he would be company for him.

But it was hard to find anything good about the situation: now that Jerell was there the feeling of panic had returned, worse than ever, and with it a sensation of leaden misery. Watching Reagan and Jerell follow Rhys, as they enthused about the place, Tyler sat on the bed feeling defeated. He reached into his rucksack, his hand dipping in beneath some clothes and DVDs, but as he rooted around; he couldn't find it. Panicked, Tyler tipped the bag's contents out carefully onto the bed, glancing towards the doorway as he made sure that no-one was around to see what he was doing. Spreading the stuff out on his bed, and lifting the clothes and DVDs out of the way, all that remained were his phone, old house keys and his wallet. As his hand searched for the cold metal of the gun that he had been hiding for the past two weeks, he realised with dread that it had gone, someone had taken it. It had to have been Jerell.

Tyler had gone to the river that night, holding the gun wrapped in the T-shirt tightly, ready to throw it as far as he could into the Thames just as Jerell had instructed. But something had stopped him. Somewhere deep inside, he had thought that if he kept the gun hidden, then the next time Jerell tried to force himself on him he would have some way of protecting himself. He had stuffed the gun back inside his rucksack and had hurried home. Jerell had been so caught up with dealing with Tyler's mother, that when Tyler had returned Jerell hadn't noticed him sneaking his bag, containing the gun, upstairs to his room.

Tyler had hidden the gun beside his bed, in easy reach. That night, when Tyler had lain in his bed, he had let his arm hang down the side of the mattress as he felt around for it, wanting to touch it. Just feeling the weapon had made him feel safer. Tyler wasn't sure that he would have the guts to use it, if it came to it. He had never held a gun until that night, and he had no idea if he would be able to pull the trigger if he needed to. The fact that he had defied Jerell's orders, mixed with the security of knowing that he had the gun as back up, had made him feel like he had regained a tiny bit of control. And now, to his dismay, it was gone. Tyler fought to hold back tears. If Jerell had found it, he hadn't said anything. But Tyler knew how Jerell liked to play games with people and watch them sweat. It gave him a kick. Maybe Jerell was biding his time and thinking up some way of punishing Tyler for disobeying him and not dumping the gun. Tyler would be in big trouble for this.

As he sat in his new bedroom, in the biggest, grandest house he had been in, all he could think was how he would give anything to be as far away as possible.

Chapter 19

"I can tell something's up, Jamie, so you may as well just spit it out, mate," Gary said, as he tried to get whatever it was that was bothering Jamie out into the open. The lad had come back a few hours ago with a face that could have turned the milk in his tea sour, and Gary couldn't fathom what the matter was. Jamie had been fine when he had left this morning; more than fine, in fact, the boy had been over the moon with his offer of running the garage. Gary hadn't expected Jamie to come back from his trip looking miserable; something had wiped the smile off his face.

"It's nothing, Gary; let's just drop it, alright." Jamie needed to get his head sorted out, and telling Gary what was going on in his mind would only further confuse the whole situation. There were some things that Jamie had never discussed with Gary. And right now, Jamie didn't want to explain what was bothering him.

After following the kid home, Jamie had driven around for almost an hour. Maybe it was shock, but the hour had gone by in seconds and now seemed like a blur. The drive hadn't helped: his head was as jumbled up now as it had been then. He was at a loss as to what he should do. Jamie was convinced that what he suspected was true, and it was a major fucking nightmare.

"Is it the garage? I know what a pair of doughnuts Gavin and Shay can be, Jamie. I won't give it a second thought if they've been fucking things up down there on us. I know I said I want to hand over the responsibility to you, Jamie, but that doesn't mean you have to sort it out all on your own, I still want to be kept in the loop." Gary leant forward in the armchair. He watched Jamie as he sat in the other one, and stared at the TV screen with a face like thunder. The last thing in the world that Gary wanted to do to the lad was burden him with a business and if that were what this mood was about, Gary wanted to know. He had assumed that Jamie would have been over the moon about being given free rein of the garage, now he wasn't so sure that he had done the right thing; maybe he had misread the situation.

"No, Gary, it's got nothing to do with Gavin and Shay. If anything they have both come up trumps these past few weeks." Realising that Gary was only worried about him, which was fair enough, Jamie wished he hadn't come back to the house while he was still so rattled. Gary didn't need this drama; he had enough on his plate to deal with. Not wishing to cause his friend any unnecessary stress, Jamie tried to think of a way to diffuse the situation. Seeing the concern on Gary's face, he wished he had gone somewhere else.

"Well, if it ain't them, what the fuck's going on?" Gary racked his brain to think what could have put Jamie in such a bad mood in such a short space of time. He had gone out this morning as happy as Larry but had come home with a mood that would rival the anti-Christ's.

"Seriously, Gary, it's nothing. Please, just drop it. It's just stuff, my stuff, and it's private. I don't really want to get into it, to be honest. It's got nothing to do with you or the boys or the garage, so you don't need to be worrying yourself." Jamie sounded like he was at the end of his tether. Gary knew he would be wise to leave the subject alone.

Jamie didn't want to talk about it, but he didn't know what to do with himself either; getting out of the house was on the top of his list, though, as he was going stir-crazy pretending to ignore Gary's concerned glances. He rang Les and asked him to come back over to Gary's; Jamie told him that he needed to go out to do a few more errands.

Les was at the house within minutes, seemingly more than happy to be of use to Gary. Jamie quickly left, needing to get out and get some fresh air in his lungs, while he thought about what was going on. Wanting to walk off his agitation, he left his car behind. He hadn't planned to return to the flat, but he ended up standing outside the building. The cold concrete walls were a suitable match for his mood. It was so miserable; so bleak. The place was like a magnet to him. It was sucking him back with a destructive invisible force, drawing him towards it against his better judgement.

He needed to know, though. He had to be certain.

As Jamie walked slowly up the stairwell, he tried to control his heart that was now thudding loudly in his chest. It was beating so hard that he thought it may burst.

On the second floor walkway, everything looked exactly as he remembered. He was fifteen again.

He stood outside the white front door; the gold of its numeral was tarnished. The front of the letterbox was still hanging off. He thought about knocking on the door, wondering who would open it. His lifted his hand but let it drop. He would be walking in blind. He didn't have a clue who, or what, he would be faced with. Deciding to play it more carefully, he reached into his pocket and took out a key. He figured security in this place had never been a top priority; no-one would have had the brains or the inclination to change the locks.

Placing the key in the lock, he turned it. Hearing the click as it unlocked, he gently pushed the front door ajar, hearing the creak he remembered as he did so.

As he crept through the hallway, he smelt cat piss, dirt and a lingering staleness, the combination both sickening and nostalgic.

The kitchen was still a health hazard, he noted, as he peered into the small room as he passed it; even rats would choose to avoid it.

Going into the lounge, he stepped back and let out a gasp. This was not what he had expected to find.

***

Sitting in the lounge, he couldn't believe how little had changed. Even the mould had continued to grow in the same corner, except now the dark patch was much larger and had spread onto the ceiling.

The old carpet was bald in places; it had been on its way out even then, but now he could see the creaky edges of floorboards, poking out in places though the large holes.

It was like being in a time warp.

The old grandfather clock ticked loudly on the wall, the only thing to break the deathly silence: that and the sound of struggling, raspy breathing.

As the minutes ticked by, Jamie leant his head back and just sat there watching her. The concern that he had felt when he had first seen her lying in a bloody heap on the floor had thrown him. He had told himself for years that she was dead to him. He guessed that if he had been happy to see her, lying on the floor, dead as he had first thought when he had seen her twisted body lying there, then he would have been more screwed up than he had imagined. It was human nature to panic, and to feel concerned, he thought as he sat there mulling over his feelings. He had learned something about himself tonight, which was a revelation. Even when it came to this woman whom he despised so much, he was still capable of being human.

His concern had dissipated as he noted the rise and fall of her breath and realised that she wasn't dead. He had sat there patiently since, waiting for her to come around from her unconscious state.

She was a shocking sight, a bloody mess lying there battered and bruised in the dingy room. Between the swelling and the blood, her face was barely recognisable. It was hard to say whether she had aged.

The sun was going down, the room darkening. But Jamie didn't get up out of his chair to switch on the light, he just sat there as darkness fell, watching her.

He closed his eyes for a few minutes, exhausted. Resting his head against the back of the chair, he continued to wait.

Waking in complete darkness, Jamie realised he must have slept. He could hear a quiet moaning from the floor. He listened to the noise of her slowly start to try and sit herself up.

She groaned in pain, as she tried to hoist herself into a sitting position. Every bone in her body had taken a battering, she thought, wincing at every movement she made.

She turned her head towards the figure sitting in the darkness, expecting it to be Jerell, and praying that he would show some mercy and leave her be. She wouldn't be able to take another beating.

Switching on the lamp on the table next to him, Jamie watched the confusion set in, as her eyes flickered in shock as she slowly recognised his familiar face staring back at her, a ghost from her past.

She couldn't believe what she was seeing was real: she must be disorientated after the ordeal. *It couldn't be him.*

Just when she thought that today couldn't get worse Jamie leant forward in his chair and spoke.

"Hello Mum."

Chapter 20

Louise was not happy. Tonight was the third time that week she had stayed at the new house with Reagan, and the third time that week that she had laid awake and listened to the sound of Tyler's sobbing through the wall from the next-door bedroom. This was too much, she thought; something wasn't right.

Louise's flat wasn't a patch on this place. This house was wall-to-wall comfort, and snuggling up to Reagan each night had sounded like bliss compared to sleeping back at hers all alone. But so far she hadn't managed to get one decent night's sleep since she had been here.

Even though she had got used to her own space over time, it could be lonely; the live-in tenants that she shared the place with came in the form of about five hundred skunk plants, which didn't make for stimulating conversation. Although there had been more than a few occasions, through boredom, that she had chatted to the plants as if they were listening to her. If anyone had seen her they would have thought she was a fruit loop.

Louise struggled to properly relax at home, especially when she was alone at night. It was like living inside a ticking time bomb; any minute the police could raid the place, or rival dealers could try to break in and damage the place. She never felt completely at ease. She knew rationally that Jerell was too shrewd a businessman to let anything like that occur, he covered all angles and they all worked so hard to ensure that no one was ever on to what they were up to, but some nights she had been unable to sleep through the worry of *what-ifs*. Ultimately if anyone did get suspicious and raid the place, she was the live-in tenant, she would be the one to take the fall.

Her main living space was two downstairs rooms and a small bathroom. Louise's compact lounge was also her bedroom, thanks to the sofa bed that Jerell had provided for her, and next to the lounge was a tiny kitchenette. It was a good job that she wasn't claustrophobic, she had often mused, as she could touch the two opposite walls simultaneously if she stood in the middle of the kitchen. Reagan and Jerell had insisted that only two other boys, Ritchie and Michael, were allowed to go to the house. They helped bag all the gear up and organise the distribution so that Jerell's other boys could make the drops. Apart from those two and Louise, no-one else was allowed to go near the place. Jerell had made sure that the utility bills and rent were paid for up front, before they were even due. He had also instructed that there was never allowed to be loud music or noise coming from there, he wanted the place to be low-key; he didn't want to draw attention to the place and get people's suspicions roused. He had no time for people poking their noses in on his business. Louise's role in the whole operation was a bloody hard task, and she also knew she played her part well, so well in fact that she made it look easy, as Louise often liked to say to Reagan. Women were multi-task masters.

Jerell paid Louise well in return for her hard graft; he knew that she was integral to their operation, and her doing her role without any fuss made his life easier. She was respected as a main player, and she felt empowered by the fact that they couldn't run things without her.

Louise had been over the moon when Reagan had told her that as long as Ritchie or Michael helped her out over there by taking watch for the odd night, then she could stay with him. It was nice having a boyfriend who didn't live in her pocket like some boys wanted to. The odd night of staying here had turned into almost half a week now, and if it hadn't been for her being kept awake worrying about Tyler, it would have been perfect.

"Reagan," Louise nudged his arm. "Are you awake?"

Reagan awoke to the sound of Louise's concerned whisper.

"I can hear him crying again," Louise said.

Tyler had seemed so jumpy and timid lately; it was out of character, and she didn't know what to do to help. She had no idea what was upsetting him so much that he was spending his nights crying himself to sleep. Maybe Reagan

had been right, maybe he was just homesick, but surely all this crying each

night was a bit much? Louise had tried on a few occasions to question Reagan

about what was going on, but he had shrugged off her curiosity by saying that

it was probably nothing, before he swiftly changed the subject. She felt like

maybe she was making a big deal out of it, but her intuition kept niggling

away, telling her that there was more to this than met the eye.

"Hear who crying?" Reagan asked vaguely, as he turned towards her, still half-

asleep; he could make out her silhouette, as she sat up.

"Tyler!" Louise answered despairingly; didn't he pay attention to anything she

said? "He's crying again, listen. Can't you hear him?"

Reagan could hear faint sobs coming through the wall. "Jesus, Louise, you

must have ears like a frigging bat to hear that!" He tried to play down Louise's

concerns, but he too felt sorry for the kid.

"He's just homesick, Louise, like I told ya; leave it be, yeah? He'll only be

embarrassed if you mention it to him. He's twelve; he needs to overcome it

himself, doesn't he? Don't go babying him, or he'll never grow up."

Reagan felt awful lying to Louise, but she would go mental if she found out

that he knew about the abuse. He recognised that he was a coward for not doing more to help the poor kid himself. Reagan knew why the boy spent his

nights crying himself to sleep. Jerell hadn't been discreet in covering up the

little visits he had been paying to Tyler's bedroom since they had moved in.

Jerell acted like he no longer cared that Reagan suspected his dirty secret, in

fact Reagan wondered if Jerell purposely flaunted what he was doing. It was

like he got a kick out of seeing the disapproval in Reagan's eyes and was

challenging him to see if he had the bottle to do anything about it. Which they

both knew Reagan didn't.

Just the thought of what Jerell was up to sickened him; Reagan remembered

that feeling of lying in bed at night and feeling terrified that at any moment

his door would slowly creep open. He had spent countless nights as a

frightened boy just lying there staring at the door handle and willing it not to

move.

Reagan had noticed that Jerell didn't go to Tyler's room when there were

others about, so as long as the house was busy, Tyler was safe. Because of

this, Reagan tried his best to keep as many people in the house for as long as

he possibly could. The boys couldn't get enough of the place, so it hadn't been

a hard task. They carried on as they had done on the estate. They turned up at

all hours of the day and night and sat around chilling out, listening to their

tunes and generally making the place their own. They always used the back entrance now, so as not to cause any more attention out on the close. They even had a large garden to park their bikes in; it was perfect.

Reagan wanted to help Tyler without the boy cottoning on to the fact that he knew what was happening. He made it his mission to send Tyler out every day, running errands, anything to put some time and distance between him and Jerell. He had even used his powers of persuasion to get Jerell to agree to let Louise sleep over sometimes, thinking that the more people he could get to stay at the house at one time the better, anything to deter Jerell from getting the opportunity to try anything on with Tyler. He had thought that Tyler's saving grace would be the fact that Rhys had moved in too, as the prospect of Jerell getting Tyler on his own would be harder seeing as Rhys' room was just across the hallway. But hearing the boy crying himself to sleep, Reagan knew that Jerell was still finding a way to get to him somehow.

"Poor kid, he must really be missing his mum to be this upset," Louise said sadly; she hoped the boy would get over it soon, she wanted to help him and had thought that if she could speak to him, reassure him, then he wouldn't feel so alone. But Reagan had constantly insisted that her getting involved would just cause Tyler to feel awkward about the whole situation, so she had reluctantly done as she was asked, and had left the situation well alone, but as the nights went on she was finding it harder to just ignore him.

"Forget it, Louise. Let's just get some shut eye, yeah? I'm knackered," Reagan said. There was nothing he could do for Tyler. Not tonight, anyway. It had been a long day, and Louise had worn him out when they had finally got into bed. Feeling the warmth of the cosy duvet around him, and the heat of Louise's soft skin next to him, Reagan closed his eyes, hoping that Louise would drop the conversation as he was desperate to get a few more hours of kip in before the morning.

Louise laid in the darkness for what seemed like ages, thinking about Tyler. She knew what it was like to be homesick. She had been just fourteen when she had been taken into care. She had had no one to talk to about how sad she had been or the loneliness she had felt.

Even now, Louise couldn't believe the way that things had turned out. It still pained her that her mum had chosen her boyfriend, Greg, over her daughter, her own flesh and blood. When Louise had finally managed to pluck up the courage to confide in her mother about her boyfriend's wandering hands whenever her mother wasn't looking, her mother's reaction had been the last thing Louise had anticipated. Greg was as slimy as they came, and Louise could never work out what her mum saw in him; it was fear of being on her own, she guessed. Greg leered at Louise at every chance he got, and the leers had quickly turned to gropes. At first he had been so subtle that she had thought that the times he had brushed up or pressed against her in the kitchen were accidents: but it kept on happening, and he stopped being so discreet. The more he realised that she was too timid to do anything about it, the worse it became. Rubbing her legs, groping her breasts... it was just a sick game to him; he enjoyed tormenting her. Greg had gone mad when Louise's mum told him of Louise's accusations. Louise had watched him brainwash her mum in front of her, as he went beyond denying the allegations and somehow managed to persuade her naive mum that Louise was a liar; he should have won an Oscar for his acting skill. He had been so convincing and the rage he displayed once he got started with his rant about how jealous she was and how she was obviously trying to wreck their relationship, meant that Louise hadn't stood a chance. "If you believe that screwed up little cow over me, then I'm off," he had warned her mum, looking disgusted at the allegations. On seeing his angry reaction, and knowing that his threat was genuine, backing down, Louise's mum had done the very last thing that Louise would ever have expected: she had chosen to believe him over her own daughter. Louise remembered the fucked-up conversation with her mum that followed. The words stung her even now. She had sat Louise down and told her that Greg was a good man and even if what Louise had told her was true, she couldn't blame him, he was only human after all: her daughter had a figure to die for and it probably didn't help that Louise often walked about the place in skimpy little bed shorts either. What man could resist the odd glance if she would walk about the place flaunting her body in his face? But as for touching her, there was no way: Greg wouldn't do that. "You can't go around making shit like this up, Louise love; you could cause a lot of trouble making up this kind of lie." As her mum had looked at her in disappointment, Greg had stood behind her, grinning at her triumphantly like the cat that had got the cream. Louise had never felt so frustrated in her life. There had been no consoling her after that, she had no-one to talk to, no-one that she could trust and she had quickly started to take her rage out on everyone and anyone that she then came into contact with. Unable to bear Greg's despicable advances and the way he laughed in her face any longer, Louise spent as much time as she could away from her home just so that she could avoid him. Seeing as nobody seemed to give two shits about her, she started bunking off school and hanging out with her mates and when that didn't ease the hurt of her mum's disloyalty, she started heavily smoking and drinking, anything that would help her block out the pain. Finally, her cries for attention were answered; her mum could no longer cope with her troublesome daughter and she had been taken into care. By then, Louise no longer gave a shit; she didn't mind where she lived, as long as it was far away from her mum and Greg.

Louise listened to Reagan breathe deeply beside her, he had seemingly fallen back to sleep almost immediately, unlike herself: insomnia often kept her awake late into the night. Wide awake, she tossed and turned, sick of being alone with thoughts of her mother and Greg. She could still hear the muffled sounds of Tyler's weeping, and she was debating what to do about it; weighing up her choices, she decided that surely checking whether the poor kid was alright couldn't be anywhere near as bad as ignoring him, she couldn't just leave him to deal with his misery all by himself.

Pulling back the duvet cover, she snuck out of the big double bed and left her boyfriend gently snoring in the land of nod. She pulled Reagan's large robe around her, grateful for its warmth as she glanced back over to the occupied bed, double-checking that Reagan hadn't stirred. He wouldn't be happy with her 'interfering'. As quietly as she could manage, she closed the bedroom door behind her so as not to wake him.

Louise crept across the vast landing and gently pushed open Tyler's door. The last thing she wanted to do was alarm him by bursting in while he was crying, and she didn't fancy waking anyone else up either.

She strained her eyes to see through the darkness. She assumed that Tyler had heard her come in as the crying she had heard for the past half an hour had stopped the second she opened the door.

"Tyler? Are you okay love?" Louise whispered in the direction of the bed.

"I'm fine, Louise." Tyler's voice sounded muffled, as if he had buried himself under the covers, and stilted. *He was embarrassed, after all.* Louise's heart went out to him.

"Do you fancy coming downstairs, Ty? We could have a sneaky hot chocolate. I can't sleep either." Louise thought that she would try a different approach so that Tyler wouldn't feel humiliated by her finding him in this state, and if she made out it was her who couldn't sleep, he would feel like he was doing her a favour by joining her. The past week that Louise had stayed here she had taken a real liking to Tyler. From all the conversations that Louise had had with him, he seemed like a sweet kid, there was something vulnerable about him that made her want to look after him like a big sister would.

"No, I'm okay, thanks. Go back to bed, Louise."

But Louise had had enough of tip-toeing around the situation. She wasn't going anywhere until she knew the poor kid was okay. She felt that she knew exactly what he was going through; she needed to let him to realise that he wasn't alone. Sometimes just knowing that someone had your back was all it took. She was here now; they were both wide awake; she was going to take the opportunity to have a little chat with Tyler. Reagan would understand that she wasn't snooping; she genuinely cared. Switching on the light, Louise's concerned expression turned to one of horror, as she realised Tyler wasn't alone in his bed. She stared, dumbstruck, at the scene in front of her.

"What the f..?" Louise didn't get a chance to finish the sentence.

"Get out of here." Jerell yanked the bed covers over him, but not before Louise had seen his naked body and Tyler's small and equally naked one beneath it.

Jerell glared at Louise, fuming that she had caught him. He should never have let the silly bitch stay over; she was too nosey for her own good.

Tyler had tears streaming down his cheeks, and his face was flushed; he didn't meet Louise's gaze. She looked from the distraught boy, straight into the evil face of Jerell. She just stood like a statue, unable to know what to say or do.

"I said get the fuck out of here, Louise," Jerell threatened.

Stepping back clumsily, Louise left the room, tears stinging her eyes from what she had witnessed.

The commotion had woken Reagan. Seeing Louise rush back into the room, he was aware something bad had happened.

"Babe, what's going on?" Reagan turned the bedside lamp on and got out of bed. Taking his girlfriend in his arms, he had a horrible feeling he knew what was coming.

"It's Jerell." Her voice was shaking, tears running down her cheeks. "He's in there, with Tyler." She nodded in the direction of Tyler's bedroom, unable to put what she had seen into words. *Oh my god, poor Tyler*, she thought, as Reagan held her tightly, trying to calm her. It was no wonder the kid spent his nights crying. Louise felt bile in the back of her throat at the thought of what Jerell had been doing.

Reagan didn't know what to say. He knew that if Louise had seen Jerell with Tyler, she was going to be in trouble. Reagan knew what the man was capable of, and there was no way that he would let her leave the house knowing what she now knew. He would want to ensure that she kept her mouth firmly shut.

Reagan had to get her out of the house. Gathering up her clothes from the floor, he thrust them into Louise's arms. "You need to get out of here. Now, Louise, right now," he ordered, imagining that they only had a few seconds before Jerell would be storming through the door. Reagan couldn't envisage him being lenient about Louise knowing what he did with underage boys. There was no way that he would trust her not to talk, and God knows what lengths he would go to, to preserve her silence.

Louise could tell by Reagan's urgent tone that she should do what he said; the panic in his eyes told her that the danger was real. There was no time to waste.

Grabbing the rest of her stuff, she ran out of the room and down the stairs. She was on the bottom step when she heard Tyler's bedroom door open. Louise had no intention of waiting around to see what he was going to do to her now that she knew his secret. Her hands shook violently as she tried to reach up and undo the bolt securing the front door.

"Where is she?" Jerell sounded livid, and Louise was petrified at what he would do to her. She glanced up the stairs to the landing, checking that Jerell wasn't on his way down to her. She was a jabbering mess and it felt like time had slowed down. The more she panicked, the more everything seemed to move in slow motion. Finally, she managed to undo the security chain. As she pulled open the heavy front door, she heard the sound of footsteps on the stairs. She didn't look back; she couldn't get out of there quick enough.

She realised, as she ran down the street, trying to keep hold of her clothes and bag, that she was still wearing Reagan's dressing gown. It was the middle of the night, so there was no-one else around. But even if it had been broad daylight she wouldn't have cared, she would have ran out of there completely naked if it had meant that she had been able to escape from the disgusting

Jerell.

Chapter 21

"You ain't changed much, have you, Mum?" Jamie couldn't muster up an ounce of sympathy for the wreck of a woman sprawled on the floor in front of him. He guessed that she must have finally got herself a fella, and judging by the state of her, she had pushed whoever the poor mug was, way over the edge. The familiar feeling of revulsion flowed through him as he looked at her.

"That's fucking charming, Jamie, that is. I'm lying 'ere, just had the bleeding crap beaten out of me, and you don't even help me up." Maura glared back at him in defiance, pulling herself forward as she struggled to sit up. She winced at the sharp pain in her foot, the agony almost taking her breath away, although there was no way she would show it: not to him.

Jamie unzipped his hoodie and threw it to her; the hideous sight of his mother sitting there almost naked in front of him, with everything hanging out, was making him want to be sick.

Maura draped the top over her shoulders and pulled the zip up. She felt less vulnerable having covered her breasts, it was hardly dignified to come to on the lounge floor, battered and naked to the sight of her long-lost son sitting there looking like he didn't have a care in the world. She saw Jamie turning his nose up as he watched her, his lips curling nastily, and she could see the hate that he felt for her still, even after all these years, festering there in his cold stare. The little freckle-faced boy with the fiery temper had finally returned. The familiarity of him sitting here in the room made it feel as though the years they had been separated hadn't taken place. He had turned out to be a good-looking little sod, she thought. She remembered vaguely that his father had been tall and handsome too, with the same steely eyes that Jamie had also inherited. Maura was blonde, but not the sort of attractive blonde that people went to the hairdressers and paid good money. Hers was a mousy, dull kind of blonde, and most of the time her hair was so greasy she could have fried chips in it.

She hadn't seen Jamie for ten years, and she wondered, if she thought he looked different, what he must be thinking about her. The years hadn't been good to her; she was under no illusions about that. She had put on weight; three dress sizes, she calculated. Her skin was old and tired-looking, she was wrinkled and saggy, and of course having just had the shit kicked out of her probably hadn't helped her in the looks department. This was not the ideal reunion. She knew that she must look a right state, and she could imagine what Jamie was thinking when he looked at her, she could see it in his eyes even now, his expression that signified he thought he was above all of this, and more significantly like he was above her, just like he always had.

"You got a fucking cheek, sitting there looking down your nose at me, boy," Maura scolded as she returned his glare, in defiance.

Maura had not expected to set eyes on Jamie again. He had no right to sit there judging and condemning. He knew nothing about her anymore; he had no idea how difficult her life was. He had just swanned off after reading her the riot act about her parenting and seemingly hadn't so much as given her a second thought since. He hadn't given two shits about his three siblings, either. He was a selfish little bastard.

Jamie's eyes bore into hers, she felt like he could almost see into her soul.

"Why the fuck are you here, Jamie?" she asked. "How did you get in? If I remember rightly you packed your bags and fucked off a long time ago. You left me and the kids to rot. So why the fuck have you come back now?"

Maura reached for a cigarette from the table beside her, her hands trembling as she picked up the lighter. She fought to stop her body shaking; there was no way that she was going to give Jamie the satisfaction of seeing her suffering any more than he had. She lit it and welcomed the deep breath of smoke as she inhaled it down into her lungs. She held it in for a few seconds before blowing it back out. Instantly calmer, she wondered if she could get her hands on a bottle of vodka for pain relief. Seeing how swollen and awkwardly twisted her ankle looked, she knew that she needed a trip to A and E, it was without doubt broken.

"Where's Kevin?" Jamie asked, as he watched his pathetic excuse of a mother puff away on her cigarette as if her life depended on it. She was the same as ever, albeit fatter and older. She looked ragged and worn out, old beyond her years. The blood and the bruises probably added to her already dishevelled appearance. One thing was for certain, she was still a fucking mess. Jamie reckoned if he had seen her sitting on a park bench down at Larkhall Park, she wouldn't look out of place against all the alcoholics that hung out down there, pissing their lives away.

"Kevin? Is that all you care about, that little bastard?" Maura laughed in disbelief. Jamie could pretend he was interested in his brother, but he had walked out on him too.

"Well, I didn't come back here for you, did I?" Jamie said sarcastically.

"Well, he ain't here no more, is he," Maura said. She stubbed out her fag in the ashtray. She thought about getting up, but even sitting she felt dizzy: if she stumbled over on her arse, he would have a right bloody laugh at her expense. Lighting another fag, she decided to stay put.

She wanted to know why Jamie had come back for the boy and why he had done it today. First Jerell wanted the kid and now Jamie.

"I don't know why you're so interested in finding him. After you fucked off and left us, we never mentioned your name again. He don't even know he's got a brother," Maura said, rubbing in the fact that Jamie meant nothing to her youngest son: the boy didn't even know he existed.

Jamie couldn't believe it; how could she keep something like that from her own kid, just because she was pissed off with him leaving.

"Oh, and your beloved brother ain't called Kevin anymore, either." Maura was enjoying shocking Jamie now she had got started. "He goes by the name of Tyler; he says Kevin's a gay name. Gay? Imagine that. I give him a good old-fashioned proper name and he goes and changes it because he thinks it's gay. Tyler... what sort of a name's that? Mind you, I guess it could be a lot worse, some of those kids in that gang he's got himself involved with have got the most stupid names I've ever heard. They think they're real gangsters, those boys do. One of them's half the size of Tyler and calls himself Psycho. Psycho! Can you believe it? The stupid bloody kid probably can't even spell the word."

Listening to his mother, it was like the past ten years had never happened. Nothing had changed; once she got started with her rants and her opinions, she couldn't seem to stop. Jamie let her carry on. She would tell him everything that he needed to know and he would barely have to endure a two-way conversation with the manky old cow.

"He's only gone and got himself in with some right bloody head-case now though! He blooming went and brought the fucking nutcase to this place. I did nothing but put myself out for the pair of them, gave that big black bastard a roof over his head for the last two weeks and look where it got me, the fucker wiped the floor with me today, and what did I do to deserve that huh?" She grimaced, trying to block out the pain that shot through her foot as she spoke.

Jamie sat up, alert. Was she talking about Jerell?

"He told me he was taking Tyler with him... fucking told me. I'm only the boy's mother, ain't I? But no, apparently I don't get a say. Cheeky fucker hasn't even left me the money he promised for taking him." She regretted her last words as Jamie's body language changed as he shifted forward in his chair; she wished she had kept her mouth shut.

"What money 'for taking him'?" Jamie hoped to God that she wasn't implying what he thought she was.

She decided that there was no point in lying to the boy; she might as well come clean. Besides, he could sit there looking down at her, all high and mighty, but this was none of his business. He could shove his opinions, as far as she was concerned: he had lost his right to have a say in what she did, in what any of them did, when he walked out and turned his back on them all.

"You haven't even bothered to ask about your sisters," she said, deliberately hoping to change the subject. "They both buggered of an' all. Pair of moody cows; barely get a phone call from either of them these days. As soon as they both managed to get themselves fellas, they fucked off out of here. It's like I don't bleeding exist, and after all I've done for the bleeding lot of ya."

His mother's babbling didn't fool Jamie. He couldn't give a shit about his sisters, they were cut from the same cloth as she was, but if they had both managed to get away from her then good – there might be some hope for them. Bringing the conversation back to the subject, Jamie said: "What was the money for?"

Maura stared down at her hands, feeling fidgety. She would normally smoke when she was rattled, but she had just chain-smoked two cigarettes, and her throat felt raw. She didn't fancy a third. But on the floor, unable to get up, she felt in need of something to help her.

Jamie had always had a temper, and with him looking down at her now, obviously thoroughly pissed off with her, she felt defenceless. Picking up her cigarette packet, she took a cigarette out and lit up; she wanted something to hold between her fingers, something she could focus her attention on, that might help her calm her nerves.

"Look," she said, "I know what you're thinking, but he was going to take him anyway, I didn't have no choice. So I told him, I wanted some money, to make it worth my while like. I only asked for three grand; it wasn't like I wanted much."

Jamie stared at her. Like a malignant tumour, his mother destroyed everything that she came into contact with. What sort of a woman sold her own kid?

"Where's he taken him?" Jamie fought the urge to kick the living shit out of her himself. Forcing himself to keep his cool, he sought to get as much information as he could from her. Once she told him where he could find his brother, he would be gone. This time, he really would never set eyes on his mother agian.

"He didn't say," Maura said, "just something about moving into some new place, and Tyler would be better off with him; fucking bloke thinks he's all that and then some."

"That's just fucking great." Jamie was back to square one if she didn't know where Tyler was. That had been his only lead. "You do know what that man is capable of, don't you, Mother?" Jamie felt the pent-up anger that he'd been holding back start to build once more.

"Course I do, the man's a fucking animal," she protested. "Look at the state of me. Hitting a woman, it's fucking disgraceful."

Jamie shook his head and leant forward on his chair. "The man you were going to happily sell your child to for a few poxy grand is a paedophile." Surely if his mother had known what Jerell was, even she wouldn't have let him take his brother? The memory of walking into that flat on the day of the shooting flew through Jamie's mind. He painfully recalled the look of fear and humiliation in Tyler's eyes, as they had all stood there for those few seconds while it dawned on them all what it was that had happened before they had burst in.

Looking slightly shamefaced, Maura continued to try to justify herself.

"He's a nonce? Well, I didn't know that, did I? I ain't been here too much the past two weeks. I didn't notice anything like that going on." Maura realised as soon as she said the words how terrible they sounded. She was digging herself a deeper hole.

Now Jamie knew Tyler had already been left in the hands of that filthy nutcase for over two weeks, and his so-called mum hadn't given so much as two shits about him. The poor kid had probably spent his childhood being neglected by their waster of a mother. Jamie wished that he hadn't left it so long to come back. Just thinking about Tyler's innocent little eyes as a tiny baby and the way he had stared up at Jamie, like he was the small boy's whole world, made Jamie feel like he was just as bad as their useless mother. He had left Tyler in the hands of this despicable woman, and now he was in the hands of a fucking animal. After the shooting, Gary had instructed Jamie to leave Jerell alone. But there was no way that Jamie could do that now, not when the man had taken his brother. Jamie needed to find Tyler and fast; he had to be in danger, and Jamie prayed that he hadn't suffered anymore. He needed to get Tyler away from Jerell.

"Are you sure you have no idea where they could have they gone?" Jamie used every bit of willpower he had to keep his voice controlled when he spoke; his priority was Tyler. He knew that getting Tyler away from the man would be no easy task, as he would have to do it alone. There was no way that he could bring the boys into it again, especially after what had happened to Gary.

"I don't know, he didn't say," she said, without meeting his eyes. Jamie realised that she didn't have a clue where Tyler was, not the faintest idea, and she barely had the decency to look embarrassed about it. It was only now, with Jamie talking to her in his bolshie tone, that she realised how bad a mother she was making herself look. "I know what you're thinking, Jamie, but it's not like that, I am a good mum. I've sacrificed everything for you kids. Carried each one of you in my belly for nine months, I did, and all you lot have done ever since is suck the life out of me in return."

Jamie couldn't find any more words; there was nothing left to say. Getting up from the chair, he felt an urgent need to get out of the flat; the walls were closing in, suffocating him. He needed to find his brother.

"Where do you think you're going, Jamie?" Maura demanded, as he walked to the door. "I need to go to the hospital. Take me, would ya? I think my foot's in a bad way, Jamie. I think I broke it when that bastard threw me down the stairs." She was full of self-pity, she could see that Jamie didn't have the time of day for her, but she had hoped that he would have dropped her at A and E. There was no way she would be able to hobble out of here on her own, and she had not a penny to her name to get herself a cab, after spending the last of it at her local the previous night. Pleased when Jamie changed direction and walked towards her, she was glad to see that he was at least going to do that much for her, the last thing she wanted to do was call an ambulance and have all the neighbours around here coming out to have a gawp at her. It was clear by the state she was in that she had taken a pasting; she didn't want the nosey bastards around here gossiping about her any more than they already did. The smile that had briefly passed her lips in thanks to him as he approached her was quickly wiped off her face as soon as it appeared. Jamie placed his size nine shoes over her broken foot and leant all his body weight on it, staring at her face as it twisted in agony as he bent down and unzipped the hoodie she was wearing, tearing it from her as she screamed like a wounded animal in crucifying pain. She felt her limp foot crunch beneath the force of Jamie's shoes.

"Goodbye, you nasty cunt," he spat before turning on his heel and walking out of the lounge, leaving his mother weeping in pain on the floor.

Chapter 22

"Oh yeah, I can see her now." Gavin shoved Shay out of the way to get a

better look at the pretty blonde that he kept harping on about. Gavin pressed

his face to the garage window, and could just about see the girl loitering

outside, as she peeped out from behind the silver people carrier parked just

down the road. She looked shifty, like she was up to no good, but even from

this distance he could tell from her slim long legs and the long blonde hair

that peeped out from her tatty black coat she was wearing that she was a

looker.

"That's the second day on the trot she's been out there, it's like she's

watching us. I wonder what she wants," Shay said, as Gavin turned around

and shot him a suspicious look.

"She's not one of yours, is she?" Gavin knew too well the drama that Shay

constantly got into when it came to the women in his life.

Shay took another look out the window. She didn't look familiar. If she wore

the right outfit she would be the type of bird that he'd go for, but he didn't

really rule anything out, there weren't many woman who didn't fall into the category of 'his type'. It was hard to tell, though, as she was too far down the road for him to get a proper look; he couldn't really see her face.

"Nah, nothing to do with me, I would have remembered her," Shay replied, although he was not strictly sure that this was true. He racked his brain to remember the details of the past few weeks. There hadn't been too many women, which made a change, because he had been so busy at the garage.

"Maybe she's just waiting for someone," Shay reasoned, although he was unsure if this was the case why she had just spent the past two days peering at the garage as if she was spying on them. It didn't add up.

"It's fucking freezing out there, Shay; besides, who the hell waits for someone out on the street for two days? She don't look like she's dolled up enough to be on the game, and not being funny, this road ain't really the right place for someone looking to drum up a bit of business, it's way too quiet. Nah, she looks like she's hiding. She's up to something." Gavin shook his head, unconvinced by Shay's apparent innocence; he would put money on the girl having some connection with him.

"Here, Shay," Gavin said. He grinned, making out like he had sussed what the girl was up to. "What if she's some drunken shag that you managed to get up the duff, huh? And now she's out there watching you. Finally after all these years she's managed to track you down so that she can tell you that you're her baby-daddy." Gavin laughed as he watched panic spread across Shay's face; he enjoyed winding his mate up. "Just think, there could be a little Tulisa-Chardonnay out there toddling around the place looking for her da-da, or even better how about a little Shay-Junior. Maybe that bird out there wants you to cough up for the last five years of child maintenance that you owe her," Gavin added for effect, as he played on his mate's worst fears. Gavin knew what Shay was like, and even though he was a total dog when it came to women, Gavin also knew from conversations that they had in the past that his mate was far from stupid when it came to that kind of thing. Shay had told him that no matter what, he always wore protection: he never wanted some girl to catch him out by getting herself in the club. He said he was too young to settle down, that he couldn't imagine the monotony of shagging the same old bird every night for the rest of his life. No matter how fit the bird, or how drunken Shay was, he had a little saying that never failed to make Gavin laugh: 'don't be a fool, wrap up your tool.'

"Nah, honest, she ain't got anything to do with me, Gavin. I ain't seen her before." Shay glanced out of the window. He would have remembered a girl like that.

"Maybe one of us should go out there and see if she is okay?" Gavin asked.

They had finished their work for today. The diary that Jamie had asked them to clear was sorted, he and Shay had worked their arses off for the past few days to get all the jobs that had been booked in completed, and this morning's book-ins had been the last of the remaining legitimate jobs that they had needed to get finished. All they had to do now was to wait for the next lot of merchandise that Jamie was organising, and they could get moving on their new contact. Gavin was looking forward to getting stuck in; shifting luxury motors always gave him a buzz. Nicking them; fixing them up; he loved every part of it. It was more satisfying than the poxy MOTs they had been doing, they had had bloody oil changes and tyre pressure tests coming out of their ears lately, and the days had done nothing but drag with the boredom of it all. This girl might relieve it.

"Go on, then, you go and ask her." Shay nudged his mate. Even though he was also dying to find out what the girl wanted, there was no way that he was going to go over to her after all the shit that Gavin had just filled his head with. "If she so much as even mentions my name, Gav, don't you dare let on that I'm here, okay?"

Gavin laughed, his wind-up was paying off; Shay was shitting himself. Still chuckling at Shay freaking out, Gavin wiped his hands on his overalls before heading out to see the girl. The way she kept staring from behind the car was unnerving, and he was sure that she wanted something. There was only one way to find out.

Shay watched Gavin approach the girl. Her body language made it clear that she realised she had been spotted. Shay could tell that she wanted to do a runner as Gavin walked towards her. He watched with interest as she looked around nervously, like she was debating on legging it; she was clearly nervous about something. Shay couldn't see Gavin's face as he spoke to the girl, he had his back to him, but it had been a few minutes now of them talking and the girl was still there, so Shay figured that was a good sign.

"Shit," Shay shouted, as Gavin and the girl walked together towards the garage. Shay couldn't read Gavin's expression. He felt knots tighten in his stomach, as he wondered why Gavin was bringing the bird back here. Shay couldn't mask his curiosity as Gavin, followed by the girl, came through the big doors.

The girl glanced around the garage, familiarising herself with her new surroundings. It wasn't what she had expected. She had imagined it to be classy, with lots of high-end motors dotted about the place and a bit of a buzz going on. She couldn't hide her disappointment as she took in the dreariness of the place, it seemed like any other small-time garage, and she wondered if she had made the wrong decision. She pulled her hood off her head as the warmth of the place hit her. She let her blonde hair fall down over her shoulders, and even with no make-up on, and the look of worry etched on her forehead, it took everything Gavin and Shay had not to stand there and gawp at the stunning girl, who was now wrinkling her nose up at the place.

Realising that Shay was unable to control his stare, and had seemingly stopped worrying about whether he was a father, Gavin quickly shot him a look, hoping that it would help him to snap out of it.

"Go and whack the kettle on, mate, I said we'd make her a nice hot cuppa while she waits. The poor girl's bloody freezing."

Shay raised his eyebrows at Gavin; he was dying to know what the girl was here for, he could see that Gavin was enjoying making him suffer by not giving anything away. He glared at Gavin but got nothing in return but a vacant stare.

"Do you take sugar?" Shay asked the girl, before adding politely: "sorry, I didn't catch your name." He remembered that Gavin hadn't mentioned it, and Shay could see that he was relishing keeping him guessing, clearly amused that he had rattled Shay's cage.

"Just one, please," the girl replied, following the two men to the back office, glad that she was able to shelter her body from the bitter cold. Her hands were blue; she had to stuff them deep into her pockets for hours, trying unsuccessfully to warm them. "My name's Louise," she added, as she looked back over to Gavin, as if to seek permission that she was able to say why she was here. "And I'm looking for Jamie Finch."

Chapter 23

"Get your arses back out there, and don't even tink about coming back 'ere til you have some news for me," Jerell roared. He stood in the doorway, furious at the cheek of Rhys and a couple of the other boys who had just sat down on the sofa, like he owed them a rest.

"Jerell, man, we've searched everywhere, we're running out of places to look." Rhys was exasperated. He was so tired that he could have had a kip standing up.

Jerell hadn't let them have any respite since the drama with Louise, two days ago, and they were all knackered from searching for her. Rhys was so tired that he couldn't think straight, he would never even dream of arguing with Jerell normally.

Seeing Jerell clench his fists at the boy's response, Reagan stepped in to try and cool the situation down.

"Have you tried Louise's mum's place?" Reagan was mindful that to an outsider he sounded like he was being helpful, but he knew Louise better than any one of these boys, and her mum's house would be the last place on this earth Louise would go to. He just wished that she would get in touch with him, so that he could speak to her about what she had seen.

"Yeah, there are a couple of boys on it already, they're watching the front, and a couple are keeping an eye on the other house too. Ritchie and Michael are there, so if she did show her face, they would tell us straight away," Rhys replied, feeling hard done by that he was going to have to go back out into the freezing cold looking for the girl, when all he wanted to do right now was get some shut eye. He didn't even know why he was looking for Louise; he had heard a commotion the other night but he had been half-asleep, and by the time he had got to the landing to see what the noise was about, Jerell was having a pop at Reagan and Louise had legged it. Whatever it was that she had done, Rhys was glad he wasn't in her shoes; he had never seen Jerell so angry.

Reagan agreed with Rhys; they had all searched long and hard the past few days and, like Rhys had said, Ritchie and Michael were staying on at the house until this mess was cleared up, and they were both doing their best to keep it running as efficiently as Louise had done. The boys needed a break. Reagan looked at Jerell to make a decision.

"Get back out there and keep looking, boy," Jerell ordered. He didn't like the way that Rhys had talked back to him, the boy was getting too big for his boots, and if he thought that he could use this place as a doss house while that girl was on the missing list he had another think coming.

Reagan watched the boys as they wearily left. He prepared to try to reason with Jerell again.

"You don't know Louise like I do, Jerell. She ain't going to say nothing. I promise you, she'll be shitting herself thinking about what you're going to do when you catch up with her."

Reagan was desperate to convince Jerell that even though no-one had seen Louise for two days, she would just be lying low while she sorted her head out. She wasn't a silly girl, and even though what she had caught Jerell doing with Tyler must have come as a horrendous shock, Reagan was certain that she just needed time to calm down, she wouldn't blab about it, he would put his life on it because, like himself, she would be more than aware that Jerell would kill her if she talked.

Reagan just wanted to know that Louise was alright. He hadn't seen or heard from her since that night, and he had thought that by now she would have made some kind of contact with him, but there had been nothing. Jerell had insisted that he hand over his mobile, so that he could keep tabs on it. But there had been no phone call, no text message: nothing.

Jerell was fuming that Louise had taken off; the last thing that he wanted was her spreading his business about the place: or, worse still, the silly bitch doing something really stupid like getting the authorities involved.

"Shitting herself? So she should be." Jerell was going to give her a beating when he found her. She couldn't leave whenever she felt like it, she had responsibilities, and her not sticking around after what she had seen him doing with Tyler confirmed to Jerell that she would cause him a whole world of trouble. Jerell had seen the disgust and hate in the girl's eyes when she had stared across the room at him, shocked, as he lay in Tyler's bed looking like a rabbit that had been caught in the headlights. Jerell knew very well that people feared notorious gangsters, drug dealers, rude boys, but kiddie-fiddlers were not something that people tolerated. If anyone found out about his secret he would be crucified. He was in no doubt that the girl would cause him problems. They had searched everywhere they could think of for her. At first they had assumed that they would find her at her house, but she hadn't turned up there. Jerell had every one of his boys keeping a look-out for her; he had offered a grand to the boy that found out where she was; that sort of money, to kids around here, would be more than enough to dissipate any of the loyalty that the boys would be feeling towards the girl, she may be one of them, but money always clouded people's judgement, and he knew the boys would be doing everything they could to find her. So far no-one had seen or heard from her, though. It seemed she had disappeared.

Rubbing his temples, Jerell rocked back and forth on the chair. His body was bursting with agitation, and he couldn't settle. If Louise went around shooting her pretty little mouth off, he could end up with the police or social services swarming around like flies to a pile of steaming shit, and he would end up losing everything. Jerell would not be a sitting target. He made a decision.

"We need to get rid of da boy." Jerell felt calmer after he had spoken. He needed to remain in control and finally after the past two days of tormenting himself with worry, and searching the whole of Lambeth for the daft bitch, he decided that he had no choice but to play it safe.

"What do you mean: get rid of the boy?" Reagan asked.

Reagan knew that Jerell was desperate; for the past few days he had been a nightmare. He was bad enough at the best of times, with his constant paranoia, but when Jerell got something in his head that made him feel on edge, he was beyond reasoning with. No-one had been able to say anything without getting their heads bitten off, and the atmosphere in the house had been bleak.

Reagan was exhausted and worried sick about Louise, but he had tried, as always, to keep things running as smoothly as possible, and he had even had a crack at trying to stop the rumours that had started flying around amongst the others. Everyone wanted to know what had happened to make Louise do a runner, and what had made Jerell get so het up about? The more that Reagan tried to diminish the rumours, however, the more the others thought that he was hiding something and became even more suspicious. So in the end Reagan had given up; he would let them believe that she was robbing Jerell blind behind his back: anything was better than the truth getting out.

Jerell looked deep in thought, but Reagan could see that now he had made a decision he was back in control.

"If there is no boy here, then what can anyone do if they do come looking, huh?" Jerell said. "No-one can prove a thing if there's no kid here. We hush the others up, you talk to the boys; no-one's going to say jack shit. Tyler's walking, talking evidence."

Reagan nodded. He was pleased that Jerell seemed to be finally getting his wits about him again and agreed that getting Tyler away was not such a bad idea. The poor little sod had turned into a quivering wreck. He wasn't eating or sleeping, and he had just been sitting in his room for the last forty-eight hours staring at his four walls whenever Reagan had popped his head in. It saddened Reagan to see that it was too late for the poor kid now. Reagan hadn't stopped Jerell from getting to him, and the boy seemed broken inside. Reagan couldn't help but feel responsible, he should have done more. He knew that Jerell had been vicious to the boy, and that Tyler was petrified of the man. Getting the kid away from here would be a good thing, and after everything that had happened Reagan felt that he owed it to Tyler to be the one that got him out of here.

"Where are we going to take him?" Reagan hoped that he would be able to be the one that took the kid; he didn't want to give Jerell the opportunity to inflict one more second of pain on the boy.

"Take him?" Jerell asked, realising that he and Reagan were not on the same page. He leant forward and spoke in a serious tone. "We ain't taking dat boy nowhere, Reagan. I want him gone. Dealt wid, good and proper. You get me? That boy is nothing but a liability." Jerell's eyes were bloodshot from lack of sleep and smoking gear, making him look more menacing than usual, and Regan knew that he was deadly serious.

Reagan tried to hide his shock. Tyler was just a scared kid. Even if Jerell let him walk out of here, Reagan knew that Tyler wouldn't breathe a word to a living soul: he was far too frightened of Jerell.

"Nah, man, we can't do that to the poor fucker... he's just a kid, Jerell. He ain't done nothing to us." Reagan was out of his depth. Everything was getting too much. Jerell was more and more unpredictable, and Reagan was disgusted that he had let things get this far out of control. He was appalled that he had sat back and let this monster abuse Tyler. And now Jerell was sitting here casually smoking a spliff, ordering a hit on a twelve-year-old boy. Reagan felt sick. What the fuck was he doing; this was crazy. When this had all started, the idea had been to make money and gain kudos on the estate. This wasn't what he had signed up for.

"What's the matter? You not got the bollocks you born with, boy?" Jerell asked, as he watched the fear grow on Reagan's face, as he realised that Jerell was really going to do this. "You don't have to be the one to do it, if you don't think you can handle it, Reagan. There are plenty more boys out there that will be more than happy to show me that they're ready to up their game, and prove themselves to me by getting rid of the kid, you know? You just say the word if you think you can't deal with it."

Jerell was talking down to Reagan, making him feel belittled, whilst he challenged him. He always had a way of getting to Reagan. The room was eerily quiet, as Jerell waited for the answer that Reagan knew his fate depended on. If Jerell could do away with a kid to ensure his silence, then he wasn't safe either. None of them were. He had no choice but to agree to get rid of Tyler; otherwise he could end up dead too.

"When?" Reagan returned Jerell's cold stare, thoughts of Tyler in his room oblivious to what was being planned, racing through his mind.

"The sooner the better." Jerell lit another joint and stretched out his legs as he inhaled long tokes of the spliff, continuing to stare at Reagan, not taking his eyes off the boy as he sussed out if he was up to the task. He studied him, taking in his every movement.

Reagan tried to remain calm, keeping his expression neutral and his body language relaxed so that Jerell would have no idea that his heart was banging in his chest. He put his hand out for Jerell to pass the joint.

"I'm listening," he said.

Chapter 24

Gavin was waiting outside the garage when Jamie pulled up in his car. Gavin wanted a heads up on the girl. He was hoping Jamie would be able to shed a bit of light on what this Louise wanted, as she hadn't giving anything away about herself so far.

"Bloody hell, mate; that was record timing," Gavin joked, as Jamie jumped out of the motor and walked briskly over. "I only rang a few minutes ago."

Jamie was obviously in a hurry to see the girl. Gavin had left her inside to finish her tea, while Shay bored the arse off her, spinning a few of his lines, ever a sucker for a beauty. The minute Shay had clocked her, his testosterone had kicked in and all thoughts of him worrying about being a newly found baby-daddy had gone straight out the window, instantly forgotten. The way Shay was drooling over the poor girl when Gavin had left them to it, he had looked like he would have happily impregnated her with octuplets had she asked him to.

The girl hadn't had a chance to get a word in with Shay banging on, but Gavin still thought that she was acting shiftily. She seemed nervous and on edge, and she was being cagey about why she was at the garage.

When Gavin had rung Jamie to tell him that a girl was insisting on talking to him and only him, he had expected a reaction, but Jamie had gone silent on the other end of the phone and then asked him to keep her there until he arrived. So far, Jamie hadn't given Gavin any clues about what the girl might want.

Gavin and Shay were extremely curious. Jamie had never mentioned seeing a girl, let alone one he would allow to come to the garage; there had to be something going on.

"Who is she then?" Jamie asked.

"You tell me," Gavin answered. "All she said was that her name's Louise and she must talk to you, right now. Tell you what, Jamie, she's a proper sort an' all.... a blonde." Gavin could see the confusion in Jamie's eyes, surely even someone as cold as him would remember a beautiful blonde girl called Louise. Gavin was trying his hardest to read Jamie, but as always it was an impossible task; Jamie was a master at keeping his business private. Gavin found it a bit weird that a girl had turned up out of the blue, asking for Jamie, but wouldn't say what it was about and insisted that she could only talk to him. Then Jamie turned up five minutes later, like a bat out of hell, and looking equally as shifty. Yet still Gavin had no answers and he knew he should give up trying to get them.

"Come on, she's out the back, probably dying of boredom listening to Shay droning on, poor girl." Gavin walked back through to the office, Jamie following.

"Here she is." Gavin announced to Jamie, as they stepped into the office, interrupting Shay mid-sentence.

Gavin looked from Louise to Jamie, trying to gauge their initial reactions and hoping that there would be a clue as to what was going on.

Seeing Jamie's puzzled expression Louise spoke up. "We haven't met, but you're the man I need to speak to. You're Jamie Finch yeah?" Her voice held more confidence than her body language had earlier implied.

Jamie didn't know who she was or what she wanted, but he agreed with what Gavin had been saying: the girl was stunning. Her young-looking skin was flawless, and she had the most gorgeous bright green eyes Jamie had ever seen. Pretty was an understatement.

"Speak to me about what?" Jamie asked.

"Jerell Morgan." Louise watched the recognition flash in Jamie's eyes.

"For fuck's sake, not this again," Shay interrupted. Gary had been through the mill because of Jerell, and they didn't need any more drama because of him.

Holding his hands up, to quieten Shay, Jamie understood why Louise was here. "Will you boys give us a few minutes?"

Gavin and Shay looked dubiously at one another before reluctantly leaving. They knew that Jamie wasn't asking, he was telling.

"What the fuck's going on? Shay whispered to Gavin.

Gavin shrugged. Since Gary had been shot, Jamie had been a different man. He was riddled with frustration, wanting retribution for Gary, but Gary had insisted that they all leave well alone. Jamie must be seething about the whole situation, and now Gavin wondered if Jamie had been planning something all along. Maybe the girl was in on it? Gavin should have known that Jamie was too hot-headed not to have reacted, and he had a feeling that Jamie had no intention of letting the situation go without a fight.

"I'm fucked if I know, mate," Gavin said. "But whatever it is, if that girl has got any connection to Jerell Morgan, you can bet your life it's all going to kick off again. Whatever you do, not a word of this gets out to Gary or Les. You got me, Shay? It's the last thing Gary needs right now, and besides, Jamie knows what he's doing, let's just wait and see what the girl says to him, yeah?"

In the office, Jamie handed Louise a fresh mug of tea and sat opposite her. Taking a sip of her drink, as she held his eye, he noted how composed she was; it was rare to see such self-assurance in a girl so young.

"Someone told you that I was looking for Jerell, did they?" Jamie broke the silence between them, as he swirled the coffee in his mug.

"I've got a mate who told me I should come and see you. He said that you've been putting the word about that you're looking for Jerell?" Louise hoped she had found the right person; otherwise the past two days would have been a waste of time.

"And what: you know where he is?" Jamie didn't want to say too much. The girl looked honest, but he wasn't falling for some pretty blonde fluttering her eyelashes, throwing him off guard, if this was a set up. He had been putting the word out on Jerell ever since his mother had told him that Tyler was with him, but what if Jerell had found out that Jamie was looking for him? Maybe the girl had been sent to dig for information, or to set him up.

Jamie had asked a few of his contacts, but until Louise had turned up, no-one had said they had seen Jerell.

"I do know where he is. He's got a new place." Louise matched Jamie's frosty tone. She had expected him to be happy that she had information for him, but his face gave nothing away.

Jamie took a sip of coffee, giving himself the extra few seconds to weigh things up. He was always wary of new people. "So why are you telling me this, Louise, what's in it for you?"

The girl would be stupid to go up against Jerell by dishing out information on him to someone she didn't know. People didn't go round doing good deeds out of the goodness of their hearts; there was always something in it for them.

"I think that Jerell's after me," Louise said, and Jamie noted a quiver in her voice. She had hidden it until now, but she could no longer disguise her fear. "I've been running for two days. I couldn't even stay with my mate; Jerell would have found me. I have nowhere to go, Jerell knows everybody I know and will catch up with me eventually. I'm on my own, and I can't go back. Not while he's probably trying to find me. I had to sleep in a shop doorway last night. I'm desperate." Jamie could hear the indignation in her voice as she carried on talking, clearly relieved to be able to unburden herself. "I can't go back there, not after what I've seen, Jerell won't trust me not to talk. I know what he's like. I got away, luckily enough, otherwise who knows what he would have done to me to make sure I kept my mouth shut." Louise took another sip of tea, grateful that Jamie seemed to be listening, and more importantly to understand where she was coming from. "I went and saw an old mate of mine, Steve Allen, he used to be a runner in a gang that I know, but he soon moved on, doing his own stuff over in Brixton. He said he knew you, Jamie, and that you might be able to help me. He said I could trust you."

Her story seemed to add up. Jamie had seen Steve four days before and had told him that if he had any information on Jerell he would make it worth his while. Steve was as trustworthy as they came; although he dabbled in a lot of shit with a lot of dodgy people now, Jamie knew that he wouldn't stitch him up.

"He said he didn't know why you wanted to find Jerell, but he reckoned from the way you were talking, you had a score to settle with him. So here I am; you want to know where you can find Jerell and I can tell you," she said simply.

"Why do you think that he might be after you?" Jamie asked. Louise seemed like a decent girl, it seemed strange that Jerell should want to harm her.

"I've seen things... things that he doesn't want anyone to know about." Louise's voice was soft. She let the silent tears that she had been trying to hold back fall, unable to hide them for a second longer. It was the first time

that she had let herself cry, since she had seen poor Tyler's petrified face the

other night, when he had been pinned down by Jerell.

Jamie bristled at her words. He knew things too. Things that he didn't want to

know, things that kept him awake at night and made him worried sick in the

day.

Louise seemed like she was telling him the truth, but he didn't want to give

too much away to her, not until he was certain that he could trust her.

"I really need your help, Jamie." Louise put her head in her hands.

Jamie let the girl get her grief out of her system. He could see she needed to

get everything off her chest. She was scared of Jerell; that much was clear,

and her story seemed genuine.

Once she had calmed down enough to speak clearly and calmly, Louise

explained how she had spent the past months working for Jerell. She told

Jamie how Jerell controlled all the kids that he had working for him. Louise

said how she knew he would be looking for her; he would be panicking about

what she might do or say. She was petrified by the rumours about what he

had done to the last person that had opened his mouth. Apparently he had

cut some grass' head off with a machete. Louise had heard he had been like a man possessed, and she knew that he was capable of doing the same to her; he was out of control.

Louise couldn't bring herself to think about Reagan. He sickened her. She had seen that look in his eyes that night: he had known all along. Just the thought of lying beside Reagan in bed each night, while he pretended that nothing had been going on between that vile man and poor Tyler made her feel physically sick.

"What is it that he doesn't want anyone else to know?" Jamie interrupted her thoughts, as he tried to encourage the information out of her, seeing as she wasn't exactly willing to tell him whatever it was that she had on Jerell. He had a good idea that he already knew what she was going to say, but he needed to hear it from her.

Louise shook her head. She was unable to put what she had seen into words, she was still shocked and disgusted by it, and frightened out of her wits that if she told anyone Jerell would find out.

"If you're looking for Jerell, I'll take you to him. But only on the condition you deal with him properly." Louise looked Jamie in the eye. She was laying her cards on the table. "He's been doing bad things..." Unable to continue, Louise hung her head.

Jamie knew that he wasn't going to get her to say much more; she was beside herself with worry. Not wanting to miss his opportunity, he asked her the question that he had been dying to have an answer to since she had first spoken Jerell's name.

"Is there a boy with him, Louise? He's only twelve, and his name's Kevin, I mean Tyler." Jamie saw the shocked expression spread across Louise's face, confirming his fears.

But Louise was confused as well as shocked; how did Jamie know about Tyler?

"That's who I'm looking for Louise: Tyler. I was told Jerell has him, and I need to find him; he's not safe." Jamie explained to the bewildered-looking girl.

"I know. I know Tyler." Louise felt dizzy from trying to digest what she had heard.

Jamie breathed a sigh of relief. She knew Tyler. Now he would find out where he was, and he would be able to help his brother. "Is he okay, Louise?"

Louise didn't know how to answer that; the boy would be far from okay after everything he had suffered, but he wasn't dead if that was what Jamie wanted to know.

"Is he okay, Louise?" Jamie felt his chest tighten. He couldn't imagine how he would react if he was too late and something had already happened.

"It depends on what you consider to be okay." Louise shrugged sadly. Unable to help her bluntness, she added: "He's alive, if that's what you mean."

Louise could see that Jamie was trying to keep himself together, as she was. There was a scared look on his face. She felt better that she had someone to talk to, someone who was on her side. The relief was too much for her, she burst into tears. The loud sob escaped her mouth, as if the worry and distress she had been hiding inside had been like water in a dam that had finally given in under the pressure, her tears now bursting out, unable to be contained any longer.

Jamie crouched at her side. He placed his arm around her and felt her body shake. "It's alright, Louise. You don't have to say another word. I know about Tyler. I know." Jamie felt rage seer through his body at the thought of what Louise must have seen.

The girl looked drained, and after her telling him that she had been sleeping rough, he figured that she must also be starving hungry and very tired. But there was no time to spare to help her now. Jamie needed to get to Tyler fast: he was his priority.

"Louise, I'm going to need you to take me to Tyler and Jerell. Do you think that you're going to be able to do that? We don't have much time. If Jerell is het up about you getting the police involved or something, Tyler may have a noose around his neck, who knows what Jerell would do to him to make sure that he doesn't get found out?"

A teary Louise looked up at Jamie, as the implications of what he was saying sunk in: although she had been thinking much the same thing. She knew what Jerell could be like. He tormented himself and everyone around him with his paranoia. He would be climbing the walls.

"Of course I'll take you to him." Louise was grateful that Jamie was on her side, he looked like he could handle himself. There was something about the way that he spoke to her; he had an air of confidence. If he could get Tyler away from that animal, that was good enough for her. But handle Jerell Morgan? She wasn't so sure. No-one she knew had gone up against him and won. "Jerell isn't going to just let you walk in and take him, though."

"Don't you worry yourself about Jerell, Louise. He should have been dealt with ages ago. You show me where he is; I'll do the rest."

Louise prayed that he wouldn't be too late.

Chapter 25

Reagan's palms were sweaty and his T-shirt stuck to his back. As he made his way over to the car, he felt like he was having an out-of-body experience. His feet were just about walking, but he felt like he wasn't really here. It was a surreal feeling, like he was in a trance. He could almost feel Jerell's eyes burn into him, as he watched him from the lounge window, as he and Tyler walked down the driveway towards the car.

"Where are we going?" Tyler was seemingly oblivious to Reagan's mood. He had been stuck in his bedroom for the past two days, and was happy to get out. He had started to feel like he was going mad up in his room all by himself, and if getting out of the place, even for a little while, meant getting away from Jerell then even better.

"I thought we'd go for a bit of a spin and get ourselves a burger, Ty. Change of scenery for you," Reagan replied, like he was doing Tyler a favour, hating himself for being so gutless. "You must be starving; I haven't seen you eat a thing for days."

Tyler shrugged, as if it wasn't such a big deal, but he was indeed famished, he hadn't eaten anything for two days because he hadn't wanted to come downstairs and face any of them. His belly was hurting from the hunger pangs and even this short walk from the house to the car had made him light-headed.

Reagan opened the doors to the Corsa, and Tyler sat in the front passenger seat. Even though he was grateful to Reagan for taking him out of the house and getting him something to eat, he felt wary. Why was Reagan being nice: was he feeling guilty? Reagan was the closest person to Jerell; Tyler wondered if he knew what Jerell had been doing to him.

Tyler hadn't seen Jerell for two days but he had heard him shouting at Reagan, about Louise. Apparently she had done a runner after finding Jerell in his room. Jerell was furious with the girl. Tyler hadn't been able to make out his exact words, but he was sure that, even though Reagan hadn't said anything about it to him, he must know what Jerell had been doing.

Tyler hadn't been able to forget the expression on Louise's face when she had turned on his bedroom light. He constantly replayed the look on her face. She had looked so shocked and disgusted. It wasn't the look of someone who had known already, so maybe Reagan didn't know either, Tyler rationalised. But he couldn't be sure. He was so confused. He had gone over every conversation that he'd ever had with Reagan, analysing every look, every comment, until his mind was whirling. Right now, all he knew for sure was that he had never felt so alone in his life. And as much as he wanted to trust Reagan, he couldn't find it in him.

It saddened Tyler that he had nobody to turn to. He had thought that joining a gang like the Larkhall Boys would change his life for the better and for a while it had. He had made more money than most grown-ups that he knew, let alone kids, and despite the constant ribbing from the other boys at first, Tyler had believed that he had made some real friends, and there had been times that he would have even classed those friends as his family. But now he wasn't so sure. When Jerell had sent the other boys all out to look for Louise the other day, Tyler had overheard Rhys having a conversation with one of the other boys, on the landing. Tyler had strained to listen to the boy's whispering, which he was sure was about him. He hadn't wanted to leave his bedroom; his sanctuary. He couldn't face the others. He felt mortified by the shame of it all. As Tyler put his ear against his bedroom door to hear the murmurs, it became obvious that none of the boys knew exactly why Louise had gone.

"The first one of us that finds her gets a grand. A thousand pounds, blood! That sort of cash would pay for my new sound system for my motor, innit. Whatever Louise has done to Jerell, it ain't got shit to do with me, let the girl

sort her own beef with him, she'd serve me up just the same, make no odds,"
Tyler had heard Rhys say.

Tyler had realised then that if Rhys, whom he had thought of as one of his
friends, could turn like that so quickly against Louise, someone who was
respected more than he was by the group as a whole, then he didn't stand a
chance. These kids weren't his family, and they certainly weren't his friends.

He was on his own.

For Tyler, the only good thing to come out of the search for Louise was that
Jerell had been so caught up with it all, that he had left Tyler alone ever since.

As much as Tyler really did need someone on his side right now, as much as he
wanted to believe that Reagan was there for him, something stopped him
from trusting him.

Driving along, Reagan wiped his sweaty face; he glanced over to Tyler, who
was clutching his wallet tightly to his stomach, like it was his comforter.

"You didn't need to bring your wallet, Ty, the grub's on me, mate. My shout."
Reagan tried to lighten the mood.

"Thanks, Reagan," Tyler said, grateful for the kindness Reagan was showing,
despite his own doubts.

"I always have my wallet on me." Tyler shrugged, as if it wasn't important.

Reagan tried to concentrate on the road, as he thought where to get food. That would drag things out and give him time to get his head around what Jerell had instructed him to do.

They drove on in silence.

At the drive-thru, Reagan ordered too much food for two people. He wasn't hungry himself, but he sat patiently in the car, half-heartedly picking at a few of the chips, while Tyler devoured his meal and most of Reagan's.

"Here," Reagan stuffed a straw into a coke and handed it to Tyler, "something to wash your food down, Ty."

"Are you alright, Reagan?" Tyler looked up from his second Big Mac, a dollop of tomato ketchup dripping down his chin as he spoke. He took the drink. "You haven't eaten much, and you look really weird." Tyler had been so distracted by hunger he had only just noticed that Reagan had barely touched the food. "I thought that you wanted something to eat?"

Tyler noticed that Reagan was sweating profusely and now Tyler thought about it, he had been acting strangely since they had got in the car.

"I think my eyes are just bigger than my belly, Ty, I really fancied some grub earlier, but I've totally lost my appetite, and now you mention it, I do feel a bit off colour." Reagan did feel physically sick at the thought of what was to come.

Tyler wasn't convinced that Reagan's problem was solely physical. So much had happened lately, forcing him to grow up quickly. He was no longer a gullible kid. He had become suspicious of everyone and everything; nothing was as it seemed.

"Did you have to bribe Rhys to lend you his motor?" Tyler asked the question because he knew how Rhys was about his car, and he wondered how Reagan had managed to borrow it; it was Rhys' pride and joy, and he didn't let anyone drive it.

"Rhys must have been feeling generous, I guess." Reagan regretted his answer immediately, knowing that he hadn't sounded the least bit convincing. Tyler knew Rhys better than to think the boy would do anyone a favour. Rhys was a selfish little sod at the best of times. Jerell had told Rhys they were borrowing his car, and Reagan had actually been impressed with Rhys for initially standing up for himself and saying no to letting him drive the car. The boy was so adamant that no-one was taking it without his say so, and even when Jerell shouted at him, Rhys had stood his ground and said that he wouldn't let them. It was only when Jerell started to manipulate him, saying how much he had done for the boy and how much he had given him, pointing at the roof he had put over his head and talking about all the money he had put in the boy's pocket that the dynamics changed. Rhys had realised the bigger picture: even if he had insisted that they couldn't take his motor, Jerell would have done it anyway. It's what he did. So, to save face, and to make it look like he was coming good for Jerell, Rhys had given in.

"Don't go driving it like a bitch, Reagan," Rhys had warned, before throwing him his car keys.

Chucking the food wrappers into the passenger footwell for now, Reagan switched the headlights on to counteract the encroaching darkness. As he drove, his thoughts turned to Louise. He hoped she was okay. It worried him that she hadn't got in contact with him, but he guessed that if she was even half as scared as he imagined her to be then he would be the last person she contacted, as he lived in the same house as Jerell.

Tyler looked out of the window at the cars whizzing by. Everyone seemed to be rushing: in a hurry to get home, he expected. His vision blurred from the glare of the other cars' lights. His head felt too heavy for his body. He leaned against the window and rested, the glass cool against his cheek. With his stomach full, and the past few days catching up with him, Tyler drifted off to sleep.

Reagan glanced across at the kid slumped against the door. The poor boy trusted him; he had no idea what Jerell had sent him to do.

As he turned his attention back to the road, Reagan wondered what he had become. This was one of Jerell's tests; if Reagan didn't sort out Tyler, Jerell wouldn't have anything to hold over his head; ultimately, Reagan wouldn't be safe. He understood that. He was out of his depth, but he knew that if he wasn't the one to get rid of Tyler, Jerell would do it himself, and without a shadow of a doubt, what he did would be far more brutal than Reagan was capable of imagining.

Chapter 26

Reagan parked on Wandsworth Road, beside the entrance to Larkhall Park. From this day on, this familiar place was going to be somewhere that he would avoid like the plague.

Reagan sat back in the driver's seat, appreciating the silence. Next to him, Tyler slept. Reagan pulled the sleeves of his jumper over his hands to shield them from the cold. Even with the heater turned up full whack, it was freezing. He looked out of the window, noting that the rush-hour traffic was dying down; most of the evening's commuters were already at home.

He watched as a tall, lanky man, wearing a suit and carrying a briefcase, strolled towards him. The man had a bounce to his step and a smile on his face. He looked like he didn't have a care in the world. Reagan would put money on it that the bloke was going home after a 'hard' day pen-pushing at the office. He expected that the bloke lived in one of the over-priced town houses around the corner. He probably had a beautiful wife waiting for him. Reagan could see it now, there would be a proper home-cooked dinner on the table, and he probably had a couple of little sprogs that were all tucked up asleep in their beds. The bloke didn't know he was born; he had no idea how lucky he was to be walking in his shoes, with the life he lived. He was oblivious

to the world that Reagan came from, he thought jealously, as the man strolled

merrily past the car, swinging his briefcase as he went.

It pissed Reagan off that money had so much influence. Too little or too much

determined just how far you could go in life. Without money you were

practically invisible. Around here there were clusters of shitty council estates,

grey towers of concrete that conveniently stacked up the dregs of society on

top of each other all in one place. Yet only minutes away from these slums,

which he had come from, there were million-pound houses where people like

that bloke lived the dream, and a dream was all it would ever be for the likes

of Reagan.

Glancing at his watch, he saw it was almost seven.

Reagan watched Tyler sleeping. His worries seemed to have disappeared from

his face, the boy's constant frown smoothed away.

Reagan didn't want to get out of the car, but he knew that he couldn't delay

what needed to be done any longer.

"Ty, wake up." Reagan nudged Tyler's arm to rouse the boy.

"What's up?" Tyler asked as he gathered his bearings and realised that he was still inside the car, with Reagan. He must have been knackered, he thought to himself sleepily; if Reagan hadn't woken him he could have slept for a week.

"Where are we?" Tyler asked curiously, trying to work out, through the darkness, which street they were in.

"We're at Larkhall, Ty. I thought we could go for a little walk," Reagan said, and then clocking Tyler's concerned expression, he added: "I thought you might need to talk, you know..."

When he had woken, Tyler hadn't recognised the place, normally he went into the park from the other entrance on his BMX, and he had never had any reason to come as far up as this way. Tyler knew the park like the back of his hand. They were called the Larkhall Boys because of the amount of time they all spent there doing the drops for Jerell and Reagan. It was their territory. They did loads of drops at Myatt Fields and Brockwell Park too, but Larkhall was their manor.

Turning up here wasn't unusual in itself, but 'going for a walk' in Larkhall with Reagan 'to chat', wasn't something that Tyler felt comfortable with, especially as it was freezing cold. But then, when he thought about it, Tyler decided that maybe it was a good thing. Even Reagan suggesting that they talk about stuff meant a lot to Tyler. He needed to get everything off his chest, and maybe Reagan would help him to sort his head out, he really couldn't cope with holding everything inside himself anymore.

However, after trudging around the park in silence for about ten minutes, Tyler was having second thoughts. It was dark, and there were hardly any people about. A couple of kids had ridden past on their BMXs but Reagan and Tyler hadn't recognised them, and a few people had been walking their dogs, but other than that it was eerily quiet. Reagan hadn't said a word, which Tyler was starting to think was strange.

Tyler could tell that Reagan was uneasy about something; he was walking fast, and his body was tense. Tyler started to question whether maybe he was in trouble; maybe he had pissed Reagan off. But he couldn't remember doing or saying anything that might have annoyed Reagan, and besides, he had been fine when they were in the car a few minutes earlier. Tyler wondered if Reagan was just waiting for him to start off the conversation in his own time, maybe he thought that he was struggling to find the words.

"I'm not gay, you know," Tyler said, as he trudged a foot or so behind, Reagan desperately trying to match his quick pace. Tyler would hate it if people thought that he was gay.

"I know you ain't gay, you plank," Reagan said. He tried to laugh off Tyler's statement. He tried to block out the fact that he had felt the same emotions that Tyler was feeling, all those years ago when he had been confused about his own abuser.

"He makes me do stuff." Tyler's voice was quiet.

Reagan felt his back straighten with tension. He couldn't deal with this; he hadn't expected Tyler to want to talk about what had happened; it sent Reagan's mind all over the place.

Tyler took Reagan's silence as his cue to continue. "He scares me, Reagan, when he does these things. He makes me do stuff to him and he says that if I don't do what he tells me, he'll really hurt me." Tyler paused, thinking about the threats that Jerell had made. "He told me about some boy, some young kid back in Jamaica. He said that he'd blabbed his mouth off to his mum about what Jerell had tried to do to him. When Jerell got hold of the kid again, before he came over to England, he told me that he had shoved a broken bottle up inside the kid's arse and cut up all his insides. Jerell said that the boy's body will never be found; he'd got away with it. He said he'd do the same to me if I talked, Reagan, said I had to let him do what he wanted." Tyler was crying now, an unwelcome, steady flow of hot tears trickling down his cheeks. He wanted Reagan to listen; to understand; to take him seriously.

Angry with himself for crying, he wiped the tears away with the sleeve of his jumper, but he felt relieved that he had finally told his secret out loud.

Tyler noticed that Reagan's walk had slowed; he was clearly listening. They had reached a quiet, secluded area of the woods, enclosed by trees. There was no-one else around.

Reagan was wondering if Jerell's story was true; he was capable of doing something so horrific, Reagan had witnessed first-hand how cold and callous the man could be. The sight of the severed Polish man's head, which Jerell had hacked off in front of Reagan and a few of the other boys in the old dusty warehouse, had been the first time that Reagan had seen anyone murdered. It had been brutal and had remained an unwelcome vision in Reagan's mind that he knew he would never be able to shake off. How he was going to be able to do what Jerell expected now, he had no idea.

Reagan was a few steps ahead of Tyler; he stopped and stood still, facing the other way. He didn't have much time to strike; the more Tyler spoke, the less Reagan felt that he could go through with the undertaking. His head was telling him to do as Jerell had instructed him before he completely lost his nerve, but his heart was saying that he should be helping the boy. Reagan thought how brave Tyler had been to speak out about what Jerell had done.

Even now as an adult, talking about his own abuse was something that Reagan was unable to do.

"You can't even look at me, can you, Reagan?" Tyler asked, ashamed that he had been so honest. Maybe Reagan hadn't known about what Jerell was doing afterall.

Reagan was still facing away from him; he was standing like a statue, his back dead straight. He hadn't said a word. Tyler couldn't blame him; he must be sickened by what he had just heard. Tyler sat on a mound of grass, nervously picking strands with his fingers, as he waited for Reagan to say something.

Reagan reached under his jumper. The gun Jerell had given him was tucked into the waistband of his jeans. Earlier on, thoughts of doing a runner with Tyler, in Rhys' car, had crossed his mind, but Reagan knew that there was no point trying to escape, Jerell would eventually catch up with him. Tears sliding down his face, his hands shaking, Reagan slowly turned and faced the boy. This is what it had come to, he thought sadly. He had worked hard to impress Jerell and had quickly climbed to the top of his game: the money, the power, it had all been his. And this was the cost. The rise and fall; you always pay the price in the end.

Tyler glanced up, expecting to see a look of disgust on Reagan's face. Instead, his eyes met the barrel of the gun.

"No, Reagan, please." Tyler realised what this outing had been about. Jerell had kept his promise, it seemed, Tyler wouldn't be able to tell a soul now.

Chapter 27

"Are you sure it was him?" Jamie asked Louise again, hoping that she had been right about her sighting. They had been heading over to Jerell's house, when she said that she had spotted the bright yellow Corsa belonging to one of his boys driving in the opposite direction.

Louise nodded. The car was so gaudy it stood out like a sore thumb, and Louise had recognised it as soon as she had seen it. Rhys' car was one of a kind; it had been modified so much beyond its original state that there wasn't another one around that remotely resembled it. Louise had ducked down initially, when she had first seen the car drive towards them on the other side of the road. She hadn't wanted to chance being spotted by any of Jerell's boys, she was sure that they would be looking for her, Jerell never let anything go. Too inquisitive for her own good, though, she had taken a peek in the car's direction, unable to help herself. The last thing she had expected was to see Reagan in the driver's seat. Luckily, he had seemed too distracted, staring at the road ahead, to notice her puzzled face staring straight at him.

"And you definitely think it was Tyler that you saw?" Jamie repeated.

Louise wasn't a hundred percent sure that it had been Tyler, Reagan had been driving so fast, and the surprise of seeing him had thrown her, so she had only managed to get a quick glimpse in the passenger side. She could almost swear that it had been Tyler's little face that she had seen squashed up against the window, though.

"I'm certain it was Tyler," she said, trying to sound convincing. She hoped that forcing Jamie to do a dramatic U-turn in the middle of the busy Clapham Road, and almost killing them both in the process, as another car had been forced to swerve out of their way, would be worth it. But she was almost certain that it had been Tyler she had seen.

"And you definitely don't think that Jerell was with them?" Jamie continued to interrogate Louise, trying to determine who else had been in the car, to work out what he might be up against once he caught up with them.

"No, it looked like there was just the driver and Tyler," Louise answered.

"Did you recognise the driver?" Jamie realised that he sounded like he was reeling off the Spanish inquisition to the poor girl, but he had to find out whom Tyler was with.

"It was just another one of Jerell's skivvies, his name's Reagan. He's probably been sent out on an errand. He's not anyone to worry about. The bloke's fucking gutless." She surprised herself that she had managed to voice Reagan's name out loud without spitting.

They had been tailing Rhys' Corsa for the past ten minutes, and although Jamie's car was much faster than the boy-racer car that they were following, Jamie had deliberately held back behind a few cars, so that they wouldn't be spotted. The last thing he wanted was for the lad that was driving to think that he was being chased and to speed off in a bid to try to lose them. Jamie's plan was to drop back, until he knew for certain that Tyler was definitely in the car. He hoped that at least this way, he would get the opportunity to get to Tyler without the drama of dealing with Jerell at the same time. This way, things should be a lot less messy.

"Jesus Christ!" Louise watched, horrified, as the yellow car swerved, dipping in and out amongst the traffic.

"He's probably pissed, or on something," Jamie said, "either that or having some kind of epileptic fit at the wheel."

"He hasn't passed his test," Louise said.

The car snaked from one side of the road to the other. Reagan's driving was so bad that Louise was surprised he hadn't been pulled over by the police. He clearly wasn't the competent driver he had made himself out to be. He had boasted to her the other night that he had only needed two driving lessons to get him started off, and that after that he had taught himself to drive whilst out joyriding; he said he was like a pro.

Louise wondered what the hell Reagan was up to; it just didn't add up. She knew better than anyone how precious Rhys was about his poxy car: the boy never stopped harping on about it. The fact that Reagan was driving it only confirmed Louise's suspicions that there was something going on. There was no way Rhys would have handed over his prize possession willingly, knowing that Reagan hadn't even passed his driving test. And why did he have Tyler with him?

Apart from the constant questions, Jamie hadn't said much else to Louise. He didn't really speak much, she found. However, the bouts of silence were refreshing rather than awkward. She was normally surrounded by gobby little shits, who were fluent in bullshit and eager to run their mouths off to anyone who would listen. Jamie's quietness was endearing and alluring, it gave him an air of mystery. He reminded her of someone from a film, one of those strong, silent types.

Louise still didn't even know why Jamie was actually looking for Tyler. Jerell, she could understand, there were a lot of people who had a score to settle with him, but why Tyler?

"So, how do you know Tyler?" Louise didn't want to sound like she was prying into his business, but her curiosity was once again getting the better of her. She seemed to remember Jamie giving off the impression earlier that he already knew Tyler was in danger, but he still hadn't let on how he actually knew him or why he was trying to find him. Jamie seemed like a man who knew exactly what he was doing; his competence made Louise feel like she was in safe hands. Whatever this bloke's reasons were for trying to find Tyler, he was on his side and that was all that mattered. Jamie was the only real hope that Tyler had of getting away from Jerell, she suspected.

Jamie shifted in his seat, not taking his eyes off the road. "It's a long story." He cut the conversation dead with his abruptness. He had only known Louise for about half an hour, and as nice as she seemed, Jamie just didn't want to get into the whole thing with her.

Louise picked up on Jamie's caginess and, not wanting to push the discussion any further, she let the matter drop. Glancing past the two cars in front of them, she made out the back of Reagan's head.

Louise despised Reagan now. The more she had thought about it over the past few days, after replaying all the conversations that she had with him about Tyler, the more she was convinced that he had known all along what had been happening to him. To her, Reagan was as bad as Jerell. How anybody could turn a blind eye and allow someone to abuse a child, Louise would never

know. As far as she was concerned, they were both equally sick in the head.

She shuddered at the thought of what had been going on just a few feet away

from where she slept. Just thinking about what Jerell had been doing to that

boy disgusted her. Reagan was nothing to her now. She had been through

worse things in her life, and this was something that she had decided that she

was just going to have to draw a line under. The only thing that she was really

fuming about was the fact that she had been gullible enough to let her guard

down; she couldn't believe that she had fallen for yet another loser. She

should have known that Reagan had been too good to be true. From now on,

she would go it alone. No more men; they couldn't be trusted.

"For fuck's sake," Jamie shouted. He put his foot on the brake and the car

screeched to a halt. Up ahead, a skip lorry had pulled out into the middle of

the road and almost collided with the car in front of them. Jamie had seen the

car slam its brakes on and he had managed to follow suit just in the nick of

time, luckily, or else him and Louise would both be joining the big dribbling

dog that was sat in the boot of the four wheel drive in front of them. The lorry

was taking its time to reverse into a side road. Jamie watched irritably, willing

the driver to hurry up so that they could pass by; he had already lost sight of the car Reagan had been driving, and every second counted as far as Jamie was concerned.

Jamie tapped his fingers impatiently on the steering wheel. Then, after a few more minutes of watching the incompetent lorry driver slowly backing up, he whacked his hand down hard on the horn, his tolerance had long gone.

"Keep your fucking hair on, mate." The bald driver leant out of his window and shouted in response to the honk. His wheels slammed into the curb. He pulled back out onto the main road again, lining up the car to give the corner another attempt.

Jamie restrained himself from punching the steering wheel. If it hadn't been for Louise sitting next to him, he would have really lost his temper.

The car in front of them was completely blocking his way. Jamie would have tried to nip around the side but could only wait for the lorry to move so that the road was clear.

"Some people shouldn't be allowed on the fucking roads," Jamie muttered angrily. He glared at the lorry driver as he finally moved past him. He drove further onwards down the road, but there was no sign of the bright yellow car.

"I can't see them," Louise said, searching the road ahead for a sign of Reagan. They had travelled almost a mile further up Wandsworth Road and the car was nowhere to be seen.

"Keep looking, Louise; check the side roads. They may have turned off somewhere." Jamie was furious; they had followed them all this way and been so close behind. They couldn't have lost them now.

Louise could see at least fifteen cars ahead of them, and Rhys' Corsa wasn't one of them. Where the fuck had they gone?

Jamie continued to drive, but he knew it was pointless: they had lost them. Pulling into a Sainsbury's petrol station, Jamie tried to decide what to do. He should have fucking battered that bloody lorry driver for blocking up the road. There was nothing more they could do now, there was no point driving around looking for them, they could be anywhere in London by now. The best thing to do, Jamie decided, was to revert back to the original plan of going straight to the main man himself; it was their only lead on Tyler's whereabouts. Wherever the boy was now, it would only be a matter of time before he went back there anyway, Jamie reasoned to himself. They needed to go to Jerell's house.

Hearing Louise's stomach grumble, Jamie realised that she probably hadn't eaten all day. The lads had told him that she had been waiting around outside the garage for the past couple of days. And chances were, if she had slept rough the previous night, she would be starving.

"Do you fancy some food from in there?" Jamie nodded over to the garage-forecourt shop.

"A sandwich would be good," Louise replied; she didn't want to put him out, but at the same time she was really hungry.

Jamie got out of the car and jogged into the shop. He bought a selection of sandwiches, a bottle of water and an orange juice; he figured that if she was hungry and thirsty, then she would probably wasn't going to be too fussy about what he had picked anyway.

"Right then, get that down ya," Jamie said, when he returned a few minutes later, and passed the carrier bag of food to her.

As Jamie drove the other way along the Wandsworth Road, Louise tucked into one of the sandwiches, barely chewing it in her hunger and washing it down with orange juice. As she unwrapped a second, Jamie glanced at her.

"What?" she asked. "I'm bloody starving." She laughed, realising that she must sound like a greedy pig; she had been shovelling the food into her mouth so fast that it had barely touched the sides. She didn't normally eat like an animal, but the last time she had any food had been the day before, and the fact that she had fished a half-eaten breakfast wrap out of the bin outside McDonalds was information that she would be keeping to herself.

All Louise had thought about up until now had been Tyler; she had pushed her own situation – the fact of having no money on her, nowhere to stay and Jerell Morgan searching for her – to the back of her mind. Right now it seemed too much to cope with; concentrating on Tyler was a welcome release from her problems.

As they sat at a set of traffic lights, Louise caught a glimpse of a bright yellow car parked on one of the side roads. "I think that's them." Louise sounded hopeful, not quite believing she might have spotted them just when they had both been ready to give up.

"Union Road." Jamie wondered if Louise would recognise the name. "It leads to Larkhall Park."

"Of course." Reagan must be doing a drop: the boys used Larkhall for them.

"Do you know where they might be?" Jamie knew how large the park was.

Louise shook her head, regretfully. It was a large park, and the boys did drops all over the place; it would be like looking for a needle in a haystack.

"They're going to come back this way at some point," she reasoned, thinking that searching the park might mean that they missed each other if they did come back this way. They could be lurking anywhere in there, it depended on what sort of drop they were doing.

"We can't take the risk of waiting about; what if someone sees us or, more importantly, sees you? Jerell will be down here in a shot. We need to keep moving. Come on." Getting out of the car, Jamie walked fast; he was not prepared to lose Tyler a second time.

Chapter 28

"Shoot me then," Tyler said, with the newly found recognition that he no longer cared if he lived or died. The realisation had hit him while Reagan had been pointing the gun at him. Tyler could see everything for what it was. He was no longer scared. After everything he had been through, Reagan – his friend – had just committed the ultimate betrayal, stooping lower than Tyler could ever have imagined.

"Go on, Reagan, if Jerell's told you to kill me, then you'd better get on with it. He'll slaughter you if you don't go through with this. You know that, don't you?" Tyler had been pushed to his limit already; Reagan setting him up like this was the final nail in his coffin. Whatever happened now, Tyler would accept his fate, but he would also have his say.

Reagan's hand trembled; tears trickled down his cheeks. It was hard for Tyler to imagine that he had once looked up to the man.

"Why are you crying, Reagan? Only pussies cry. That's what you taught me, remember?" Tyler mocked, angrier with every passing second. "Come on, Reagan, stop being a pussy and pull the trigger," Tyler challenged.

Reagan shook his head. A stream of snot hung from one nostril, and he wiped it away with the back of his hand; his other was holding the gun.

"I'm sorry, Tyler, really, I am." Reagan's finger gently pressed against the trigger. He couldn't bring himself to squeeze it.

Reagan was clearly losing his nerve; he looked like one of those deranged people on a documentary about mental people; like he was having a breakdown, Tyler thought.

"What are you sorry for, Reagan? Sorry you're about to plant a bullet in my skull? Sorry you knew what that fucking paedo was doing and that you did nothing to help?" Tyler threw the question out there, wanting to find out how much Reagan had known. Reagan at least had the good grace to briefly look away at the question, and the fleeting movement told Tyler everything he needed to know.

"You knew all along, didn't you?"

"I didn't know at first, Tyler, I swear." Reagan snivelled, as he tried to explain, knowing he sounded pathetic. "I had an idea, but I wasn't sure."

Tyler shook his head in disappointment. "You're weak, Reagan, weak and pathetic. Jerell may as well shove his hand up your fucking arse and use you as a puppet. That's all you are to him. You're a puppet on a fucking string, and he's the one controlling you. What about Louise, huh? He doesn't give a shit about her. What do you think he's going to do to her when he catches up with her?"

"I don't know." Reagan spoke quietly. He knew that Tyler was talking sense.

Tyler laughed. "You don't know? Going by this fucked-up situation, I'd say he's pretty much going to want to do away with her an' all. He ain't gunna leave it to chance that one day she might blab her mouth off to someone about me. Jerell doesn't give a shit who he tramples on. Me, Louise... It'll only be a matter of time until he comes for you too. You hadn't thought of that, had you?" Tyler felt empowered by the fact that he could see everything playing out so clearly. Even if Louise and he were off the scene, there would still be one person left who knew the truth about Jerell. Having a gun shoved in his face had given Tyler a voice and, knowing it was do or die, he carried on talking. "Do you think that he trusts you enough not to talk? I mean, this is Mr Fucking Paranoid that we're talking about here," Tyler continued.

There was a silence.

"Go on. Shoot me," Tyler said. "Shoot me, and then when you find Louise, shoot her too. Then who knows, one night you'll be lying asleep in your bed and someone will sneak into your room and blow your brains out all over your pillow. Might be Jerell himself that does that deed. We'll all be brown bread, and Jerell's dirty little secret will be buried nicely along with us. Until Jerell finds another young boy." Tyler's eyes flashed with rage. How dare Reagan do this to him, and for what: so he could be that fucking man's scapegoat?

"Come on then, Reagan, fucking shoot me," Tyler shouted now.

"I can't," Reagan cried. "I can't. I'm so sorry, Tyler. Please… I don't know what I was thinking." Reagan dropped the gun and fell to the ground, sobbing uncontrollably. He didn't know who he was anymore. He was bawling, speaking incoherently.

Tyler grabbed his chance and picked up the gun. Then he ran as fast as he could, and he didn't look back.

Chapter 29

"This is pointless," Louise exclaimed, after she had been trudging around the park, following Jamie, for the best part of an hour. It was icy cold, white frosty clouds of her breath accompanied her words, hitting the night air as she spoke.

"If we haven't found them by now, then we're probably not going to." Louise hated stating the obvious, but she couldn't help feeling like they were on a wild-goose chase. Her feet were throbbing from all the walking they had done and it probably didn't help that she hadn't taken her shoes off for almost forty-eight hours. Louise wasn't cut out for living on the streets, and she hadn't even found a place to stay tonight. "They're probably not even here anymore," she reasoned.

Jamie had a stubborn look on his face that indicated he wasn't ready to give up looking. Louise understood that he desperately wanted to find Tyler, and she did too, but the chances were that he and Reagan had been and gone, and she and Jamie were now walking aimlessly around the park wasting time that they didn't have.

"Why don't we go back to your car?" Louise persisted. "We can see if their car's still there. If it is, it's only going to be a matter of time before they come back to it; we've been here ages."

As much as he hated the idea of giving up, Jamie knew that Louise had a point. They could search this park all night, and there was still a chance that they would miss Tyler, the place was too big. If they were doing a drop, as Louise thought they were, they wouldn't be lurking around somewhere waiting to be found, they would be on the move too.

"Okay, Louise." Jamie sighed. "Let's go back to the motor."

Louise was relieved. She thought that they should have stayed in the car from the start but, as she was slowly learning, Jamie was the boss and he called the shots.

They hadn't seen many people in the park. Which was to be expected, Jamie thought, seeing as it had gone eight o'clock, and the park was almost in darkness. The temperature had dropped too; Jamie could hear Louise's teeth chattering as they walked in silence.

"Are you alright?" Jamie asked. The girl hadn't moaned once about the cold, or how tired she must be, and Jamie was impressed. Most girls would be feeling hard done by and going on about stuff like that by now.

"Yeah, I'm fine," Louise said, as she hugged her arms around herself to try and keep warm, she was looking forward to getting back to Jamie's car and blasting her cold hands with the heater, anything that would help to stop herself from shivering.

They walked fast and within minutes they were back at the entrance to the park, where they had pulled up earlier.

"Looks like you were right then," Jamie said, as he indicated the empty space where the Corsa had been parked. Somehow Reagan and Tyler had managed to get back here and drive away without Jamie and Louise spotting them.

"Bloody hell," Louise said. "What a waste of time that was then." They should have stayed in the car.

"Come on, get in." Jamie was in no mood to hear 'I told you so'. "I want you to show me Jerell's place; chances are they've gone back there. Then I'm going to drop you at my mate's house. You need a hot cup of tea and a warm bed; you're going to end up with flippin' pneumonia otherwise." Jamie looked concerned. Louise hadn't made a fuss, but he could tell by her drooping eyes that she was exhausted.

"What, you're not going to let me come in with you? You can't go in on your

own, Jamie. Jerell's a psycho; you don't know him like I do." Louise felt scared

as she spoke.

"Trust me, Louise. I know exactly what I'm dealing with. I'll be going in there

alone." He started the engine and concentrated on driving. Louise could tell

that once again the conversation was over. Jamie had a way of cutting her

dead when he didn't want to discuss things further; it was starting to do

Louise's head in. He was bloody stubborn.

"Who's your friend then?" Louise hoped she wouldn't be left with that bloody

Shay again. He was harmless enough, she guessed, but she didn't fancy

another session of him talking about nothing but himself.

"Gary. He's a nice bloke; he's got a spare room. He won't mind you being

there for a night."

Louise didn't want to intrude on some poor bloke she didn't know. But then,

she didn't have much choice. It wasn't like she had any other option.

***

Letting himself in with the key that Gary had given him, Jamie walked quietly

through the hallway, Louise cautiously following. Jamie had pre-warned her that Gary was recovering from surgery, and Jamie wanted to keep the noise down in case he was in bed.

He shouldn't have worried; as he opened the lounge door, he saw Gary and Les sprawled out on the settee like an old married couple, Gary had a blanket over his legs and they were both cradling mugs of tea.

"Oh, I didn't know you were bringing someone back," Gary said, sitting up, surprised to see a beautiful girl standing behind Jamie. Gary had never had the privilege of meeting any girlfriend of Jamie's, the boy was so private that Gary had never even heard him even mention that he was seeing anyone. And he certainly hadn't expected him to bring somebody back to his own house. The girl looked nice, though, Gary thought, quite young, but nice all the same.

Realising that Gary assumed Louise was his girlfriend, Jamie immediately put him right; Louise would be cringing at the thought of an old git like him being mistaken for her boyfriend. "This is my friend Louise, Gary; she's got herself in a bit of bother. I said it would be okay to put her up here for the night: she can have my room. I wouldn't ask, only it's getting late and she hasn't got anywhere else to go." Jamie wished he had rung Gary beforehand, and felt bad that he was putting him on the spot, whilst Louise was standing there no doubt feeling awkward.

"Of course, Jamie, that's fine with me," Gary said, not batting an eyelid. Jamie wouldn't ask for a favour unless he really needed one, and as always Gary was happy to help him out. He had seemed to have so much on his mind lately. Maybe this girl had something to do with it.

Les, however, scoffed at Gary being so accommodating whenever it came to Jamie.

"Well, it's not really ideal letting someone stay at the moment, is it, Jamie? I mean, Gary's only just back on his feet." Les was fuming. Jamie was taking the piss bringing some stranger to Gary's house without warning and expecting him to put the girl up was out of order, especially in Gary's condition. Jamie was a selfish bastard.

"No, no. Don't be silly, Les. Any friend of Jamie's is a friend of mine. And if she needs a place to stay for the night, she's more than welcome," Gary insisted. "Take a seat, love." Gary wanted to make the girl feel comfortable.

Louise sat on the chair nearest to her. Gary, who could tell that she was cold as her nose was red, asked if she wanted a cup of tea. Louise nodded gratefully. She had never known why English people drank so much tea, but right now, she could understand it. A nice cup of tea would really help warm her up.

"Bung the kettle on, will you, Les," Gary said, ignoring Les' grumpy face.

Les stomped to the kitchen, like a child that had just had his toys taken away from him.

Jamie shook his head at the man's temper tantrum, but kept his thoughts to himself. He didn't want to cause Gary any grief, especially when he was being so good by allowing Louise to stay the night.

"Gary, I've got to go out for a bit. Is it okay for Louise to stay here?" Jamie knew that he was taking the mickey out of Gary's kind nature, but he didn't have any choice. He needed to get over to Jerell's to see if Tyler was okay, and he didn't want to get anyone else involved this time. He had to sort this mess out once and for all.

"No worries," Gary said, "as long as you don't mind watching *The Apprentice*, Louise. That Alan Sugar cracks me up, ruthless old bastard he is." Gary laughed and smiled over at Louise.

Seeing Louise return the smile, Jamie was relieved to see that she looked happy enough in Gary's company.

"Les," Gary shouted in the direction of the kitchen. "See if there's any of that cake left out there, would ya? Bring Louise in a nice big slice with her tea, yeah?" Gary winked at Jamie; they both knew that Les would be rolling his eyes to the heavens out in the kitchen. He wasn't happy unless he was moaning, and where Jamie was concerned he was always moaning. Jamie could imagine Les slamming around out there. He could be a diva when he put his mind to it; Mariah Carey, eat your heart out.

"Right then." Jamie felt less guilty at leaving Louise with Gary and vice versa. "I'll leave you two to it. If you get tired, Louise, have a sleep in my bed."

Louise blushed as Gary raised his eyebrows at Jamie's suggestion, and not wanting to give the man any ideas, Jamie added: "I'll take the sofa."

Stepping out into the dark streets, Jamie walked to his car, leaving the warmth of Gary's cosy house behind him.

Chapter 30

Jamie parked in the next street to the house that Louise had pointed out as belonging to Jerell, and decided to do the rest of the journey on foot. Now he was alone he sprinted, desperately wanting to get to Jerell's house. He prayed that Tyler would be there; that he would be okay.

***

The house was peaceful. Jerell had spent the last two hours smoking weed whilst listening to tunes on the stereo. He was chilled out; for the first time in ages he had the place to himself; for once he truly appreciated the stillness around him.

The boys had been told in no uncertain terms that they were not to return to the house unless they had Louise in tow, so for now Jerell was just going to lay back and chill, while he waited for the boys to fetch the girl to him. There weren't too many places that she could be; it would only be a matter of time until somebody found her. His boys were like sniffer dogs, it wouldn't take them long to get her out from wherever she was hiding.

After the way Louise had run rings around him by disappearing, and disrespecting him, Jerell felt that he had been left with no choice but to make an example of her. These boys couldn't be getting ideas in their heads about going up against him. He needed to retain control.

Forgetting his troubles for now, though, he closed his eyes, and let the music transport him, as it always did, to thoughts of home. The reggae sounds had a way of soothing his soul. He settled back in the chair and got swept away by the musical vibes.

Tonight his happy thoughts of home were overcast by difficult feelings about his grandma. Jerell had been in England for almost six months, and he knew that she would be worried. She was the only person that had been there for him no matter what, and he was ridden with guilt for leaving her without saying goodbye, but he knew if he had, she would have begged him not to go.

He decided that first thing tomorrow he would call her, and ease the worry that he undoubtedly had put her through. Finally making a decision, he felt the weight he'd been carrying lift from his shoulders; at last he could relax.

***

Clad in black clothing, the shadowy figure who had been hidden by the darkness of the night watched him through the window, pleased that Jerell Morgan seemed to be alone. It was time to strike.

Tyler scaled the drainpipe that hung down the side wall next to his bedroom window. He was panting and aware of the gun in the waistband of his jeans digging into his thigh as he climbed. He had been out of breath from running all the way from the park; fuelled by adrenaline, and thoughts of getting his own revenge, he had managed to make it back here in good time.

Someone else was watching, concealed by darkness. Jamie, who had been hiding against the tall fence, crept towards the back gate, keeping his body pressed against the wood; he was hoping to stay undetected in the shadows. On reaching the back gate, he gently lifted the handle and slid his body inside through the gap.

Upstairs, Tyler was tip-toeing along the landing, aware that even the slightest creak of a floor board would alert Jerell to the fact that there was someone inside the house. Nothing got past him. Tyler didn't want to give the man a head start; he was counting on the fact that catching him off guard would be the only way that he could get his revenge.

Jamie, finding the back door ajar, crept in and through the kitchen. So far there had been no sign of Jerell, or anyone else for that matter. He made his way to the stairway, assuming that because the house was in darkness Jerell was in bed.

The lounge was dark; the only light that broke up the blackness was a tiny blue one that flickered dimly on the stereo in the corner of the room, as the voice of Bob Marley filled the air. Jerell was lying on the sofa with his mouth hung open, as he breathed deeply in slumber.

Thinking he heard a noise, Tyler stopped at the top of the stairs and hid down on the floor behind the banister. Crouching down, he remained still. Maybe Jerell had heard him. Getting out the gun and holding it tightly, he got himself ready in case he needed to use it, as he heard faint footsteps sneaking up the stairs towards him.

Tiptoeing as carefully as he could, Jamie was also holding a gun in front of him. Gary would have gone mental if Jamie had told him that he was coming back here on his own to find Jerell; because he didn't know the full story, Jamie was convinced that Gary wouldn't understand, and he would go ape-shit if he found out that Jamie had taken his Smith and Wesson out of the safe in the garage. Jamie had loaded it earlier, when he had met Louise down there. He imagined that Jerell would be tooled up.

Jamie had reached the top of the stairs, and turned the corner, when he almost tripped over himself. The kid crouching down on the hallway had scared the shit out of him.

The small petrified boy lurking in the shadows was Tyler. Jamie felt a massive wave of relief surge through him that he had finally found him, until he saw that Tyler was pointing a gun straight at him.

"Don't move another step," Tyler said. He felt his hands go clammy with fear. Realising that it wasn't Jerell who had come up the stairs, Tyler continued to hold his gun tightly as he stared at the man standing before him. He looked familiar, but Tyler couldn't place him.

"Put the gun down, Tyler... please, I'm not going to hurt you," Jamie said, shocked at the sight of the kid before him; even through the shadows, with only the moonlight coming through the skylight above them, Jamie could see that Tyler looked skinny and terrified. "I've come to help you, Tyler," Jamie whispered nervously, hoping that Tyler would believe him, not only did Jamie not fancy getting shot by the kid, he was also worried that Jerell would hear any noise they made, and would come up the stairs to investigate. Jamie knew that Jerell was in the house; he needed to keep Tyler calm if they were both going to make it out of here alive.

Although his body was shaking, Tyler didn't put down the gun. He didn't know who this bloke was: why should he trust him? Although he looked really familiar... His mind whirled.

Then it dawned on him. He had been one of the men who had barged into

Reagan's flat. One of them had been shot. Maybe this man was only here for

Jerell, hoping for revenge.

Jamie could see a flicker of doubt cross the boy's mind, but Tyler didn't waver

as he continued to point the gun at Jamie while he kept his eyes locked onto

his.

"I'm here to help you, Tyler." Jamie couldn't have been any more sincere. He

could still see traces of the little chubby baby brother that he had left behind,

in Tyler's cold, hardened face. He couldn't begin to imagine what this poor kid

had been through, and he felt partly responsible. He should never have left

him. Things may have been different if Jamie had been there when Tyler was

growing up. He couldn't turn back the clock, but he hoped that in time Tyler

would let him make it up to him. Jamie was pained by the fact that this boy

crouching in front of him, holding the gun out so bravely, had no idea who

Jamie was; he didn't even know that Jamie existed.

"I promise you, Tyler; you can trust me. Put down the gun."

Tyler saw tears in the man's eyes. He had no idea what was going on, today

had turned into an extremely fucked-up day.

Tyler lowered the gun as Jamie gave him a smile, thankful that he believed him.

Seconds later, the sound of a gunshot rang out downstairs, making both Jamie and Tyler jump.

Jamie instructed Tyler to stay where he was as he ran down the stairs. Rushing into the room that he thought the sound had come from, Jamie froze. He could see a silhouette. Someone was standing holding a gun, pointing it at a figure lying on a sofa: Jerell.

Jerell was writhing on the settee. He had woken up to pain searing through him, realising instantly that he had been shot.

"What the fuck have you done?" he screamed. The pain was excruciating, making him flush hot and cold. Shock was setting in. He had thought of himself as indestructible, this was his worst nightmare.

Unable to stay away as Jamie had told him, Tyler crept into the room to see what all the commotion was about. Seeing a familiar figure standing in the room, he switched the light on and gasped loudly.

"Mum?" Jamie and Tyler said in unison. Tyler swung his head towards Jamie in surprise.

Maura Finch looked like she had done ten rounds with Mike Tyson. Her right leg was in plaster from the toes to the knee. Her face was battered almost beyond recognition: her eyes dark purple, her lips swollen. And right now, she looked like a woman possessed.

"Not so cocky now, is he?" Maura laughed manically, emphasising the word cocky. The boys both looked at Jerell. A thick pool of blood seeped out from around the groin area of his jeans, indicating where she had shot Jerell.

Tyler recognised the gun as the one that Jerell had told him to dump. His mother had obviously taken it.

Aiming the gun at Jerell, Maura fired, straight into the howling man's chest. She would love to leave him lying there bleeding to death from having his dick blasted off, but she wasn't taking any chances. Jerell was the sort of jammy bloke that might survive an attack like this; she could imagine him rising from his death bed like the frigging Terminator.

The second bullet tore through Jerell's chest. He stopped breathing on impact.

'Redemption Song' played out in the background. Bob Marley's lyrics about freeing yourself from evil were not lost on Jamie.

Jamie and Tyler stared at their demented-looking mother in disbelief. She didn't take her eyes off Jerell's body, as she stood there seemingly in a trance.

"No one fucks with me or mine," Maura said, to no-one in particular.

Chapter 31

"Stay still. One movement and you'll be seen."

Jamie was the mastermind once again, and as always when he put a plan together he wanted it executed exactly as he intended. Everyone had been briefed, there were to be no fuck-ups. Jamie had worked hard to see that this all went exactly to the letter; it was important.

The room was dark; the only sound heavy breathing.

Hearing a car pull up outside, Jamie felt his heart beating fast; they had to pull this off. Jamie was relying on being able to hear the door open when he entered; otherwise this had been for nothing. Shay and Gavin were on the other side of the room, waiting until Jamie gave a signal.

A key turned in the front door. Voices could be heard in the hallway, chatting quietly at first, but louder as they came closer.

The lounge door opened. The timing was crucial.

"Now," Jamie said, as he, Gary and Les jumped from behind the curtains, while the walk-in cupboard door across the room simultaneously burst open, as Shay and Gavin almost fell over each other in their hurry to jump out from where they had been hiding.

"Happy birthday," they all shouted to a gobsmacked-looking Tyler who had just walked into the room, closely followed by a smiling Louise. She was glad that the men had managed to pull off the surprise that Jamie had organised. Tyler looked dumbfounded as he realised what was going on.

Jamie wondered whether they should have jumped out like that, Tyler looked like he had seen a ghost, still understandably jumpy from all that had happened.

Jamie needn't have worried; the look on Tyler's face, as he took in the balloons and decorations, was enough to make even these tough men feel teary.

"Wow," he said in awe, as a massive grin spread across his face. "Is this all for me?" Tyler had never had a party, not even when he had been little, and he couldn't believe that they had gone to all this trouble for him. He had been through so much and was still getting over the shock of finding out that Jamie was his brother. He would never forgive his mother for keeping the secret from him for all these years. Jamie had become his best friend, and Tyler loved the funny stories that Jamie had told him about when he had been a baby. He had never realised that he had been loved so much.

Jamie laughed at the boy's modesty. "Of course it's all for you, mate, you don't see any of us turning thirteen anytime soon, do ya?" Jamie pointed at the 'Happy Birthday' banners that were dotted around the walls, all brightly displaying the number thirteen on them, before he quickly added: "well, Shay might just about pass for thirteen, the way he acts, but you'd have to be pretty blind not to clock his stubbly moosh and the suitcases under his eyes."

"Oi," Shay said, and laughed, his mouth full of sausage roll; he was happy that now the birthday boy had arrived he could finally tuck into some food. Unable to wait another second, he had started to help himself.

"Come on then, Tyler, take a seat. You've got a mountain of presents to open, you know." Gary beamed from his seat at the table. He was still taking it easy, even though he had almost fully recovered. He didn't want to push himself. Even jumping out from behind the curtains had taken it out of him. He had been happy to have Tyler's surprise party at his house, though. Jamie was like a son to him, and Gary would do everything he could to help him with Tyler.

Tyler made his way over to the table, where Les handed him a plate of goodies to eat, and Gavin gathered up the boy's cards for him to open.

"Are you alright?" Jamie asked Louise, who was getting a cold drink.

"How could I not be… look at his face, he's made up." Louise nodded at a grinning Tyler, as he tore into his presents. She stepped back a bit, Jamie was standing in such close proximity to her, she was paranoid he would read her thoughts. Her pulse had quickened and she fought to stop herself from blushing as he stood close to her, chatting. Jamie was a good man, one of the best in fact, and what he had done for Tyler had proved that. Looking around at the men in the room, Louise felt emotional. This was far from a traditional family set-up, but she couldn't think of anyone better to look after Tyler. Now that Tyler had moved in with Jamie, Louise had never seen the boy so happy: he was a changed kid.

"Any news on your re-housing?" Jamie asked.

Gary letting Louise stay had been a weight off Jamie's mind, but he knew that even though she and Gary got on well, she was eager to move into a place of her own. She was used to her independence. After telling the council that her house had been taken over by squatters while she had been staying with friends, the local authority had offered to re-house her. The police had investigated the claims of squatters moving into her flat and had declared the place a crime scene when they had discovered the drugs factory.

"Yes, actually, there is." Louise beamed; she had been told the news that afternoon. She was excited to start her new life. Thoughts of Jerell, Reagan and the others had been put to the back of her mind. She was never going back to that life. No more gangs; no more drama, she had started looking at recruitment websites in search of a job. "I've been offered a little place just around the corner, actually."

Jamie was pleased. Louise was a nice girl and if she lived nearby, Tyler would be able to spend time with her; they had a strong bond, and Jamie could see that Louise cared about him.

"What about you; did you speak to the doctors about your mum?" Louise asked.

Jamie tried not to flinch; he didn't like it when people referred to Maura as his mum.

The past few weeks had been a nightmare for them all. But now Jerell was dead, hopefully they could put this all behind them and finally get on with their lives.

"The doctor said that she's going to be assessed by a psychiatrist next week, to see if she is able to be tried for Jerell's murder, but they reckon she won't go to trial," Jamie said. "The doctor said she spends her days talking gibberish to herself and trying to cave her head in by banging it against the walls of her room. They've got her under twenty-four hour surveillance."

Tyler had told Jamie that the gun their mother had used for Jerell's murder had been the one that Tyler was supposed to dump for him; the gun that Tyler had then hid, which had since gone missing. It had been their mother who had taken it. Not only did she have Jerell's gun on her when she was arrested, but the police had also found the original property details from the estate agents on her, which explained how she knew where to find him. Jamie had a feeling that Maura's attack on Jerell had been more on her part, for his attack on her, than about getting revenge for what the man had done to her youngest son. Jamie knew that he wouldn't be seeing his mother ever again, and he had a feeling that Tyler felt the same.

"What's this?" Tyler called to Jamie, as he ripped the wrapping on the final present he had to open; it was from his brother. Inside was a pair of navy-blue overalls and steel-toe-capped boots; they were not the clothes that Tyler would have chosen to wear.

"Well..." Jamie walked over to Tyler and grinned at his unimpressed face. "We've all been talking, and we think that you've got what it takes to train as a mechanic."

"So we want to offer you an apprenticeship at the garage," Les chipped in. He had taken a shine to the boy, even though he was Jamie's brother.

"How would you like to come and work for us on Saturdays? It won't interfere with your school work, and we'll put a bit of money in your pocket for all your hard graft," Gary added.

"The only downfall is you'll have to get used to Gavin's smelly arse if you get stuck in the workshop with him," Shay ribbed his friend.

"And if any of Shay's 'lady friends' turn up, you'll have to hide him in a cupboard until they're gone." Gavin laughed, although he was only half-joking. Shay nudged him. Gavin had done that twice for Shay in the past few years, unbeknown to Gary and Jamie.

Tyler looked at them all smiling at him and Jamie waiting patiently, clearly hoping that he would say yes.

"I can't..." he said, sadly, dropping his head.

Louise exchanged a confused look with Jamie. She had been sure Tyler would go for it, when Jamie had suggested it to them all.

Then, raising his head and laughing loudly, Tyler quickly finished the sentence:

"I can't ...thank you enough. I'd love to!" Jumping up, Tyler gave Jamie a hug.

Thirteen he may be, but on that one day he didn't care how old he was as he

cuddled his brother.

Also Available from this author

"Rotten to the Core"

Casey Kelleher

Billy O'Connell may have been just a boy when Den Shaw crossed him and his family, but the bad news for Den was; little boys eventually grow into men.
A mutilated corpse turns up in a skip one morning, tortured and almost unrecognisable. Billy has bided his time, ten whole years of hurt, and now justice, as far as he is concerned, has finally been done.

Jay Shaw only looks out for himself, His old man had taught him that much at least. When his father is found murdered Jay knows in his gut who is to blame, but nothing is ever proven. Billy may hate him with a vengeance but the feeling is most definitely mutual. Jay is as nasty and conniving as his father before him: They say the apple doesn't fall far from the tree, and this one is Rotten to the Core.

Kate O'Connell is a decent girl considering the rough area that she has grown up in, and the fact that her brother Billy is so fiercely protective of her. How she has managed to keep her secret from him for so long she has no idea. She is pregnant and Jay is the father.
Caught up in the vicious feud she finds herself having to make a choice, between the man she loves and her fiercely protective brother.

It's a decision that could cost Kate her life.

CPSIA information can be obtained at www.ICGtesting.com
Printed in the USA
LVOW101925291112

309388LV00006B/732/P